...der, ...g re... ...ently, I've been a writer... many readers. But ...riters' conference or a b... ...ally had a chance encounter with a reader.

One evening my husband and I were out walking two of our dogs. We'd gone about a mile when I spotted a young woman sitting alone on a bench reading. Naturally, I checked out the book—I always do. Much to my surprise, it was my book—*Lilly's Law*, my first Flipside! My initial impulse was to rush over and autograph it. Which I didn't, of course, because sensibility, my husband and two big dogs held me back.

Instead, I watched her read for a few minutes. Watched her face and saw pretty much the same expression we all have when we read. Nothing good, nothing bad. But then she laughed out loud, and when the laugh was gone her smile remained a while longer. For those few minutes, I had made a difference. I made her laugh, maybe even feel a little better, and it's such a privilege to be able to do that for someone I've never met.

It is also a privilege to be back with you again, and I'd like to thank Wanda Ottewell and everybody at Harlequin for allowing me to write this book for you.

Wishing you love and laughter!

Dianne

P.S. For a different kind of read, try my new Medical Romance novel, from Harlequin Mills & Boon, coming in May 2005. You'll find it available for order at www.eHarlequin.com.

"Do you listen to her show? Valentine McCarthy's?"

Roxy's heart skipped a beat at Ned's question. She *never* admitted to being her alter ego. "I've heard she's really good. Cute. Smart. Nice voice. Great wardrobe. Good shoes. Very successful." She couldn't help applauding herself.

"Clearly you don't listen to her much, do you?"

She got caught up in Ned's eyes, forgetting who, what, when and where for a second. He was so hot. But then his words registered. He obviously was *not* a fan of her show.

"I listen sometimes," Roxy said carefully. "She's good entertainment. And popular."

Ned laughed. "Well, you're right about that. She's popular. I guess that's the way she wants to waste her Ph.D."

"Waste?"

"Hack advice." His voice was dismissive.

"Entertainment." Funny, he wasn't looking quite so attractive right now.

"Bad entertainment."

That's what he thought? "So would I be wrong in assuming you're not a big Val fan?"

"Nope. Just listen when I can't sleep."

Great. She had just spent all this time ogling a guy who hated half of who she was. Not the best forecast for a relationship.

Playing Games

Dianne Drake

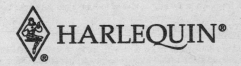

HARLEQUIN®

TORONTO • NEW YORK • LONDON
AMSTERDAM • PARIS • SYDNEY • HAMBURG
STOCKHOLM • ATHENS • TOKYO • MILAN • MADRID
PRAGUE • WARSAW • BUDAPEST • AUCKLAND

ISBN 0-373-44206-8

PLAYING GAMES

This edition published by arrangement with Harlequin Books S.A.

® and TM are trademarks of the publisher. Trademarks indicated with
® are registered in the United States Patent and Trademark Office, the
Canadian Trade Marks Office and in other countries.

www.eHarlequin.com

Printed in U.S.A.

ABOUT THE AUTHOR

What's life without a few pets? Dianne Drake and her hubby Joel have seven—four dogs and three cats, all rescued strays. In the few spare minutes her animals grant her, Dianne goes to the Indianapolis Symphony, the Indianapolis Colts NFL team, the Indiana Pacers NBA team—can you tell she lives in Indianapolis? And occasionally, she and Joel sneak away and do something really special, like take in a hockey game.

Books by Dianne Drake

HARLEQUIN FLIPSIDE
16—LILLY'S LAW

HARLEQUIN DUETS
58—THE DOCTOR DILEMMA
106—ISN'T IT ROMANTIC?

Don't miss any of our special offers. Write to us at the following address for information on our newest releases.

Harlequin Reader Service
U.S.: 3010 Walden Ave., P.O. Box 1325, Buffalo, NY 14269
Canadian: P.O. Box 609, Fort Erie, Ont. L2A 5X3

To Janie, the real spunk behind the
heroine in this book

1

"WELCOME TO MIDNIGHT SPECIAL, sugars. Are you ready for something special? Because if you are, you've certainly come to the right place. Doctor Val has something *extra-specially* special for you tonight."

Roxy Rose gave her sound engineer, Doyle Hopps, the nod, and the program started on cue with caller number one, a thirty-something hubby-done-her-wrong from Olympia. Make that cheating husband number fifty-six for the week. Roxy always counted them—the cheating husbands. Just in case she landed a book deal somewhere down the line she wanted to be accurate. Not that she was planning on writing a book, like that obnoxious Doctor Edward Craig seemed to do about every two minutes. But she wasn't ruling out anything because her career was on a big-time growth curve lately, and all those hanky-panky-ing husbands and two-timing boyfriends came in at a whopping fifty percent share of the calls.

Love 'em, hate 'em…she definitely counted on that loose zipper legion for some nice, fat ratings. And either way, Roxy needed them. They were one of the main reasons she was eyebrow-deep in building her new dream home…a million dollars' worth of cement, steel and glass, along with a to-die-for panorama of Puget Sound.

"Eighteen years, Doctor Val. That's how long I've been

with him. I've kept myself up physically, stayed good in bed…at least I thought I was good in bed, until he started hunting down other beds. I've held down a full-time job, raised the kids. For eighteen *long* years. Then I find out he's cheating on me. And it's not like she's some younger bimbo. She's older…my age, and married, with four kids. So what's he seeing in her? I mean, if she was twenty with a tight ass, I might be able to understand it, but she's not!"

Astrid hit the bleep button as the *a* word popped out, then gave Roxy the thumbs-up to indicate she'd caught it. They were on a seven-second delay for such slippages.

Nodding, Roxy returned the thumbs-up to her friend. Best friend, actually. Astrid Billings—long auburn hair, figure of a goddess, the one who really looked like what Val sounded like—had come with the show when Roxy had inherited it from her predecessor.

"Whoa," Roxy said, her Doctor Valentine drawl slow and Southern, even though she was Seattle-born and raised and didn't have a drawl, slow, fast or otherwise. "Just calm down, now. Okay? Take a deep breath and pour yourself a big ol' glass of wine. In fact, why don't all of you go ahead and do the same." Roxy nodded at Doyle to cue up the music, then purred into the microphone, "Be right back. Don't you go away. Valentine's counting on you." Settling back into her chair, she took off her headset and gave Doyle the *I need a drink in a bad way right now* sign— the invisible cup tilting to her mouth, then tilting and tilt-ing and tilting for emphasis. Unfortunately, Roxy's invisible cup wasn't filled with wine. Never was on air, hardly ever was in real life.

"Anything in particular?" Doyle asked from his booth.

"Anything wet. Other than that, I'm not picky." Roxy looked at the monitor for the seconds left in this break. A one-minute break already one-quarter gone, meaning she didn't have time to get it for herself. Or she would have.

"Told you we needed a wet bar in here, Rox," he said, grinning through the glass at her. His booth was large, full of all kinds of gizmos and gadgets. Hers was tiny, big enough for a desk and not much else. "A pitcher of margaritas right now sounds pretty good to me."

"Yeah, and with margaritas, you get Roxy dancing on the desk. Tap water's okay."

"Tap water...*boring.* You need to live a little, Rox. I keep telling you there's more to life than business, and I, for one, would appreciate a good desk-dancin' from you."

"You got it. Tap or ballet?" Roxy laughed. Doyle was so close to hitting the nail on the head about her boring life that it wasn't funny. Two hours on air was all anybody heard, but she managed her own Valentine publicity, hunted down sponsors, and lately, went cruising for a syndication deal. So her two hours really translated into at least fourteen. And then she slept. Oh, and did some house designing.

"I was thinking something in veils, or less. Little cymbals on your fingers."

Astrid stuck her head into the booth and held up a can and a red plastic cup full of ice. "Hey, Rox. Before you put on your dancing shoes, or veils, is orange soda okay? They're out of root beer and the tap water's looking pretty brown."

"Orange is just dandy," Roxy said cheerfully, glancing back over at Doyle for the count. "Sorry. Guess the veils will have to wait."

"Promises, promises." Doyle held up three fingers on his pudgy right hand and made a zero sign with his left. "Thirty. And I ain't lettin' you off the hook for those cymbals."

Short, a speck on the plump side, with long, scraggly brown hair always hanging out of a Seattle Mariner cap, in the control booth he knew his stuff like nobody else in the business. Like Astrid, he'd been with Roxy from the show's get-go, grabbed off a sideline grunt job and given his domain on the boards. Roxy, Astrid and Doyle…the three of them together, thick and thin, yada, yada. And Roxy never forgot that. For all her quirks, she was loyal.

"I'll put them on my to-do list right after tweaking the master bath."

"Not the house again!" Doyle cracked, covering his face with his hands. "Please God, anything but the house."

"Like you won't be parking it out there when I get my entertainment room set up. Big projection TV, a sound system that'll make you eat your heart out…"

"And you in veils…"

"We don't talk veils until we talk about my house plans, and I got into some new ones today, in case you're interested." Which Roxy knew he wasn't, but he sure liked teasing her about them. "And I'm thinking they could be the ones. Some pretty neat stuff."

"Twenty. And I doubt it, Rox. Not with the way you're killing every single architect in the greater Seattle area who comes within a mile of you and your house plans. Fifteen."

Well, maybe she'd fired a few. Two, three? Definitely not more than five. But they couldn't get it right. She wanted minimal with a homey feel. They couldn't manage both in the same blueprint, and the homey part always got left out. So she was doing it on her own now, with the help of a CAD—computer assisted design—program and some old Bob Vila tapes. Plus in her spare time she stayed glued to Home and Garden TV, making up a wish list. Her house on her own beach would be nothing short of perfect. "Just cutting through the middle men. That's all." And sure, somewhere down the line when she roughed out exactly what she wanted, she'd go architect shopping for someone to whip it into proper form, find the general contractor, and all the rest of it. *After* she was finished with her own preliminaries.

"Cutting up the middle men's more like it." Doyle gave

her the ten sign—ten chubby fingers wiggling at her. "And just when I thought you were working out your control issues. Eight, seven, six..."

"It's not a control issue, Doyle." Well, maybe. But she *was* working on it. "It's just that I'm the only one who knows everything all the time." Grinning, Roxy winked at Astrid, who'd returned to the producer booth, then acknowledged Doyle's cue. "Valentine McCarthy back with you now, feeling so nice and mellow with a wonderful glass of..." She looked at her orange soda. "Chardonnay. Do you have your glass of wine, sugar?" she asked her caller.

"Bourbon," the caller replied flatly.

Doyle tapped on the window between their booths and she glanced over. Plastered to the glass was a cardboard sign reading Control Freak with a dozen exclamation points after it.

She stuck out her tongue at Doyle, then without missing a beat went right back to her caller. "Well, whatever works best for you. Make it a double, if you have to, and while you're doing that let me tell you what I think about your bed-hopping hubby. First, I think his cheating on you is only a fling. Usually is. Just sex. Men don't leave their wives for older women with kids, unless there's a whole lot of money involved. So, does she have money?"

"Not that I know of. She's a waitress, I think."

"Good, that means it's just sex. He's simply out for some exercise. And since he's real busy exercising his male muscle in all the wrong places, you've got a decision to make. Unless you want to go through life getting taken advantage of by a bed-buzzing jerk, you can either kick him out or keep him. Either way, you've got to learn how to respect yourself so you'll believe you don't deserve what he's doing to you.

"So like I said, you can dump the bum. Hold your head

high, walk out that door, take everything you can get your little hands on, and don't look back. He's not worth it. And believe me when I tell you that, because this is an area where Valentine knows what she's talking about." Except when Roxy walked out that marriage door, the only thing in her little hands was the iron resolve to do better without him than she'd done with him. It was all she wanted, all she took. He got the three-legged card table, the brick and board bookshelves—no books, couldn't afford them— and the lumpy mattress on the lumpy floor. A good deal for Roxy all the way around.

She drew in a deep breath, preparing herself to take the other approach—something she always did since most callers didn't want advice, but rather validation for something they wanted to do or had already done. "Or here's another plan that just might work for you. If you love him—and I think you do or you wouldn't be calling trying to figure out how to fix this thing—and you want to keep him around, I think you should teach him a lesson. Revenge is so sweet. Good for the feminine ego, and if you do it the right way he won't go wandering off again." She glanced over at Astrid and smiled. "So which is it?"

"Keep him, give him another chance."

A keeper. Not necessarily *her* personal choice. "And would you like to get even with him? Teach him a lesson that really counts? One he'll remember before he drops his drawers anyplace but home?" In the next booth, Astrid was already *visibly* fretting about the imminent advice. Roxy feigned an innocent shrug. It was Friday night, after all. *Somebody* needed some Friday-night fun. "Because if you do, I've got just the right plan. One he won't be forgetting for a long, long time. I promise you."

"Yesh…"

Just great. One caller half-soused. She couldn't blame her because that's sure what *she'd* do if she had to go public with her life. *Her life…* If she took that public, her listeners would be getting all liquored up from boredom. "So are you ready to start teaching, 'cause this is guaranteed to be a mighty fun lesson."

"Yesh…because I don't want to be pushed around by him anymore. And if I confront him, tell him what I know, he'll just say he's sorry, beg me to forgive him, then we'll be fine until he starts sneaking out again."

On that count, the caller was right. And Roxy was getting herself worked up for some good, on-air two-timer throttling. "You're right. There sure will be a next time. If he gets away with it this time, he'll figure he can go out and do it all over again. Once he's had seconds, he'll want thirds and fourths and it'll never stop."

"So tell me what to do, Doctor Val. I want to get even with the jerk, and I definitely want to teach him a lesson."

Roxy took a drink of her orange soda, then laughed into the microphone. It was a throaty, deep, practiced laugh. A pseudo laugh, one that fit her pseudonym—Doctor Valentine McCarthy. Valentine was her real middle name, McCarthy her married name, although she'd dropped it right after the divorce and hung out her license to practice as Doctor Roxanna Rose, Ph.D. But she liked hiding behind her pseudonym, liked hiding behind her husky pseudo voice, too. And it fit the raven-haired, brown-eyed radio shrink who came out at midnight, talked sex for two hours, then went away to be just plain Roxy again. Make that Roxy with the bright, sunny laugh—cropped-cut, blond-haired, blue-eyed girl next door that she was. Not a thing like her pseudo self, *thank heavens.*

All things considered though, it worked out pretty well. For both of them.

"Well, my advice is simple. Do unto hubby as hubby would do, and apparently has done, unto you. Have yourself a little fling, too. Then let him know about it. Does his honey have a hunky hubby? Maybe *he'd* like to get in on some good extracurricular activity, since his little woman is already getting it on her own. Or does your hubby have a lonely hubba-hubba back at his office, down at the lodge, maybe his best friend? If he does, I say go for a young one if you have a choice—they're so eager and willing to please when it comes to a more experienced woman.

"And that's what you are. More experienced, not older. Also, finding yourself a younger man will definitely let your hubby know that you're not over the hill or otherwise checked at the door, that there's still some mighty good grazing left, even if he isn't the grazer. Oh, and leave the clues, so he'll find them. Be obvious. He deserves it."

"And if I do all of this, Doctor Val, do you think he'll leave me?"

"Honestly, he could. I've gotta be truthful about that. But if he leaves because you're doing unto him, then he wasn't going to stay around, anyway. And if he does leave, you've got options, 'cause you can do a whole lot better. But if he doesn't, I'll bet he'll think twice before he wanders off again, knowing you might be wandering off right behind him. Bottom line, dish the dirt, but have a little fun while you're dishing it. Two more can play at hubby's game besides hubby and his mistress. And call me back, will you? Let me know if it was good for you."

Roxy cued Doyle to bring up the program music. "That answer got me all hot and bothered, thinking about all the exciting possibilities that are waiting for us out there if we care enough to go out and hunt them down. So let me go cool off for a minute, then I'll be right back." She went to break. Two minutes this time.

"Her husband?" Astrid screamed over the microphone into the booth. "You told her to go out and have an affair with her husband's mistress's husband? Come on, Rox. What's wrong with you? That's crazy, even for you!"

"*You* come on, Astrid. When you were dating that guy, Buford, last year, and found out he was sleeping with three other women besides you, didn't you want some revenge? I mean, who was it that stalked him at night and poured syrup and feathers all over his car?"

"Burton, and yes, I wanted revenge. I'll admit it. But that was different. And my revenge could be fixed at a car wash."

"Yeah, you left him the ten-dollar bill under the windshield wiper, you wimp. But what I'm saying here is that the emotion's the same. We get wronged, we want to fight back, whether it's with the guy's girlfriend's hubby or a bottle of syrup. Same thing. And I just gave her an interesting way to fight back. Which she's *not* going to do, Astrid. Human nature. She wants to fix her marriage, not make it worse. But I'm betting she'll let him know, one way or another, that she knows what he's doing. And if her marriage can be worked out, that's the start of it."

"And what if she takes your advice?"

Roxy wrinkled her nose. "Then she might just have some fun. And guess what, I'll bet no one's turning me off at the break right now and going over to that all-night sports talk show. When they're talking home run, they mean home run, but when Valentine talks home run, her callers know exactly what she means."

"I love it when you two fight." Doyle chuckled. "I think people would pay big bucks to see you do it in person…in syrup and feathers."

"Somebody gag him," Roxy yelled, glancing up at the computer screen, checking for the name of the illustrious Doctor Edward Craig. Not there yet. Kind of a surprise because the spicier calls always brought him out.

"Gag *you*, next time you pull something like that," Astrid muttered. "And next time you want something to drink, get it yourself."

"She's baiting him," Doyle quipped. "That doctor dude. That's just her way of asking him to come out and play."

"And he's ringing the bell right now," Astrid announced over her microphone. Part of her job was to screen the calls—letting in the good, keeping out the bad. And her order was to always move the self-important Doctor Edward Craig right to the top of the call-in queue. Not because Roxy particularly liked him, because she didn't. But the ratings! He brought 'em, she loved 'em. A match made in broadcaster's heaven.

"So maybe I bait him a little…."

"A little?" Doyle sputtered. "Honey, you throw out the chum and he eats it up like a hungry shark. And you enjoy it, even if you won't admit it."

"Oh, yeah. I enjoy it all right. Just like brussels sprouts. My mom fixes me brussels sprouts when I go home and I eat them because I have to, but they give me gas." Roxy thought about Doyle's notion that she liked the great Eddie Craig's calls, then dismissed it as ludicrous. He was a sprout, that's all. Necessary, not gratifying. And he did cause a fair amount of gastric upset from time to time, even though somehow she always managed to walk away satisfied. In a professional sense, of course.

"Come on, Eddie, let's see what you've got cooking for me tonight," she said, checking his name on the monitor. Yep, he was there, first name on the top of the list, and ready to go. "Whatever it is, it's going to be way better than brussels sprouts."

"Good evening, Valentine. You're in rare form tonight."

At the sound of his voice, Roxy wrinkled her nose at Astrid. The man did come on so darn strident sometimes. Like sending her copies of the fifteen billion books he'd written—the ones still in the carton in the trunk of her car. *Unopened.* "Good evening, Doctor Craig. And let me just correct one thing you said before we go any further. I'm *always* in rare form. Not just tonight." Something about his voice, that little Boston/British accent thing he had going on, made her voice go even sexier than her normal Valentine sexy. If dark chocolate could talk, it would sound like Edward Craig.

Roxy glanced down at the dark-chocolate truffle on her desk. Every night, right about this time, she got the craving.

"Rare form, maybe. But rare doesn't necessarily mean good. Not when you do such a disservice to your listeners with your advice."

"My advice, Doctor Craig?"

"Keep it nice," Astrid warned over the headphones. "We've got a couple of potential new sponsors listening in."

Roxy slapped a sweet smile on her face just for Astrid's benefit. "My advice, Doctor Craig, is what my listeners want. Or they wouldn't call me, would they." She felt a chill, awaiting his voice. Strange effect, but it happened a lot. She chalked it up to the adrenalin rush of a battle. "So what would *you* have me do?"

"I'd have you give the previous caller sound advice instead—"

"Yeah, yeah, *Eddie*," Roxy interrupted. "We know your broken record. Get counseling, get counseling. But what good's counseling going to do a cheating husband? It's not a problem in his head. It's in his pants. Actually, let me rephrase that. There wouldn't be a problem if it *was* in his pants. You know a counselor's going to charge her a couple hundred bucks an hour, and you know as well as I do that cheating hubbys don't go to counseling. So she goes there by herself, plunks down all that money, and for what?"

"To fix her marriage."

"Might be better spent if she could *fix* her hubby. But that's not going to happen, so what I'm suggesting is an inexpensive alternative—revenge sex, *Doctor*."

"And you really believe a knee-jerk reaction like revenge sex, *Doctor*, is sound advice for working through an indiscretion? By the way, do you really think revenge sex is a good label to put on what you're advocating? That oversimplifies a serious problem."

"Knee-jerk?" Instinctively, she looked down. The left knee of her jeans had a hole in it. The right was frayed. Not exactly the Valentine image she put out there. "And whatever do you mean by *sound* advice? Personally, I think my advice *sounded* awfully good. Oh, and if you don't like to call it revenge sex, I'll be glad to go with make-good sex, getting-even sex, do-unto-cheatin'-hubby sex. Take your pick." This was getting particularly good between them tonight. Somehow she'd known it might when she'd given that little piece of revenge-sex advice to the caller.

"And you don't think the wife plays a part in the husband's actions?"

Oh, Eddie. You really opened yourself up with that one. Roxy glanced over at Astrid and winked. "A wife may play a part in the marital problems, but you and I both know it's not always marital problems that send a man into another woman's bed. So unless the wife actually drives her husband to his mistress's door, and says, 'There you go, dear. Go have a good time, and I'll be back in an hour to get you,' she's not playing a part in his cheating. It's a solo gig, Doc. He opened that door by himself, and he walked through it, and claiming she pushed him through it is a cop-out. Bottom line is, when he's cheating it's all about sex. Motivations don't matter. So if that's what it's about for him, why can't it be about that for her? I certainly think the first time he drops his pants for someone else he's inviting his wife to do the same, if that's what she wants to do."

Edward let out an impatient breath meant to be heard on air. "Having an affair because she's been hurt—what will that accomplish, *Doctor*, except to cause more hurt?"

"Sex, *Doctor*. Not an affair. And the only hurt it could

possibly cause—since she's a consenting adult—will be her husband's, who deserves to be hurt for what he's done to her. Like they say, an eye for an eye…or in this case…a romp for a romp."

"Which will drag her down to her husband's level. That, Valentine, solves nothing."

Which was true, at least in Roxy's thinking. But Roxy's thinking wasn't Valentine's, and sometimes that little tug-of-war got rough. But, all for the ratings… "Quite the contrary, Doctor. It will serve as a catharsis. Surely, as a shrink, you realize the value of a good catharsis every now and then, don't you?"

"As a *shrink*, Doctor McCarthy, surely you realize that catharsis is not an act of revenge, but an act of release—"

"And a good orgasm's not a release, Eddie? If that's what you think, then I'd say you don't get around too much, do you?"

"An emotional release," Edward said defensively, then nervously cleared his throat. "I'm talking about an emotional release, if you can forget about the sex for a minute."

"Forget about the sex?" Roxy replied in her deepest, huskiest, sexiest voice. "Doesn't sound like you've been having too much fun." Roxy smiled, impressing a mental mark in her imaginary column. "Like I said before, you must not get around, because an orgasm can be as much of an emotional release as a physical one, and there are studies to back me up on that one, *Doctor*." She added a second mark. "Think about it…Edward. Think about the last time you enjoyed that release…with another person, I mean." She scrunched her nose at Astrid, at the thought of the pompous Doctor Craig indulging in that scenario. "Wasn't it a wonderfully satisfying emotional surrender, as well as the obvious physical enjoyment?"

"It might have been, but this isn't about me, *Doctor*," he said, his voice so dark-chocolate it gave her goose bumps.

She glanced at her truffle. Never, ever until *after* Edward, but she wanted it so bad right now. "Isn't it, *Doctor?*" she purred, claiming her third mark. "It's about your ideas of right and wrong, which, like it or not, are affected by your life, your loves, your sexual experiences, and vice versa. My caller was hurt, she needed to vent, and yes, she needs to feel like she has some control in the matter. As a relationship counselor you know this, or you should. What I suggested, Eddie—a little revenge sex—gives her back some of that control. To me, that's a pretty simple solution. You know what they say about two playing that game, and maybe when her husband finds out she's been playing—and you know he'd never suspect she would, men never do—he might just rethink his playing if he wants that marriage to work out. If he doesn't and he leaves, she's better off without him."

"Adultery, Doctor McCarthy, is never the solution. Not to any problem. It's only a means to compound it."

It was time to end this now. He was drifting off into levelheaded land, where it was hard to combat his real logic with Val sense. Meaning she had to cut him off before Edward succeeded in besting Valentine. That was not what her listeners wanted.

Roxy drew in a steadying breath, and looked to Astrid for her end-the-segment signal, but instead got the stretch sign, meaning she was going to have to roll this all the way to the next commercial break. "Adultery isn't an issue for the husband, since he started it, Doctor, so don't make it an issue for the wife, too." She twisted toward Astrid, and gave her the slash-throat signal, but Astrid shook her head.' Roxy shook *her* head emphatically, but Astrid countered with a nod to which Roxy mouthed the words, "You're fired." Astrid responded with a gesture Roxy knew was coming and turned away from before she saw it.

"I wouldn't have to make it an issue for the wife, Doctor McCarthy, if you hadn't given her license to go out and do what feels good simply as a way of getting back at her husband. But you did, and now..."

"And now nothing," she countered. "It's sex, Doctor Craig. Sex for the sake of getting even. Nooky for nooky, and that's all it is, so don't blow it out of proportion, okay?" A little over the top, she thought. Roxy had personal reactions. Val didn't. Not ever. So, it was time to take a deep breath, refocus and bring Val back to the front of the line before Roxy went reactionary again and torpedoed the ratings.

"You know, Edward..." She whispered his name this time. Drew it out, turned it into husky need and silk sheets and promises. "It's Friday...a little after midnight now. You should be in bed with someone...in bed and making mad, passionate love. You should be sweaty, and gasping for air, and on the verge of an orgasm so explosive you can literally feel the earth move. And afterwards, you should be sipping champagne in a bubble bath with her...I'm assuming it's a her...and kissing her toes, feeling that familiar stirring down under the bubbles...the stirring that won't let you make it all the way back to the bed this time. But you're not. You're on the phone debating sexual advice with a radio psychologist instead of indulging in some of those mighty fine pleasures yourself...pleasures I would certainly be indulging in if I weren't working." Yeah, right. Pleasures she hadn't had since—she couldn't remember when. "So I'm wondering, Doctor Edward Craig, why aren't you?"

She shut her eyes, envisioning a wildly sexy Doctor Craig on her beach—she always envisioned him as wildly sexy— then jerked her eyes back open and glanced at Astrid, imploring her to end this thing. Which Astrid did with a slash gesture across her throat, laughing at the same time. Just in the nick of time, because that last image on the beach took deep root, wouldn't go away even when her eyes were open.

"It's not always about sex, Valentine," Edward continued. "Sometimes it's about making love. And that, my dear, is always the best sex, physically and emotionally. But we'll save those fine distinctions for another night, if that's okay with you." With that, he clicked off.

The image of him on her beach still floating around in her head, Roxy grudgingly gave him a mark for that last remark. He deserved one every now and then. After all, Edward Craig translated into good rating points.

And good fantasies, when she let him. Very good fantasies.

"Be right back, sugars," she said to her listeners. Then she grabbed the truffle, popped it into her mouth, and sank back into her chair to savor the taste.

2

Still Later, and Not a Creature Was Stirring, Except…

DRIP…DRIP…DRIP. Roxy shifted her stare from the computer screen, where she was designing the Rose Palace—her future home on the Sound—to the leaky kitchen faucet. An upright, with a nice, graceful, swan-curved neck and one handle. Drip! "Damn," she muttered. She'd called that maintenance guy about it twice now. Begged him to come de-drip the durn thing. She'd been pretty blunt about how much it was annoying her, too, and how she really needed him over there as soon as possible. Which was yesterday, when it wasn't even so much of an annoying drip as an occasional one.

So what if her call did have the dual purpose of drip-busting *and* getting an up-close and personal look at the man? Preferably from behind. Admittedly, she'd watched him a time or two. Or more. From the peephole in her door, from the elevator, in the lobby. He was the kind worth stopping and staring at. Gorgeous bod. Tight. She was betting six-pack abs under his T-shirt. A real appealing package in her 3D life—dull, dreary, dismal—even if all she got to do was look. Looking was good, though. Safe. Uninvolved. Easy.

Too bad she hadn't taken that road the first time. But the appeal of a starving artist had seemed romantic at age twenty. Wore off fast, thank heavens. Funny how her working three jobs so that he could stare out the loft window and think about painting had a way of doing that.

So now she only looked. And Mr. Handyman was a looker well worth the effort. She was thanking her leaky swan-necked for choosing to slaver at that propitious moment, even if, so far, the plumbing Galahad had not come running to her watery rescue. All things considered, she thought she'd been pretty patient about waiting for him to haul his lethally fabulous butt through her front door to obliterate that damned dribble. But now it was getting ridiculous. The drip was running amuck and Roxy was actually more interested in a solution than the butt! Such a sad state of affairs. And pathetic.

Pathetic but true, Roxy. Admit it. Here it was, 3:30 a.m., and the damnable drippity-drip was so loud she just knew her snoopy neighbor on the other side of the wall would start banging out a Beethoven symphony. From day one in her apartment—was it only a month now?—he, she or whatever had pounded whenever Roxy sneezed, blinked, or when the light in her fridge came on. She did try hard to stay mouse quiet. Didn't wear shoes, listened to music only through headphones, didn't swing from the chandelier. The wee hours had always been good to her, and getting home at two-thirty every morning all wide-eyed and raring to do anything other than sleep furnished her with oodles of time to design her new house.

Until she moved in here. And Mr. Gorgeous Handyman cruising the hall in his drop-dead tool belt didn't offset the inconvenience of having her nights interrupted by the Pounder.

Her house.... Roxy smiled, just thinking about it. It would be good. Better than that, it would be all hers with her own personal brand on every single aspect of it. She liked that, the total control, at least at this stage of the planning. The house that Roxy built, or would build, as soon as he got over here and took care of that demon drip from the very bowels of hydrous hell. It was driving her insane right now, not to mention ruining her creativity! And just when she was all set to choose between marble or granite on the...no, wait. That couldn't be right. Marble or granite dining room chairs? Where'd the bathroom vanity go?

That demented demon drip stole it!

Roxy's gaze shifted back over to the culpable faucet, the one devising its next move against her, and she scrunched her face into an I-dare-you-to-drip-one-more-time glare. Fat lot of good that did, because at that very moment the fiendish faucet morphed itself into a living, breathing entity, one blatantly defying her to do something about it. *Okay bitch, you asked for it. Take this...* Drip! One single, solitary drip! A laugh! That's what it was. The faucet Lucifer was laughing at her. Ddd...ri...ppp! This time an exclamation point after the laugh! "That does it," she snapped. Roxy stormed across the kitchen floor and smacked the faucet with her open palm. "Ouch," she squealed, pulling her hand back and shaking it. Didn't phase the drip at all. In fact, the dribbles started coming in punctuated pairs. *Drip, drip! Ha, ha, ha! Drip, drip! Ha, ha, ha! Double-drip dare ya!*

Of course, Pounder on the other side of the wall started right up.

"Now I lay me down to sleep, I pray the Lord for earplugs, please," Roxy muttered, pulling open her junk drawer to see if anything in it was up to the task of silencing the one-handled dribble monster. A wrench, a sledgehammer, a stick of dynamite! As she expected, though, there wasn't a single, solitary usable thing in there—only a red plastic flashlight with dead batteries, naturally, some emergency candles with no matches, of course, and a fistful of wooden skewer sticks, not that she'd ever skewered a thing in her life. Well, maybe Pounder once or twice...in her dreams. But nothing labeled drip-fixer.

Frustrated that a pipe wrench hadn't magically materi-alized when she needed it, Roxy started to slam the drawer shut, but caught herself in the nick of time, gently push-ing it back into its place lest the wall-banging dervish on the other side started all over. Then she glared at the dreaded wall, "I hate this place, I hate this place." Close her eyes, click her heels three times and maybe she'd land in the Rose Palace.

But mercifully, this apartment was only a temp—a ref-uge from the rodents and roaches and fleas, oh my! in her former apartment. And it was a quick hop to work as well—a stopgap until the Rose Palace was built, which she hoped wouldn't be more than a year down the road. Provided *he*, the fixer of drips, ever got his pipe wrench over here.

Drip…ka-drip…ka-drip…drrrripppp…

"Okay, that's it!" Roxy didn't care what time it was. She'd already been reasonable with the guy, it didn't work, so now it was time for him to come play on her turf dur-ing *her* hours. And she had his number. Right at the top of an important phone numbers list stuck to her fridge, just below her fave food deliveries—pizza first, then Chinese. So, *he* was about to make a little home delivery himself, substituting tool belt for pepperoni, and a pipe wrench for egg roll. It was time for Mr. Dazzling Derriere to get over there and prove just what he was good for, other than fill-ing out his jeans in some really unbelievable ways.

"Six-three-three," Roxy repeated the phone number from the list as she dialed. "You'd better be home…with *all* your tools ready to go." She drummed her fingers im-patiently on the countertop as the first four rings went by unanswered. By the sixth ring, she was tapping her right foot. "Two more rings, then I'm going to…"

"Hello." The voice was a little jagged, a little thick, a whole lot gruff. And sexier than anything she'd ever heard at 3:38 in the morning. Or any other time of the morning, for that matter. This guy could be worth two truffles, she thought. *But I'll trade you two truffles for one fixed drip.* That's how desperate she was!

"Is this building maintenance? You *are* the handyman, aren't you?" She didn't even know his name. Hadn't bothered asking. No need, since enjoying the marvelous view had been more than enough for her—until now.

"Call back in the morning."

Certainly not a very friendly response for someone who dealt with the public, Roxy thought. "In the morning I'll need an ark. You don't happen to have one handy, do you? Or some bailing buckets?"

"Huh?"

"My faucet's leaking. More like gushing all over the place. By morning my apartment's going to be flooded." Well, maybe that was a slight exaggeration, but demented drips called for desperate measures. "I need someone to come over here *right now* to fix it, before it starts leaking through the floor into the apartment below." Well, maybe another teensy, weensy exaggeration. But if that's what it would take to get him over there…

"Do you know what time it is, lady?" He was making no attempt to hide his irritation. "Because if this isn't an emergency…" Bordering on downright hostile. But still so sexy she was thinking junk food. Always the infallible substitute.

"Well…" Roxy shrugged, then looked at the bug-eyed, tail-ticking cat clock on the wall. "Yep, I know exactly what time it is. I know what time it was when I called before—both times. And I called at respectable times then—you know, during the day, when you had that message on your voice mail saying to leave a message, that you'd call right back. But that didn't work, did it? Since you never called back, and you never came over. So this time I thought if I called in the middle of the night when you'd probably be sleeping, I could wake you up and talk to you directly." Roxy shut her eyes, trying to conjure up his sleeping image. Dark and brooding, hair tousled, sheet coming up only to his waist. Strong arms, naked chest... He wasn't wearing a stitch of clothing under the sheet because men like that always slept in the nude. Or they should, anyway. Damn waste of a lot of good maleness if they didn't. God, she needed a Twinkie. "And since you're up right now, why don't you come on over here and do something about the drip? Okay?" With or without clothes.

"I'll put you on the list for first thing in the morning," he grumbled.

A turndown? He was actually refusing after she pleaded her case so eloquently? Well, that wasn't good enough. If she had to suffer the drip, so did he. Roxy gritted her teeth for the next round. "Which is when? Nine o'clock? Ten o'clock? It can't wait that long. It's already oozing through the floorboards. You'll be getting a call from my downstairs neighbor any minute."

"Then go stick your finger in the dike, lady. That'll hold it until morning."

Roxy's foot began its impatient tapping again. At this rate there really would be a flood before he got over there. "So, will a bribe work on you?" she blurted into the phone. Drip, drip. "Anything I have, short of sexual favors." Of course, if he came over there the way she'd pictured him in bed... "Just please, come and take care of it right now. Okay? Or bring me a pipe wrench so I can do it myself."

"You ever used a pipe wrench, lady?"

"Well, no. But how hard could it be? You clamp it on the pipe then twist."

"All that leaks isn't in the pipe."

"Hey, I've got plenty of Bob Vila tapes and I know how to use them." The only response to what she thought was a reasonable request was an audible, and very vexed, sigh. So she continued. "And if you let me use your tool I'll promise not to ever call you at three-thirty in the morning again."

"Three-forty," he grunted. "And no way in hell are you touching my *tool*."

Touching his tool… Boy, oh boy, the ideas that came with that. The ideas and the images. *You wish I'd touch your tool, Mr. Handyman!* "Three-forty," she agreed. "So if your tool is off-limits, that means you're coming over and doing it yourself. Right?" It was beginning to sound promising, from a purely plumbing perspective, of course.

"Who the hell are you, and where the hell do you live?"

So he wasn't very friendly. Brooding and temperamental types were good, too. Especially when they packed a pipe wrench. And right now, the wrench was all she really wanted. "Roxy Rose. Apartment five-B."

"Five minutes." Then he hung up.

Five minutes—just enough time for him to get dressed. Damn! Another fantasy shot to pieces.

On her way from the kitchen into the dining nook she used as her office, Roxy passed by a large hall mirror and stopped, then hopped up on a plastic step to appraise her face. Whoever had hung that mirror must have been hanging it for Amazon women, because in her full five-foot-two glory she could just barely see her face. In fact, the mirror chopped her off at the nose, giving her a clear shot only of her eyes and forehead. So she'd bought the step. Easy solution. Just the way she liked things—easy.

Roxy smiled at the reflection and pushed her tangle of uncombed hair back from her face. "It's a natural look, trendy-chic," she always claimed, when friends asked why it was sticking out in odd directions, different odd directions. Truth was, she didn't like the bother of fixing it, and she'd owned that disarrayed look long before it *had* become trendy-chic. "Oh well," she sighed. "It's not like this is a date." Besides, no one had ever accused her of being a trendsetter—not in Roxy-mode. Roxy was no-fuss, no-muss, no makeup, with no particular concern over it. Trendy was Val's gig, one she used for special appearances, photo shoots and the like. Geez, those mugs of her on the city buses. All over Seattle. Here a Valentine, there a Valentine, everywhere a Valentine. And all those billboards. Yikes! There were certain stretches of road she assiduously avoided because she loathed and detested being looked down upon by the pseudo-her camouflaged up to fit the public perception.

Hopping off the step, Roxy wondered if now would be a good time to get Mr. Beautiful Buns to lower the mirror, since he was already going to be there with his tools. Doesn't hurt to ask, she decided, kicking her step back to the wall. Probably wouldn't hurt to throw on a tighter T-shirt, either.

"Who's there?"

"It's three forty-five, lady. Who do you think it is?"

"Can you show me some identification please—slip it under the door?"

"Lady, the only ID I have on me is my pipe wrench. So open up or I'm going back to bed."

Smiling, she knew what ID she wanted to see. Yeah, like she'd really ask him to turn around so she could take a look. *Only in your dreams, Rox.* "Well, hold out that pipe wrench where I can see it," she said, opening the door an inch. And there it was, his tool thrust right out there at her, and right behind it bare chest. Bare chest every bit as good as his backside. The she-gods were loving her tonight because this was pure, glorious male potency at its best. "Okay, I'm going to trust that that's a pipe wrench." Not that she had even looked at the wrench.

"It's a pipe wrench, lady, so do you want me coming in

and using it, because I'm two seconds away from going back across the hall to bed. Which is where I should have stayed in the first place."

Mercy, mercy, please come in and use it. "Across the hall, as in you're my neighbor?" Through the crack in the door, Roxy's eyes wandered from his chest, down the low-riding jeans to his bare feet then back up to his chest. Hairless—somewhat surprising, since men with black hair usually had a fine mat on their chest. But his chest was boldly bare, showing off his flat, rippled stomach. *Oh, my heavens, a six-pack!* "I guess I've just been too busy to meet—"

"Your leak, lady?" he interrupted, his lack of interest in neighborly chitchat made abundantly clear by his testy intonation.

Roxy's eyes went back up to his face. Except for the furious scowl it wasn't bad—not bad at all. Probably the first time she'd looked past his...endowments, and she sure liked what she was seeing. Whiskey-brown eyes, dark eyebrows, and that nighttime shadow of stubble. *Now, that would be something real nice to wake up to.* She remembered waking up to Bruce. He looked more like the bad end of a mop in the mornings. "Please come in...um...neighbor." She unlatched the chain, opened the door and pointed to the kitchen. "It's through the living room..."

"I know where the kitchen is," he snapped, his testiness booting up another notch.

"I guess you would...did you mention your name, by the way?"

"Ned," he grunted in passing. "Ned Proctor."

"Well, Ned Proctor. Welcome to my apartment." Stepping back as he whooshed by, Roxy caught a trace of his scent. *He smells great, too. Could this get any better?* He was like a fresh splash of something bold and virile, unlike her one and only date in the past three months. What was his name? Michael? Or was it Rupert? Whichever...he'd shown up smelling like an array of discount cologne samples, and she'd sneezed her way around the first block with him before jumping out of his car and hoofing it all the way home—in the fresh air. It took a whole month for her aching sinuses to completely recover from that redolent attack.

"It's been driving me insane," she said, watching from the doorway while he tried to manipulate the faucet's single handle to stop the drip. "And that won't work. I've tried." For Ned, it was scarcely dripping now. Barely one drop every five seconds, and a puny little drip at that. An ugly plumbing conspiracy meant to make her look silly.

"You couldn't have lived with *that drip* until morning, *Mizzz* Rose?" Glancing down at the floor, he shook his head, letting out the impatient sigh she was already coming to know quite well. "It's not exactly pouring over, getting ready to flood the apartment below, is it?"

"I'm on…a project. All the dripping was breaking my concentration."

Frowning, Ned glanced across at Roxy's makeshift, make-a-house desk area next to the pantry. "It needs a washer, and I don't have a washer." He tucked his tool in the waistband of his jeans and headed for the door. "Tomorrow."

"Tomorrow? Come on, Ned. I've been calling you for days."

"One day, two times," he grunted. "And you were on the list."

"Well, I don't want to go back on the list."

"First thing in the morning."

"I sleep all morning."

"Then I guess you'll know what it's like to be awaken during a sound sleep, won't you?"

Not to be thwarted on this, the night of her bathroom design, Roxy scooted in next to Ned and yanked at the faucet handle impatiently, hoping to… Well, she wasn't sure

what she hoped to do other than what he wasn't doing—
which was fixing it. But the only thing that happened was
a drip that doubled in both frequency and resonance. "So,
now what?"

"I'd tell you to live with it, but that's not going to get
me back to bed any quicker, is it?"

"My contract said maintenance emergencies twenty-
four seven. All I need is a lousy washer."

"All you needed *was* a lousy washer, lady. Heck if I
know what it needs now, and I'm not going to find out
until morning. What time did you say you get up?"

"Ten."

"Then I'll be here at eight." He grinned at her. "G'night."

"But what about the leak?"

"Wrap a towel around it, for Pete's sake." He pulled the
pipe wrench out of his waistband and handed it to her.
"I've changed my mind…be my guest."

The wrench slipped from his hand and landed with a hol-
low thunk on the old wood-and-linoleum countertop. "Well,
now you've done it," Roxy warned, her face poker-straight.

"Done what?" he asked.

"Ten…nine…eight…seven…" Pounder next door
started up on the five count, and the beat went on for
nearly half a minute. "That," she said, smiling. "That's
what I was warning you about. And this." She opened a
drawer then shut it, not particularly loud, either. With that
came the encore, a sequence half again as long as the first
chorus, accented, at the end of the performance, by one last
clap that knocked an old, black trivet right off Roxy's wall
and into the sink. "So like I was saying, Ned," Roxy continued, without missing a beat, "it's driving me nuts—the
dripping—and I have a lot of work to do tonight, and if
you can please stop it for me, I'd be grateful."

"How often does *that* happen?" he asked, nodding at
the wall.

Roxy shrugged. "Not more than three, four times a night." Grinning, "Someone over there's a Listening Tom. Too bad for them it's only my kitchen and not my bedroom." Yeah, right. Sounds from the Roxy Rose boudoir were guaranteed to put anybody to sleep, including Roxy Rose herself.

Ned cleared his throat, turning back around to face the sink. "And what do you do every night to annoy her? Georgette Selby's her name, by the way. She's eighty-two. Sweet. Bakes chocolate chip cookies. Used to be a schoolteacher."

"Normally, it's just breathing." Roxy grabbed up the pipe wrench, but he yanked it away from her. "Once in a while I eat Twinkies, and I have this little TMJ thing in my jaw…it sort of pops occasionally."

Stepping back over to the sink, wrench in hand, Ned bumped into Roxy. "I'm going to bend down now, Miss Rose. Take a look under the sink. If you don't mind moving back…"

Did she mind stepping back to get a better look at him bending down? About as much as she minded chocolate and orgasms and lots of money. "Just trying to see what you're doing so I can do it myself next time. So tell me what you're doing," she said, struggling to reign herself back in.

"Turning off the water at the valve. That'll stop the drip and when I get back over here at seven-thirty…"

"Eight."

"*Seven*, I'll get everything fixed up the right way."

"Think it's gonna work for tonight? No more drip?" The valve handle was tight and she watched him put extra muscle into his next twist—translating into something so sexy on his backside that it almost made Roxy squirm right out of her skin. Damn those baby-making hormones, anyway. They sure were in overdrive tonight. *Success now, the rest later*, she reminded herself. "Need another…" a slight tuchus wiggle caused her to gulp "...another tool?" she sputtered. *Okay, Rox. Success now, blah, blah, blah. Remember?*

"There!" he declared, rather than answering her question. "That should hold it, temporarily." Ned's head had barely cleared the open space under the sink when the valve groaned a plumbing obscenity, then let the full force of a geyser rip, shooting water everywhere—the walls, the ceiling, Roxy, Ned. Springing to his feet, Ned yanked the faucet handle, only to have it break off in his hand. No simple fixes now. It was a full-out water cataclysm in need of some instantaneous plumbing surgery, and Ned's only surgical instrument or know-how, it seemed, was a pipe wrench that clunked to the floor when he leapt back from the deluge.

Scrambling to avoid the fat force of the spray, lest she be caught up in a full-frontal wet T-shirt look, Roxy darted into the bathroom, grabbed up an armful of towels, and dashed back into the kitchen only to find Ned standing there in the middle of Niagara Falls clutching a cell phone, staring down at his pipe wrench. "Don't just stand there," she cried. "Stop it. Turn something. Or plug something up."

Ned shrugged. "The plumber will be here in a few minutes."

Shaking her head, Roxy stared at the kitchen wall, awaiting the inevitable. And sure enough, before she could even blink, Georgette "Pounder" Selby commenced doing her thing, this time, it seemed, with two fists, and perhaps, a foot.

3

Monday Night and All Is Dry

"WELL, HE'S NOT BAD to look at, but with a pipe wrench he's lethal, and not in a good way." Three nights since the great flood and Roxy's apartment still wasn't back to normal. To his credit, Ned had sent in a water damage restoration crew, and nothing was permanently ruined. Just soggy.

"And he didn't come back after he did all that?" Astrid handed Roxy the broadcast notes for the night. Nothing out of the ordinary—a new sponsor, a proposal from station management to add another hour of programming at the top end of her show, which didn't make a whole lot of sense since her show was called *Midnight Special* and not *Eleven o'clock Special.* "They might as well make me drive-time," she snorted. Drive-time, either morning or afternoon, was a coveted slot. But a deadly one for Roxy's show since her late-night topics weren't even close to drive-time subject matter.

"They know you won't do it," Astrid said, "but they keep hoping."

"They're lucky they get two hours of me a night. And they know that!" Of course, she was lucky to get those two hours, and *she* knew *that.* Hiring someone who'd jumped right from clinical counselor to talk-show host in the blink of an eye, and without any radio experience, had been a big risk for her station owners. And now, backing her in a syndication deal, and letting her continue to broadcast from their facilities was a heck of a nice thing to do. Of course, she would own that show, with a piece of it going to Astrid and generous compensation to her station owners, so it was a win-win thing all the way around. She hoped. Gosh, did she hope.

"So you said he wasn't wearing a shirt when he came over?" Astrid waved at Doyle who was settling into his chair in the engineering booth, ready to scarf down a pizza.

"Nothing but jeans, and I swear..." she raised her hand into the air as if swearing a solemn oath "...I was good. I mean this guy is...like...the best thing you've ever had in your dreams—or fantasies—right there in my apartment in the middle of the night. And all I can do is stand there practically drooling. Not that he would have noticed." Roxy waved at Doyle, too, then sat down in her chair. Still thirty minutes until air. She spread out her latest house plans on the desk. Coming along pretty well, except that aviary where the kitchen should go. "Then I didn't even see him in the hall all weekend. Not once. I mean, he's right across from me, so I kept watching, but I don't think he even opened his door all weekend. Worse than that, he sent this big, burly plumber over—the kind whose pants didn't quite make it up to his belt line by a good four inches. Believe me, that's not the bare butt I wanted to be seeing in my kitchen. But it's fixed, so I may never see him again. The handyman, not the plumber, who I *never* want to see again."

"So unfix something," Astrid suggested. "Then call him back over."

Roxy laughed. "You've been hanging around me too long. I already did that this morning. The bedroom window doesn't seem to open anymore. Imagine that."

"Bedroom?" Astrid raised her eyebrows. "Nothing subtle about that, is there?"

"Mind if I interrupt you two with some work matters and do sound levels now?" Doyle asked, still chewing his last bite.

"Check away," Roxy answered, then laughed. "Which is what I'll be saying to Mr. Pipe Wrench in a few hours, I hope."

"In the middle of the night again?" Astrid asked.

"Best time. Just ask Doctor Val. I think for once the two of us would agree on something." Roxy folded her latest house plans and crammed them in her canvas briefcase. "I think I may have to go buy another home design program. This one seems to have some kinks in it."

"Could you squeeze in a couple of promos before we go on?" Astrid asked. Then turning to the engineering booth window, she asked Doyle, "Think we could get them in? I know I shouldn't be springing this on you at the last minute, but management wants a couple of spots to stick on in evening drive-time. They think it'll tap a new audience."

"Always drive-time," Roxy sighed. "But if it brings 'em in, what the heck."

"Just give me five, and I'll be good to go," Doyle called back.

One pizza slice left, he was obviously debating whether to cram it down or leave it for later. Knowing Doyle, he'd go for the cram and order a whole 'nother pizza for later. "Extra cheese," Roxy said. "Thin crust. I'll buy."

He winked at her before he bit into the last slice. "You bet you will, *sugar*."

"Here's the copy. Go over it a couple of times before you do it." Astrid plunked some papers down in front of Roxy.

"I prefer to *do* it spontaneously," Roxy called after her.

"Just as long as you get the name in…"

"I know. Five times."

"Seven, if you can. Plus the time it comes on."

"Like anybody listening in drive-time will still be up to hear me." These were the people who did Monday through Friday, nine to five. According to market research they were heading to bed after the eleven o'clock news, so there was no chance she was reaching the right audience with drive-time promos. But free advertising was free advertising. "So Doyle, are you ready?"

"For you, babe, I'm always ready. Let me cue up then I'll give you the count."

He was on the five count when Roxy picked up her copy and looked at it for the first time.

"One," from Doyle.

"Good evening, sugars. This is Doctor Val reminding you to tune in tonight as we talk about love, sex, and all the other little things that rock your world…and mine." Including a building maintenance man who was a solid ten on the rock scale. "I promise to have an extra-specially good show for you tonight, but you won't know how good until you turn me on." Ad-lib time because the rest of it was drivel. "And I do so want you to turn me on." Much better. Much more Val. "So stop by and check me out on *Midnight Special* at…well, midnight. The best hour of every night for *everything*. I'll be waiting for you, sugars."

Doyle gave her the cut sign, and Roxy wadded the copy and lobbed it into the trash. "I know, I only got the name in once, but they'll get the drift."

"*And I do so want you to turn me on,*" Doyle mimicked. "Doctor Val, raising erections all over the interstate. I can just see all the accident reports. So is the next promo better than this one?"

"Aren't you the critic?" Astrid snapped at Doyle.

"Hey, I call 'em as I hear 'em." Doyle gave the cue sign for the next promo just as Roxy slid the copy sideways until it flittered down into the trash can. One more ad-lib coming up, but this one all the way.

"Hello out there in rush-hour traffic. This is Doctor Val with two pieces of advice for you. One is listen to my program, *Midnight Special*. You'll be amazed what you'll hear in grown-up time when we can talk about the good things, the sexy things you'll never hear on your way home from work. And the other piece of advice is drive naked, sugars. Makes the whole experience much more fun, especially if everybody else commuting right along with you is driving naked, too. So try it, then call me tonight at midnight and let me know if it was good for you, 'cause, if I'm the one commuting next to you, I'll be watching, and it'll sure be good for me. *Midnight Special* every night at...midnight."

Roxy turned to Astrid. "Got the name in more."

"And you've got two minutes to do the right one," Astrid yelled from her glass booth. "Doyle, erase that last mess and get ready for the correct promo."

"Yeah, Doyle," Roxy said, grudgingly grabbing the copy from the trash. "Cue me up to do the really good one. The one that will put everybody to sleep."

Smiling, he gave her the sign, and Roxy read, "This is Doctor Val reminding you to listen to *Midnight Special* every weeknight at midnight. On *Midnight Special* we're full of all kinds of surprises..." She couldn't help herself. "And on *Midnight Special* we like to talk real dirty. Lots of sex on *Midnight Special*. So if you like sex, if that's what makes you hot at midnight, you'd better tune in and listen to just how hot it can get on *Midnight Special*. 'Cause sugars, Valentine gets hot every night on *Midnight Special*. That's *Midnight Special* every weeknight at midnight." She made a slashing gesture at Doyle and grinned at Astrid. "Seven times, count them. So is that better?"

"After work, the real thing. And Doyle's locking the doors so you can't get away," Astrid grumbled, sitting down in her chair.

"You didn't really expect me to stick to plain old boring, did you?" Roxy countered.

"Boring pays the—"

"I know," Roxy said. "It pays the bills, but it doesn't attract the listeners. And without listeners, there's no program, and without a program we're all slapping burgers on a grill somewhere down on the waterfront." Astrid with her business degree, Doyle with one in engineering and Roxy's in psychology—the trio couldn't flip a burger together. But the burger-flipping imagery was good, she thought. "So I do what I have to do to keep us in this job." She laughed. "And deep down you know I'm right, even though you won't admit it. So just edit it, okay? Whatever you thinks works."

"Five minutes," Doyle said.

Roxy glanced up at the clock, wondering momentarily if Doctor Craig would be calling tonight. For sure he would if her ad-libbed, driving naked promo made it out on the air. Too bad Doyle had erased it.

Then briefly, Roxy imagined Ned Proctor driving naked.

ALMOST MIDNIGHT. He was tempted to turn on the radio and listen to the reigning queen of babble, since his plan to wander across the hall and ask Roxy Rose how her plumbing was doing went down the dumper when she went out a couple of hours ago. Going back across the hall... He'd been wanting to do that for several days now, but he needed some distance between himself and that whole humiliating faucet incident. What was he thinking, anyway, strapping on a tool belt and playing handyman? "Good disguise, Ned," he muttered, plodding to the fridge for a beer. Three now, on an empty stomach, and he was getting a little buzz. But he didn't care, since all he was going to do was settle in. "Bet she really bought that handyman bit hook, line and bailing bucket," he added sarcastically.

He'd been watching *Mizzz* Rose for the past month, since she'd moved in. Quick glances in the hall mostly.

Cute as hell. Sexy, actually. She was like an approaching electrical storm, all full of spark and sizzle. And sure, she was a little off center from normal, in the sense of the women he usually dated, anyway. They were all pretty much run-of-the-mill—good-looking, a lot taller, a whole lot more sophisticated. But *Mizzz* Rose fascinated him. Had since the day Oswald, the building super, had rented her the apartment across the hall from him and she burst into it like a tornado sweeping through a wide-open Oklahoma plain.

Sure, he'd wanted an introduction to her. Just not the one he'd gotten. There was no turning back from an embarrassment like that one, and no conceivable way to undo it, except maybe switch apartments. Which was as easily said as done, since he owned the building. Unfortunately, it was full right now, with a pretty long waiting list. Nothing open except the boiler room in the basement. So he was staying put for the time being, abject humiliation notwithstanding.

"So do I avoid her, Hep?" he asked his Siamese cat. She was named after Katharine Hepburn—elegance galore with a set of big claws. "Or just pretend it didn't happen?"

Hep's answer was a guttural *I don't give a damn* growl, as she strutted through the kitchen, back arched, tail up, in search of a fluffed pillow for her nighttime nap.

"You're right. Just ignore it." Plodding back into his study with his beer and a bag of chips, Ned looked at the jumble of words on the computer screen, decided to call it a day, hit save then backed it up. No reason killing himself over this one. It wasn't like he hadn't cranked out a dozen books just like it before. Pop psychology had a way of bringing out all kinds of issues in people who'd never before had an issue until they read one of his books. To date, twelve bestsellers—the reason he could afford this building. A good investment, his financial guy had told him. Not that he wanted to be a landlord, because he didn't. But he had to do something with the money he was making. And real estate was as good as anything else. Gave him a place to live, too—an upside that didn't matter much, since he'd managed to get along for thirty-five years without getting himself too entangled in the usual trappings.

"Well, what will she be doing tonight?" he asked Hep, as he settled into his trusty ten-year-old recliner to listen to Doctor Val McCarthy. Pretty much everything that came out of her mouth was wrong. Bad psychology, bad advice, bad reasoning. But what the hell. She killed a couple of hours, and he sure liked her voice. It was a nice one to hear last thing before he nodded off.

"Welcome to *Midnight Special*, sugars. Are you ready for something special? Because if you are, you've certainly come to the right place. Doctor Val has something extra-specially special for you tonight."

"That's what she thinks," Ned snorted, stretching out in his chair and turning off the floor stand reading light.

"So tell me, what's on your mind," Val continued.

"Don't worry. I *always* do." Callers number one, two and three all rang with cheating spouses, boyfriends or both. And Val pretty much rang true with her advice, which was becoming predictable, Ned thought. Same ol' same ol'. Of course, how many ways could you spin it? You either dump them or you keep them. He chuckled. Or sleep with their significant other's significant other. That certainly wasn't a theory he'd seen in any of the books he'd read. Or written!

"Just be true to yourself," Valentine said, wrapping up a conversation he'd apparently spaced out on. But she was right. Too bad he'd missed it. "There are more big hunks out there for you if you want to go looking. Make sure you're looking in the right place, though. Someplace without a wedding ring, because if you get yourself hooked into that again, like you did last time, you'll end up like you are now, wondering why he's wandering. Now Doctor Val's gonna go treat herself to something sweet for two minutes. So sugars, I'll be right back, better than ever."

"Two minutes, Hep? So she can go look under a rock for more advice?" Chuckling, Ned grabbed his cell phone and punched in the number for *Midnight Special.* "I have a question for Doctor Val," he said, when a live voice came on. His *Ned* voice, only a little higher, because he didn't want anybody he knew hearing him call that hack. It was a little slurred, too, he noticed, thanks to that beer buzz he had going and a rasp of exhaustion. "But it doesn't involve a cheating spouse. Do you think she'll answer my question, anyway?"

"And the nature of your problem is?" the voice on the other end asked. They always qualified the callers. Some made it through, a lot didn't. He kept his fingers crossed.

"Met a woman I'd like to impress, but the first thing I ever did was pretty damned inept. Performance anxiety, I'd guess you could call it, and now I'm embarrassed to see her again. I just want to know some ways I could start it over between us. Or if I *can* start it over." Sure, he'd twist it until it sounded like this was about bad bed performance. *But never, ever let 'em know how he'd failed with a pipe wrench.* Man, oh man, talk about bored silly, doing something like this. But since Roxy wasn't home, he wouldn't get the do-over he'd been plotting all weekend in case he ran into her again. Shutting his eyes, Ned cringed.

"You'll be caller number one in the next segment," the screener told him.

"That's fast." Actually, this wasn't the call he'd intended to make. It just sort of slipped out. But what the hell! Go for it, anyway.

"Well, normally we hold that slot for someone else, a program regular, but apparently that's not happening tonight, so you're in luck. Just make sure you turn off your radio, okay? And no swearing or graphic words, because we'll have to cut you off."

Two minutes later, he got the cue. "Hello, sugar. And what can Doctor Val help you with tonight? I understand you sort of embarrassed yourself the first time you were with her and you're looking for a way to redeem yourself? Is that it?"

Ned cleared his throat, not so much because he was nervous, but because he was preparing to raise the pitch a tad more, just in case Roxy was listening. Bad with a pipe wrench *and* getting advice from a radio shrink. Two strikes for sure. "I've wanted to meet her for a while," he began. "And I finally did. But something happened, and yeah, I guess you could say I embarrassed myself."

"How? We're all on your side, so tell us the juicy."

"Let's just say it was something that comes naturally to most men, and I thought I could do it, but I found myself lacking in the skill. And she was definitely in need of that skill, but I had to call in someone else to help her out when I couldn't, well, take care of the job." Ned smiled. *Should be interesting.*

"You say you called in someone else to finish up for you?"

"That's what happened, but that's not why I called you. I just wanted your opinion on whether or not I should try it again with her. If you think she'll have me back. And how you might suggest that I go about it after humiliating myself like I did the first time."

"Well, I'm not a medical doctor, but I do know that it happens to all men at one time or another. No need to be embarrassed. And I've got to admit that Doctor Val is somewhat amazed at the lengths you'd go to for that woman of yours. Calling in someone else to finish—don't think I've ever heard that one before. But if it was between three consenting adults, I guess that's okay. I'm curious though. Since you were the one at the starting gate, wouldn't you rather be the one at the finish, too? And since you were her first choice, I'm assuming she'd like *you* to go the distance with her. So does she? Does she want you there with her at trophy time?"

"That's the problem...I really don't know. After what I did..."

"Give it another shot. I mean, this gal is really lucky to have someone so considerate, someone who cares about her pleasure and fulfillment more than he does his own. And I'm betting she'll be glad to have you back. Just make sure you take a little blue pill with you next time. Okay, sugar? Go on and knock on her door and tell her you want to give it another try."

"WHAT WAS THAT?" Roxy asked Astrid on the next break. "I mean, he's sending in the second string. Think the high and mighty Doctor Craig was listening? 'Cause I'd sure like to hear what he has to say on the subject. Especially since it's not *me* being off the wall for a change."

"He's in the queue. Just called in," Astrid said. "And he was listening. In fact, he's raring to go."

Roxy smiled. "Should be interesting."

"Twenty," Doyle called. "And if you give me the last caller's name, I'd be glad to stand in for him sometime when he needs that second string."

"I'll bet you would." Roxy laughed. "You and every other guy listening tonight, *except* Doctor Craig, who wouldn't even volunteer to stand in for himself."

"Five, four, three..." Doyle gave her the cue to go.

"Well, Doctor Craig. Welcome back. You're a little late, and I was beginning to think you were cheating on us, plying some other late-night talk show with your refutable advice."

"Not a chance, *Doctor*. Not after what I just heard. Your callers need someone to set them straight—"

He sounds a little tired, she thought. Probably exhausted himself coming up with a response. "Straight? You mean after I bend them, *Doctor?*" She glanced at her dark-chocolate truffle. Someday she was going to make that man buy her a whole box of them!

"After you bend their ears with *your* refutable advice."

"Come on, Doctor. Don't hold back. Tell me what you really think."

"I think, *Valentine,* that you wouldn't be so excited with the prospect of a pinch-hitter if you were the one committed to the regular hitter. You know, committed as in love."

Roxy leaned back in her chair and smiled at Astrid. "Sounds like you want to get into my personal life, Edward. Is that what you're trying to do? Catch a little glimpse of Valentine at home...in the bedroom?"

"Believe me, over the months I've caught that glimpse, and I threw it back."

Wow! Pretty peckish, even for him. Roxy scrunched her nose at Astrid, like she was smelling something bad. "You're forgetting, my caller was the one who'd already come up with a solution to his problem. At least his problem in the sack. And while that might not work for you, it seems to be working for him."

"If it's working so well, then why did he call you?"

"Maybe because he wants some advice on how to set things right between them, sexually."

"So you told him to go take a pill and all his sexual problems will be over."

"He wants sex, Doctor Craig. That's all he asked about. Sex. Not love everlasting or some other storybook fairy tale. He likes the gal, and he wants to know if he should try it with her again."

"I know we come from completely different disciplines, but tell me, Valentine—would you let your man line you up with someone else if he couldn't perform?"

Her man...*if only.* "You're assuming I'd get myself involved with a man who couldn't satisfy me, which is an incorrect assumption." Actually none of them had satisfied her, and she didn't mean in the physical sense. But that was none of his business. "In terms of an early relationship— mine, yours, my caller's—you simply don't know what will satisfy you. You have an idea what you'd like, what you've liked in the past, but when you're clean-slating it with someone new, it's always a great big question mark. My caller got to that great big question mark and unfortunately he turned it into a great big *huge* question mark, so I told him it's worth taking another chance on. Simple as that. Nothing ventured, nothing gained."

Roxy winked at Astrid, then continued. "Unless you're burying your head in the sand, Edward, there are signals, hunches, tinglings telling you this is someone you want to pursue. And tinglings are the best indicators. The kind that start at your toes and don't stop. Haven't you ever met a woman and started tingling right away?"

She'd certainly started tingling the instant she saw Ned Proctor standing outside her door. Maybe even before that, when he was so grumpy on the phone. Or even before that, passing in the hall, or watching him through her peephole. Whatever the case, there had been tinglings. Strong ones. Still were when she thought about him.

"But your caller wasn't talking about tinglings," he countered.

"Wasn't he? Something made him want to go back and try again, and it sure wasn't good sex since he had to bring in the second string. And since you, Edward, are always the champion of hanging around, trying to work things out, which is what I told him to do, I don't know how you could argue the point. Even though what my caller's doing isn't the way you'd do it..." Or the way *she'd* do it. "He deserves a do-over." And she was betting Doctor Edward

Craig had never, ever had a tingling or he'd know it was worth doing over.

"The way *you'd* do it, Valentine?"

Roxy leaned a little closer to the microphone. "The way I'd do it, Doctor Craig, is open to a whole lot of possibilities, many of which, I'm sure, you've never considered." Possibilities she wouldn't mind exploring with her not-so-handy handyman.

"Actually, the only one I consider is love, Valentine. That's the only thing that comes with all those possibilities you talk about."

Love? Well, that wasn't one of *her* possibilities, no way, no how. But score one for him, anyway. When he was right he was right. Even though she'd never admit it. "You almost sound like a romantic, Doctor. But of course, I know better. You write books that espouse all that academic thinking, and your readers walk away, what? Happy? Enlightened? Glad their pockets are lighter by the cost of a book? Sorry, Doc. You're still not ringing...*or tingling* my bell. And I'm sticking by what I said earlier. My caller needs to go back and try again. And take the pill with him, if that's what it takes."

"And I'm sticking by what I've said time and time again. You've skirted around the only truly important issue. But then, you always do, don't you, Valentine?"

Doyle gave Roxy the slash-throat signal, then a five count into a commercial break. Good timing. The hard and fast rule for Edward Craig's calls was that she *always* got the last word.

"What I skirt, Doctor, is being close-minded about issues my callers consider to be serious problems. That's all we have time for tonight. Thanks for calling, again." Then she was off. Truffle time!

"Whoa," Astrid said, stepping into Roxy's booth. "You two almost agreeing there?"

"Not agreeing," Roxy argued.

"But getting pretty darn close. I mean, you guys were just a couple chapters off from being on the same page. Good thing you still managed to find a way to argue about it, because the last thing our listeners need is Valentine and Edward in bed together."

"Yeah, like that's going to happen. The guy's a snore. The only thing in bed with him is a pillow."

"But it was close, Rox. You know it."

"So I agreed with him tonight…on some points. Big deal. And he was right…on some points. That caller needed a lot more than a little blue pill to fix his problems, but that's all Valentine can do—hand out the snappy fixer-upper, which is not necessarily the best one."

"Is this really about that caller?" Astrid asked. "Because you're sounding more like Roxy than Val right now."

Yeah, because she was Roxy right now. Roxy tingling over Ned. "Just tired." And full of expectations and anticipations and not sure what to do with them. "Not my usual self, I guess."

"Want me to stick in a rerun for the last half of the show so you can get out of here and go find your usual self?"

"Nope. I'm okay. Just pour me a root beer and I'll do better next segment." Roxy saw Doyle's ten-second signal and asked Astrid, "What's up next?"

"In a nutshell, big-time mamma's boy, age forty-two. She's seventy-five. He's unmarried, two of them live together. He wants a life, she won't let him have it, and *don't you dare* tell him to take his balls back from her like you did last time one of them called, okay?"

She crossed her heart, grinning. "Promise." And just when she thought she might have some fun. "Welcome to *Midnight Special*, sugar. I understand you have a little problem with your mother? So before we get started, let me just say one thing." She really hated mamma's boys. They were all whiners. Didn't listen. Made excuses. Got defensive. Horrible on the ratings. Her listeners turned them off, went to get a snack, have sex, grab a beer, or all of the above. "Mamma needs a man, junior. Even at her age, she's still got it in her. So you go out and find her one, ya hear? Find her one who will give her some good, hot mamma sex and I'll guarantee she won't be bothering you about whatever she bothers you about, and you'll be able to go out and get some good, hot junior sex for yourself."

She smiled at Astrid, giving her the thumbs-up. Val was back, all the way.

4

NIGHTS LIKE TONIGHT WERE made for the dumper, and Roxy didn't dwell on the show once it was over and she was home. Done, finito, put to bed and that was it. Edward got all the points, damn him, she got none.

"Get Eddie off the brain," she muttered, padding over to the peephole for the tenth time since she'd been home. "Time to think about you-know-who." Except you-know-who wasn't out there. Worse than that, he wasn't in her apartment. So, to call him, or not to call? She wanted to. Wanted to really bad. That's all she'd thought about all night. Probably one of the reasons why she'd hadn't ripped apart the good Doctor Craig like she should have. But now that she was on the verge of calling Ned, she was actually nervous about going through with it. Nervous, indecisive, weak-willed, just plain chicken. Which was just totally bizarre because normally if she wanted it she went after it. And she wanted it, but her feet were lead. So were her fingers. Couldn't dial the phone. Couldn't go across the hall. Couldn't even open the durn door so she could hang out in the entryway hoping he'd see her. *Hi Ned. I've just been hanging out here in the doorway for thirteen hours hoping you'd notice me sooner or later.* Go figure! No control issues here because she had no control.

"Well, no Twinkies for you tonight," she said. It was the

only decision she'd been able to make since she got home. That, and just giving it up for the night and going to bed. "Good place for us chickens, huh?" she said, plopping down in bed, and looking up at the window she'd super-glued shut earlier. "Stupid. Really stu—"

"Rrrooww!"

"What the…" Roxy jumped straight up, looked around, saw the cat. It was in the corner of her bedroom, shredding the seat cushion in her rocking chair with its claws. "Who are you?" she asked, not sure whether to get up and toss the cat out, risking the same fate as her cushion, or simply let it continue wreaking its havoc undisturbed. "Kitty, tell me. What am I supposed to do here? What's the protocol?"

The cat merely glared at her for a moment, then turned tail and lay down, apparently intent on spending the night where it was.

"You have a home, cat?" she asked. "Someone I should call?" Like it would answer her. "I'll bet someone's really missing you right now." Missing it, like missing a tooth-ache. "So why don't you run along home." Cats were supposed to be sweet and cuddly. This one had goblin eyes that glowed pure, luminescent evil in the dark. "Home, you know, the place where people feed you. Where people actually like you."

No clues on where that was, but suddenly, inspiration hit, and she wanted to kiss the kitty for it…almost. "And I know just how to find out where that is," she said, picking up her bedside phone. *Ah, the lead fingers suddenly work.* Punching the numbers she'd memorized the first time she'd dialed them, she was prepared for a ten-ring wait, but amazingly, Ned picked up on the second.

"Yeah, what do you want?" he said, his voice a little gruffer than she remembered his 3:00 a.m. voice to be last time.

"It's about a cat."

"Pet deposit's five hundred bucks," he snapped. "Write a check, leave it under the office door in the morning."

"I don't have a cat, but somebody does, somebody who's missing one. So do you know who's missing one? And what should I do about the one who broke into my apartment?"

"I suppose you want me to come over there at…"

"Three-oh-three," Roxy supplied, smiling. Providence was also smiling a little, it seemed. Serendipity in the form of one cranky cat.

"Three-oh-three…and figure out where the cat belongs. Is that correct, *Mizzz* Rose?"

So *he* remembered *her* voice. Promising…very promising. "You have a list of pet owners in the building, don't you? This one's such a sweet little kitty, and I'm sure somebody's heartbroken over losing him." Sweet as straight lemon juice with a vinegar chaser. With claws! "And while you're here, I have this window that sticks. Maybe you could bring your tools."

And come without your shirt. She glanced at the irritated feline, its claws extended a good two feet and envisioned the cat scratches the beast could rake all over Ned's chest. "Better wear your shirt," she said grudgingly. Damn that cat, anyway.

TWO HOURS' SLEEP. It bit through some of the exhaustion, but barely took care of the beer buzz. *Well, Ned, it's what you wanted.*

Problem was, he couldn't figure out why he wanted it. It wasn't like he had time for anything else. He didn't. It wasn't like he was in desperate need. He wasn't.

But simply knowing Roxy was right across the hall made him…tingle. *Thank you, Valentine, for that description. For once you were right.*

"SO WHERE'S THE CAT?" Ned growled at her from the hall-way. A softer growl than last time, though, and she liked him in soft.

He was wearing the T-shirt, smart man. Too bad, but he did have on some nice, tight jeans as the consolation prize. For the first time since, well, since she'd closed the door on Ned last Friday night after the faucet fiasco, Roxy was feeling like Roxy again. All weekend she'd drifted between edgy and wistful and downright sloppy sentimental, one emotion chasing right after the other until she'd finally opted to sleep it off. Of course, sleeping came with dream-ing, tossing, turning and a stiff neck. Which made her grumpy, which was just a hop, skip and a jump away from edgy, wistful, and downright sloppy sentimental. Round and round and round she goes... Amazing how one cranky handyman could do that to her.

"It's in my bedroom." Never in her life had an invitation been so easy! Too bad it was only about a cat. "And I sup-pose you know where it is, don't you? The bedroom, not the cat. Who's in the corner of the bedroom by the way, sitting in a rocking chair, ripping up my fake-silk cushion." Of course, having him follow her down the hall into the bed-room did have a certain appeal to it. Being carried by him down the hall and into the bedroom had an even better ap-peal, but she wasn't sure she could manage that one...yet! *But Ned, Doctor Valentine McCarthy prescribed one big, hand-some man to sweep me off my feet and carry me straight to bed.*

"So how did this alleged cat get in?" He scowled down at her, but it was only a facial rumple, with nothing in his eyes to indicate he was put out, angry or otherwise provoked.

"I don't have an *alleged* clue. I was just getting ready for bed and there he was, sitting in the chair, glaring at me. Kind of reminds me of the way you glare at me, come to think of it."

"She," Ned corrected.

"Huh?" What was that? A twinkle in his eyes? Was he actually twinkling at her, or was it the lighting?

"Nothing. Just lead me to the cat."

Well, the *getting him into the bedroom* part of the fantasy was coming true, for starters. The rest would have to take care of itself once they were there. Yeah, right. *Like I'm really Valentine.* "My window's stuck. Thought maybe you could pry it open while you're there." Suddenly, she really wanted to be Valentine. Sexy, sophisticated, no doubts in the world about what would happen next. Val would spirit him right into bed, forget the cat, and in the morning they wouldn't even have morning hair…talk about a fantasy. Although he would look absolutely magnificent in morning hair, morning stubble, morning anything. Geez…where was Doyle's "Control Freak" sign when she needed it, because right now she sure needed some control.

Especially now that Ned was giving her a twinkle. "It's at the end of the hall, the bedroom on the right, the first cat you come to." Following him into the bedroom she kicked herself every step of the way.

ALMOST, Ned thought, standing in the bedroom doorway, tool belt slung over his shoulder. He'd sure been thinking about what would happen once he crossed the threshold, but she had that Bambi in the headlights look, one he hadn't seen since he'd given Sally Ann Stojowski her first kiss, complete with tongue…they'd been thirteen at the time. But because he had ideas of something far better than a first kiss, complete with tongue, with Roxy, he decided it best to turn off that headlight. Only for now, he hoped.

"So, do you know that *alleged* cat?" Roxy asked, pointing to it sitting regally blasé amid the remnants of pillow in the corner of the bedroom.

Ned snapped off his momentary regrets and took a quick look at Hep's handiwork, cringing at the damage, since, after all, he'd been the one to slip her into Roxy's apartment. Well, maybe *slip* wasn't the best choice of words here. Earlier, just after he'd turned off that lunatic Doctor Val, and right before he'd dozed off, he'd decided to take a look at Roxy's kitchen faucet. Purely a professional house call, of course. And Hep just happened to be in his arms at the time of the *alleged* inspection. So what if he'd inadvertently left her behind, intending to go back later and get her? *Mizzz Rose, I don't suppose you've seen my cat wandering around in your bedroom, have you? I may have lost her earlier, when I was in there for professional purposes only.* Good thing she'd called him over because that was *infinitely* better than him on his hands and knees in the hallway, begging to be let in. "I know the cat," he said stiffly.

"And would you know how it got in?"

"Apparently she got in when the door was open at some point." Good evasion. Not a lie, exactly. More like the truth, in a circuitous kind of way. He stepped into the room and tossed his tool belt casually in the chair, sending the cat scampering.

"Well, gee. You'd think I'd notice something like that, wouldn't you? A cat getting in? Guess I should be more attentive when my door is open…or closed and locked. You never know who or what's wandering in or out, do you?"

"She's harmless." Except with soft, fluffy pillows, floor-length drapes, bathroom throw rugs, bath towels, cashmere, angora, wool, wooden door frames…

"So tell that to my dearly departed pillow." Roxy crossed the room and pointed to the window over the bed. "It's stuck. Guess I've never tried opening it since I moved in. Think one of your tools might do the trick?"

Man, oh man, she was cute. Standing there in her short-short jean cutoffs and T-shirt, she certainly wasn't his typical type, *or what he thought was his typical type*, but this past month, every time he'd seen her in the hall, in the foyer, from his peephole…well, suffice it to say there'd been a few typical *man* reactions. Hep was the proof of that, using his poor, innocent cat to *allegedly* worm his way into Roxy's apartment. That was some pretty hefty alleging and scheming…scheming worthy of Doctor Val. The kind she'd actually approve of, probably even make suggestions for improving upon. *Skip the cat, and curl up naked on the pillow yourself.* Actually, that thought had crossed his mind a time or two.

"I mean, I'd really like to let in some fresh air tonight, if I could get the window open."

He heard the words but his mind was still on curling up naked somewhere…anywhere in her bedroom. Nice thought. But not tonight. "Fresh air?"

"Remember…stuck window? Big tool to open it?"

"Let me see if I can jiggle it open first." *So climb on in her bed and do it…the window, not her.* Since the window was centered in the middle of Roxy's cushy king-size mattress, Ned crawled over it, then grabbed hold of the handle and gave the window a good, hard yank. One that should have opened it up straightaway, but didn't so much as budge it. One more try, one more great big nothing. Shades of the broken faucet. His second attempt at being handy was already bombing. "Must be painted shut," he said, clearing his throat uncomfortably. "Could you hand me that screwdriver from my belt?" The belt he sure wished he had on. He glanced at the chair where he'd dropped it. *Dumb, Ned. Really dumb.*

Without missing a beat, Roxy grabbed a screwdriver and bounded right into bed with him. And before he could tell her she had a Phillips head, and he needed a flat, she was wiggling in so close it didn't matter which screwdriver he had because he didn't have enough room to do anything with it, anyway. In bed with Roxy…that would have been a very nice place to be, except…well, he couldn't think of an *except*. It was a very nice place to be, period. "I need a flathead, the big one," he mumbled, sounding like a tongue-tied ten-year-old.

"The big one?" she asked.

"Uh-huh," was all he could manage. *So where's the snappy comeback when I need one?* Talk about being a Bambi in the headlights.

"Guess I need to study up on your tools, since you seem to be over here in the middle of the night using them a lot, lately. And thanks for getting that faucet fixed, by the way. No more drips." Roxy crawled back out of the bed and stood alongside it. "And my project is coming along much better because of it."

He'd taken a look at her *project*. Just briefly, since it was printed out and lying on the counter right next to her sink, and he *was*, after all, checking out the sink. For an architect, she was pretty bad. Horrible. Bizarre. What architect in their right mind would ever put a cupola *inside* the house? "So did you get that house plan done yet?"

"You saw it?"

More like was struck blind by it. "I noticed it the other night." He took the large flathead and wedged it between the window sash and the sill. "Kind of an odd place to put a cupola, but if that's what they like..."

"They who?"

"Your clients. I mean, I assumed you're an architect."

"You're observant, Ned. And my *client* decided to scrap the cupola altogether. Kind of cramped her style. Of course, I guess there's an advantage to having all the essentials in one convenient area, don't you think?"

"I've never considered a cupola an essential on an ultramodern." He laughed. "I'm a little more traditional than that." Finally, a nice conversation—one, he hoped, that would deflect her attention from his ineptitude.

"Four predictable walls, a normal roof, cement slab,"

she said. "And don't forget the white picket fence. That's the trademark of the traditionalist, isn't it?"

"Something like that." Screwdriver in place, Ned tapped it with the palm of his hand, hoping to break loose the paint that was holding the window down. But nothing chipped away, nothing even budged. So he hit it again, harder. Same results. "Really stuck," he muttered. *Cue up even more disgrace, the man still can't get the freakin' window open.* Could he do anything else wrong here? he wondered. And to think only minutes ago he'd had all kinds of expectations.

"I like the nontraditional, myself. Like that house you saw on my computer. Lots of open spaces, angles. It's going to be steel and cement. Lots of glass."

"Like an office building." He tapped again, this time with a lot more force, and the only thing that happened was the paint on the wooden window frame chipped away when the screwdriver slipped. Glancing over his shoulder to see if she was watching, which she was, he made one more addendum to his ever-increasing level of abject humiliation. By now she was probably wondering what kind of clod he'd be in bed. Actually, he was beginning to wonder that himself.

"Like a home. People always put tags on things that are outside their norm. And I try to throw away the tags. So who's to say what has to look like what? Whether a cupola belongs on an ultramodern, inside or out?"

"Your client, I suppose." He repositioned the screwdriver. "And that's all that matters, really. If that's what your client wants, then that's what your client gets. Me, however…I like traditional, and that includes the picket fence, and even the cupola…outside." Then he hit the window with such force the screwdriver slipped off the wood frame, clobbering the glass above and shattering it into hundreds of tiny, jagged shards that splayed out all over the top half of Roxy's bed. "Dammit," Ned muttered, jumping back from the flying glass.

Roxy jumped back, too, clean away from the bed. "Let me go get my vacuum cleaner. And stay right where you are. You're barefooted, and you'll cut your feet to ribbons if you get off."

Shutting his eyes, Ned expelled a hard, angry, humiliated breath. Oh, sure, he'd wanted an invitation into her bed. He'd thought about it for days. Somehow, though, a vacuum cleaner had never entered the picture.

GOOD NIGHT FOR Georgette "Pounder" next door, as it turned out. She never let up during the vacuuming, then went into overtime when Ned nailed a piece of plywood over Roxy's former window. Somewhere around 3:35 Georgette stopped, luring Roxy into a false sense of security, because somewhere around 3:37 Pounder actually came pounding on Roxy's front door. She was cute, in a granny sort of way—shorter than Roxy by a couple of inches, probably not even ninety pounds soaking wet, and with sweet, little ol' granny-gray, curly hair. "You either can the damn noise, lady," Pounder growled in a voice that certainly wasn't granny-sweet. Kind of reminded Roxy of the beasty voice in *The Exorcist.* "Or I'm havin' you thrown out on your ass. Got it?" Pounder stormed back over to her apartment muttering expletives that would make any sailor blush, leaving Roxy wondering if the chocolate chip cookies *sweet* little Georgette baked were safe for Ned to eat.

"Want some coffee?" she asked Ned, careful not to raise her voice lest Pounder came back to make good on her threat.

"Sure, if it's no trouble. I'll be done here in just a couple of minutes. And I've got some of Georgette's cookies across the hall—"

"Twinkies," Roxy interrupted. On her way to the kitchen, she took a quick detour by the dictionary. Cupola…a small structure on top of a roof or building. No way she'd designed a cupola…or had she? Taking a quick look at her house plans as she poured the coffee, Roxy saw it—a cupola in her kitchen. Cupola…cupboard? So maybe a cupola could have been a unique touch. "How do you take it?"

"Black." He dropped down onto a kitchen chair. "Find the cupola?"

"I didn't lose the cupola." Handing him his coffee, Roxy grabbed the box of Twinkies from her cupboard, not to be confused with her cupola, and tossed it onto the table. The living room would have been cozier, but the casualness of a kitchen was nice too, especially going on four in the morning without an intimate moment between them in sight. "Are you always up so late?"

"Nope. And, technically, I'm not even up right now." Ned unwrapped his first Twinkie. "And I'm not eating Twinkies with you at this ungodly hour, either."

She shoved another Twinkie at him. "So tell me about the cat drop. On purpose, I'm assuming, unless you can prove otherwise."

"If I say yes, are you going to read a whole bunch of hidden meanings into it?"

"Maybe." Roxy laughed. "If you think I should. So should I?"

"I'm not sure yet. Can I get back to you on it?"

"You know where I am, how late I'm up and apparently how to get in." Promising. He wasn't exactly leaping over the table at her, but he wasn't ruling it out, either. "But skip the cat, okay? A nice, subtle pipe wrench says it all, and it doesn't tear up my pillow. And about that window, you're not going to get in trouble for it, are you? With the building management or owner? Because if you are, I could just say I'm the one who…" Glued it shut. About as subtle as a cat. "Broke it."

"No trouble that I can't handle. So tell me, Roxy Rose,

what kind of trouble you get yourself into in the middle of the night."

Sounded promising. Shoot, it sounded downright leading. "I got grounded a few times. My parents...they didn't like me wandering around all night. I thought it was because I made too much noise, then when I was older I realized they thought I was listening at their bedroom door."

"You seem like the type who would." He grinned. "Am I right?"

Roxy grinned back. "Parents *never* have sex, Ned. Everybody knows that. So why would I want to listen at their bedroom door?"

"Curiosity." His fingers wrapped around the second Twinkie, then he shoved it at her.

"Curiosity...well, let's see. It didn't kill the cat, did it. I believe you deposited her in my bedroom." She shoved the Twinkie back.

"So do you listen at bedroom doors, Miz Rose?" Ned arched his eyebrows suggestively. "And what do you hear?"

"Only if I'm on the right side of the door, Mr. Proctor. And believe me, the only thing I've heard lately is a ferocious, growling cat. Meaning, I'm not involved, if that's what you were asking." She sure hoped he was.

He unwrapped the Twinkie, broke it in equal halves and slid Roxy's half across the table. "I was, and I'm not either...involved. And the only ferocious growling I've heard lately comes from that radio whack, Valentine McCarthy. And take it from me, a growling cat is much safer."

Roxy's heart skipped a beat. This was not where she wanted the conversation to take them. "I've heard she's supposed to be really good. Really popular. Cute. Smart. Nice voice. Great wardrobe. Good shoes. Nice hair. Very successful." So she couldn't help applauding herself. What of it?

"Then you don't listen to her too much, do you?"

Ned popping his half of the Twinkie into his mouth just

about popped her eyes right out of their sockets. Talk about sexy! The way he chewed, his jaw moving so slowly, so seductively…his eyes never leaving hers, it made her forget who, what, when and where for a second. No words, nothing except the zing of pure sexual awareness between them until he finally swallowed, then he glanced away to pick up his coffee cup, effectively breaking the Twinkie love spell he'd cast on her. "Huh?" she asked, still basking in a bit of the afterglow.

"Do you listen to her? Valentine McCarthy?"

"Uh-huh." Still basking in the heat of that moment, she needed a fan but that would be an admission she didn't want to make. "Sometimes," Roxy admitted, going for her half of the Twinkie. Nothing like drowning a few pent-up frustrations in that wonderful creamy filling. "She's pretty good entertainment. And popular." Afterglow fading now, she was about to launch into a dissertation on market shares and where her program ranked, but that might send up a red flag, and right now the only flag she wanted to send to Ned was white—surrender.

Ned laughed sharply. "Well, you're right about that one. She's popular. Her face is plastered everywhere—billboards, the sides of city buses. So I guess if that's the way she wants to waste her Ph.D."

"Waste?"

"Hack advice."

"Entertainment."

"Bad entertainment."

"So bad *you* listen to it." This was certainly disappointing. Splitting a creamy filling with a guy who hated her other half wasn't the best getting-to-know-you she'd ever had. So maybe it was a good thing they weren't meeting each other halfway across the table to explore the many uses for that creamy filling. "So would I be wrong in assuming you're not a big Val fan?" Yeah, yeah, yeah. Like she didn't already know the answer. But under that Val-hating exterior... Well, she really liked the rest of it. Hope springing almost eternal here, even if it was about to get slapped back in her face.

"Nope. I'm not a big fan. Just a curious listener when I can't sleep. She's a little too off the wall for me. She does have a certain appeal for the masses, though, I'll give her that."

Doable! Not nearly as harsh as it could have been. It kept him in the ballpark, anyway. And she was sure glad she hadn't spilled the Valentine beans yet. On the bright side, her resolve was safe with him. Career first—and Ned? She was tucking him in the TBD category—to be determined. "Because you're a traditionalist, right?" Time to put Val away for the night.

"Something like that. So tell me about this *untraditional* house you're designing."

Ned crossed one leg over the other, settling back in his chair. "You've designed others?"

"Especially lately. Seems like it's the only thing I design."

"But do you like what you do?"

"I love what I do." That wasn't a lie. "Took me a while to find my niche, and I'm really happy there." Sure, she had been a clinical psychologist for a while, and it had been a good gig. Lots of patients to see, lots of problems to counsel through. Nothing that gave her a thrill. But the first time she'd uttered "Welcome to *Midnight Special*, sugars," she'd discovered a great gig. That thrill she'd always lacked. Then, when she'd had to make the permanent choice between good and great, good got left in the dust. "For a while I thought I wanted to be firefighter, a nurse and an ice skater, in that order, then for a little while all at the same time. Then there was the Egyptologist phase, but I don't particularly like excavating and getting gritty."

"I'll admit to firefighter, Egyptologist and cowboy."

"So you could have been a firefighter on an Egyptian ranch."

"I've never mastered camel-riding."

"How did you end up…" Oops. Tactical error asking a *bad* handyman why he wanted to be a handyman. "Actually, it's none of my business. We don't need to talk about it."

Ned laughed. "You mean you're not dying to ask the handyman why he's such a klutz?"

Wow, what a nice laugh. Deep and rich and full of earthy undertones…so much so Roxy felt goose bumps start crawling up her arms. "Maybe I am. But that would be kind of rude, wouldn't it?"

"Like listening at bedroom doors?"

"Okay, so I'm asking. Why *are* you a handyman, Ned? Especially when you're not very handy. And I don't mean that in a bad way," she added quickly.

"Like hell you don't." He grinned. "And don't go turning all red."

The blush *was* creeping up. Being blond there was no way to hide it. And hers was sooo bright red. "I, um…"

Ned ripped off the lid of the Twinkie box and handed to her to use as a fan. "I'm not a handyman, by the way."

"But you have a tool belt." She fanned frantically for about ten seconds, until the heat started to subside.

"Borrowed."

"Can you get arrested for impersonating a handyman?"

"In my case, probably yes. But I own the building, since you didn't ask. And a few other properties. Oswald, the guy who runs it, also does the maintenance, but he had his appendix taken out a few weeks ago and he's still on medical leave. So I decided to do it for him."

She remembered Oswald from the day she moved in. Nice man. Scrawny, nervous type. Definitely not any tool belt potential in him. Not like with Ned. "Then I'll bet you're costing yourself a small fortune hiring someone to fix the messes you fix."

"Well, let me just say Oswald's getting a raise, now that I have a better appreciation for his talents."

He glanced over at the bug-eyed cat clock that read ten till five. "I know you're better at the wee hours than I am, but I really do have to get going. Even *bad* handymen need to catch a few zzzzs every once in awhile." Ned pushed his coffee mug aside. "Sure hope it was decaf," he said, standing.

Roxy smiled sheepishly. "Next time, I promise." And in spite of his lack of affinity for Val, she sure hoped there would be a next time. Men this easy to eat Twinkies with didn't come along very often. "But you can't go until you fess up on the cat."

"Boy, are you going to be embarrassed when you hear how logical my explanation is." He laughed. "I bet you're thinking there's some ulterior motive in it, aren't you?"

"Isn't there?"

"Hey, I was just doing my job, making sure the plumber fixed the leak. Instead of getting under the cabinet myself, I stuck my cat in there, figuring if she came out dry the leak was fixed."

"Well, gee. What an innovative use for a cat. So tell me, how did you manage to leave her here?"

His face was dead-straight while his eyes were laughing. "I thought that should have been pretty obvious to you. Couldn't tear her away from your pillow." With that, he retrieved Hep and went home.

5

What Seagulls Do on Tuesdays

"IT'S SO ISOLATED OUT HERE, and it doesn't get any better each time we come out," Astrid said, faking a shiver. "You need something civilized popping up somewhere—a Curves, a Starbucks, two Starbucks, for God's sake. I mean, privacy's nice, I'm all for it and everything, but I also like a little something around me besides…nothing." She gestured to the open expanse all the way around them. No houses in sight, no highways, not even a byway, whatever the heck a byway was. Just plain nothing. "I think I'd be scared to death living out here all by myself like you think you're going to do. Which I'm betting you won't."

"Like I *know* I'm going to do." Sitting on her own beach towel, Roxy dug her toes into the sand, wiggling them around in the warmth, then shaded her eyes with her hand and looked out over the water…a few drops of it her very own. It was a beautiful afternoon, crisp and blue. Perfect weather in an ever-changing climate, and she loved that. Loved this land. Loved the house that would someday stand on this land. Loved all the things that scared Astrid. No, she wasn't afraid of being alone out here. In fact, she looked forward to it, even welcomed it. "You're a hopeless urbanite. A hopeless chicken urbanite, and I don't expect you to understand why I'm doing this."

"Oh, I understand all right." Astrid slapped some sunscreen on her bare arms. For a September afternoon, it was warm, sunny. Not quite summer any more, not quite fall, either. An ideal day for doing what they were doing... basking. "You lost your mind, that's why you're doing this. The real estate agent was a hunk. He brought you all the way out here, seduced you, put some crazy notion in your head that sex in the sand is the best, so you bought the place. Right? He did some mighty fancy selling and you took whatever he had to offer, including this lump of godforsaken clod."

Roxy laughed. "Close. She was older, three grandkids, bonsai hobbyist, reads romance novels, talked about retiring soon."

Astrid capped the sunscreen and pulled on a wide-brimmed straw hat. "Sympathy factor? Trying to add a little something to her retirement kitty?"

"As it turned out, I added a lot. But I liked the land. Loved it. And so far I don't have a clue if sex in the sand is the best, but I'm sure hoping to find out." Maybe with Ned? Now that was something to look forward. A house *and* Ned out here. Talk about perfect.

"And you thought about it for what, two minutes, before you signed on the dotted line?"

"Five." Love at first sight. Six months later now, and still no regrets. "Would have been quicker but I couldn't find a pen."

"Like I said before, you lost your mind." Astrid lay back in the cabana chair and tipped the hat to cover her face. Sun and freckles were a disastrous combination.

"Hey, I've got to agree with Astrid on this one," Doyle slipped in. "You've never lived anyplace but in the city since I've known you, and somehow you just don't strike me as a beachy kind of gal, Rox. You're way too city for all this seclusion. You'll turn into a damned hermit."

"More like hermit crab," Astrid muttered from under her hat.

"So I used to be way too city," Roxy corrected. "What of it? This is what I've always wanted and didn't think I'd ever have. And no one was more surprised than me when I was actually able to buy this place. Now that it's mine I'm getting beachier by the day, and the city in me is beginning to convert. So if that means hermit to you…hey, I'll do hermit."

She tried to get out here every few days. Didn't always make it, and sometimes she made the hour-each-way drive only to claim five or ten minutes. Nevertheless, she always devoted some part of every day to getting herself out there on a permanent basis—whether it was being there in person so she could simply sit and dream, or staying holed up in her apartment and working on the house plans. Today it was being there with her friends—naysayers and cynics that they were—and she was wishing she'd asked Ned to come along, too. Or instead of. But she'd already asked them, and exposing him to any part of her Val side yet was way too risky, especially since Roxy genuinely liked Ned's company. And maybe she even had a few expectations of the tinglings she felt when she was with him.

"So I was thinking about putting the house on the knoll over there." Roxy pointed to a raised grassy patch at the edge of the sand. "House on the hill so I can look down on my domain." She laughed, nodding at the boulder where Doyle was perched. "Think I'll put my turret right where you are. I hear they're great for domain-surveying."

"A turret on that warehouse you're building? Excuse me, that was last week. It's an office building this week, isn't it?" Doyle asked. "For cripes sake, Rox. You're sitting on the edge of a bedroom community. Their houses are so freakin' traditional, it looks like a Norman Rockwell. And you really think they're gonna let you go ultra-whatever the hell it is you're doing?" He shook his head skeptically. "They don't even allow poppy seeds on their rolls, Rox, and you really think they're gonna allow you on their outskirts?"

"When he's right, he's right," Astrid chimed in. "That house is going to be one great big boil on somebody's butt."

"Well, like it or not, I'm taking that boil to the zoning board pretty soon," Roxy defended. And yes, it was going to be one great big struggle. The town board was already nipping at her heels, sending its pit bull, *actually more like its schnauzer,* William Parker, out every few days to issue vague warnings against what she was going to build. Yeah, right. Warnings based on rumors started by an architect she'd canned—an architect who lived in Shorecroft. Since she'd pink-slipped him, speculative tongues had been wagging nonstop, and so the village schnauzer, who also happened to be the village manager, was sicced on her. "And the ace up my sleeve is my property line—one toe beyond the Shorecroft village limits. They may have a say, but they can't stick me with community building covenants." Thank heavens!

Doyle snorted. "Sure hope you aren't holding your breath on that one, Rox. Politicians are politicians, and once they get a look at what's on your table they're going to pick it up and chuck it into the Sound, then come up with a law to cover their collective butts later."

"And that's what friends are for," Roxy snapped. "Support."

"And honesty," he snapped back. "The town who-has have a reputation that's a whole lot more irritating than a prickly heat rash, Rox. And I'll guarantee once you take those house plans to them for approval, the only thing you're going to walk away with is a great big prickle."

"Like you know."

"Like I know. I'm a small-town boy, came this close to being a who-ha, myself." He held up his hand, measured an inch with his thumb and index finger. "And if anybody knows who-ha, it's me."

"Well look, quasi-who-ha. It's not like I'm building some kind of Ripley's Believe It or Not out here. I just want a plain structure, nothing fancy, nothing even outlandish."

"Meaning you're getting rid of the estuary in the den?" Astrid laughed.

"It was an aviary in the kitchen, not an estuary in the den. And out here it's all aviary," Roxy said, looking up at the seagulls flying overhead. They knew her now. Expected her to bring cookies like she did every time she came.

"With an aviary you get bird crap," Doyle grumbled. "And I guarantee you'll be hating it out here once you've got all those birds trained, because all they'll do is eat your cookies then fly over your house—your mostly glass house in case you need reminding, Rox—and drop a big old load of appreciation down on it. Sure hope you've got a great big squeegee handy, because you'll be needing it."

"Or maybe I have a good friend with a great big squeegee who won't mind coming out here and helping me," Roxy retorted. She was thinking Ned, and not necessarily in a big squeegee sense, either.

"I'm betting after a month out here with the birds you'll be running right back to urbanity as fast as you can, kissing the sidewalk every step of the way." Doyle spread a blanket on the sand, then plopped down on it, making sure the eats were well within his reach. Lately they'd turned this weekly pilgrimage of theirs into a picnic of sorts, and he was already groping for the fried chicken before he had completely settled in.

"You can have your urbanity," Roxy commented, pulling the lid off the red-and-white bucket for him. Picnic the easy way. Grab it from the drive-through. So totally her lifestyle these days, she didn't even have to think twice. Which was one of the reasons she wanted to get out here so badly—she *wanted* to think twice. Living in the big city simply didn't nourish that. Not for her, anyway. "I'll take this any day." She glanced sideways at Doyle, who had a chicken leg in each hand, and was eating from left hand to right. Well, most of it, anyway.

"I'm getting tired of all this city Rox, country Rox nonsense. I vote we talk about your handyman," Astrid said, holding out her plate to Roxy for a breast.

"Not *my* handyman. And there's nothing to say. He likes Twinkies." She found the breast for Astrid, then dug out six more legs for Doyle and plunked them on a paper plate. "We talked all night, drank coffee, he broke my bedroom window, then he went home."

"Uh-huh," Astrid muttered. "So should I ask *how* the bedroom window got broken?"

"If I told you, you wouldn't believe it, so I'm not telling." Roxy grinned. God willing, next time maybe there would be something to tell.

"So what you *are* telling me is that you had him right where you wanted him—in the bedroom. Was he naked?"

Doyle cleared his throat, but they ignored him.

"No, don't tell me," Astrid continued. "I want to imagine it my way. Big, blond, brute of a handyman with a low-riding tool belt. Boxers under that tool belt, no shirt. Six-pack, and I ain't talking beer. *And you let him go, Rox?* Are you nuts?"

"Dark, jeans and you got it on the six-pack."

"My fantasy, not yours," Astrid snorted.

Doyle cleared his throat again. "Remember me? The one who *doesn't* do girl talk?"

"Yeah, like you don't listen to every word we say," Astrid quipped. "And love it!"

"I deserve a raise, "Doyle moaned, going for a container of baked beans. "I mean, I've heard you two talking about PMS so much I get sympathetic pains twice a month."

"Not PMS. Indigestion from the way you eat," Roxy threw in.

"Okay, okay," Doyle interrupted. "You're ganging up on me, two against one. I demand that raise now."

Roxy pointed to the empty bucket of chicken, laughing. "If I give you more money, I've got to quit buying you food. Take your pick."

"Not fair," he groaned, reaching for the coleslaw.

Roxy liked being here with her friends. Liked her camaraderie with Doyle and Astrid. But maybe next time she'd bring Ned out here. Just the two of them, alone on the beach…

"Earth to Roxy," Astrid said. "You were drifting off, and I'm betting it has something to do with the handyman."

"The handyman, and the fact that he hates Doctor Val."

Doyle let out with a low whistle. "Well, doesn't that make for a dandy relationship. So I'm assuming he does-n't know what you do with your nights?"

"Nope, he doesn't know, and I'm not going to tell him. He saw my house plans and assumes I'm a bad architect, and that's where I'm going to leave it. I mean, it's not like I'm going to marry the guy or even get involved with him on a serious level. So what's the point of saying anything? Right?"

That comment drew speculative looks from both Astrid and Doyle. "So let me get this straight," Doyle said between bites. "The dude saw your house plans—the one with the bathroom in the middle of the coat closet? And this rocket scientist handyman thinks you're a gainfully-employed architect, albeit a bad one?"

"Dining room," Roxy corrected. "Bathroom in the dining room."

"My point is, the dude's gotta know you're not an architect, Rox. Not even a bad one. Which can hang okay if all he's wanting out of you is…"

"It's not hanging okay, or any other way," Roxy snapped. "We're casual. That's it. And he's not wanting anything out of me. Nada!"

"Like you're not wanting anything out of him?" Astrid popped in.

"Like I'm not wanting anything out of him except for him to fix a few things in my apartment." Ooh, such a lie. They already knew he was fixless. No wonder she never lied—she was a complete bomb at it.

"Yeah, right. And I'm ready to give up pizza for the rest of my life." Doyle eyed the chocolate chip cookies Astrid had fixed and started scooching his hand over in the direction of the plastic container. "So are *you* one of those things that needs fixing, Rox? One of the things that needs some handyman attention?"

Roxy slapped his hand and pulled the container back, not sure she would even give Doyle a cookie after that crack. "Okay, so I'll tell him what I really do. *If* we get together again, and *if* there's a reason I need to. We've only been to bed together once so far..."

"Stop right there," Astrid sputtered. "You've only been to bed once? Am I missing something here?"

"The window he broke is over the bed."

"Which brings us back to my original question, how the heck did he break the window?"

"With his screwdriver. It slipped." Roxy grinned, releasing Doyle's cookies. Talking about Ned, thinking about Ned, she couldn't do anything *but* smile. "And before you say anything else, just let me tell you he's going to have to bring out the ball-peen hammer before we take this thing to the next level." Immediately her mind went to removing the big ball-peen hammer from his tool belt, removing the tool belt from around his waist, unzipping his jeans...

"Sounds to me like someone's taking her own advice too seriously," Doyle heckled, breaking into her fantasy just when it was getting to the good part. He grabbed his cookies, then headed back to the coleslaw. "Maybe *you* should make a call tonight and see what Doctor Val has to say about it."

Roxy already knew what Doctor Val would say. *Go for it, sugar.* And for once, she half agreed with her. The other half, the Roxy half, was the problem.

"Speaking of advice, have you got any for that?" Astrid said, pointing at the beachy area just beyond where they were picnicking. It was loaded with seagulls, maybe two hundred of them, all lining up, watching them, licking their lips—if birds had lips. "They're not getting ready to go Alfred Hitchcock on us, are they?"

Roxy pitched a grocery bag full of generic cookies at Doyle. "Go toss these out there," she said, finally settling in to eat her own lunch now that Doyle was full.

"Bird crap," he muttered.

Eyeing the chicken breast she was about to eat, then getting a case of the guilts over eating one of their very distant relatives while the gulls were watching, she dropped it back in the bucket and opted instead for coleslaw, biscuits and chocolate chip cookies. "Bird crap out there unless you don't feed them, then it'll be bird crap up here."

"I'm telling ya, I really deserve that raise," Doyle grumbled, grabbing the bag and stalking out closer to the water, where the birds were congregating.

"Dump them on the ground and run," she yelled at him just as he realized that he needed to run. And he tried. Oh, how he tried. But he just wasn't fast enough.

"I'll bet we don't have a squeegee with us, do we?" she asked, setting aside her own chocolate chip cookie for Doyle, since she was, after all, the one who'd sent him off to be gull slathered that way. Not that he'd ever go near a cookie again.

But then, a cookie was to Doyle as a pizza was to… Doyle. And he *was* Doyle, after all.

TEN-FIFTEEN, and Ned was knocking at her door. Taking a look out her peephole, Roxy's heart beat a little harder. She was already fifteen minutes late getting out of there— meaning Astrid would kill her for sure—and here he was, looking *sooo* like something worth being late over, even calling in sick for. Big what-to-do quandary, when there shouldn't even be one. She'd never skipped work before, never even been tempted. But still… *Sorry Astrid, but I've come down with a bad case of the Neds. Don't think I can even drag myself out of bed tonight. Think I might have to call the Proctor to come make a house call.*

Good idea, *except* she was bringing on another big sponsor tonight, a national dot com with some pretty hefty advertising bucks to spend on little ol' *Midnight Special*, hefty bucks that would translate into even heftier ones once she made it into syndication. Which meant she couldn't afford to have Astrid stick on a Best of Doctor Valentine rerun just so she could stay home and discover the best of Ned Proctor. Not when she needed to welcome the dot com on board personally. *Take it from Valentine, you haven't experienced one of the finer joys of life until you've had your com dotted by the best dot com in the business.*

Anyway, passing off her responsibilities wasn't the way she ran her business, and as much as the tartlet parts of her were telling her to choose the handyman, *please choose the handyman,* the business parts, which were in far bigger supply, were pushing her on out the door. Into his arms? *Wishful thinking Rox, but not hardly.* Because as she brushed into the hallway, he backed away from her.

"I've got a late appointment tonight." Sure, maybe he hadn't asked, but he was skimming her shredded-knee jeans and "Born to be King" T-shirt. Was that his eyebrow raising in speculation? A twitch of disbelief on his lips? Okay, so her attire wasn't very businesslike, but she didn't owe him an explanation. It wasn't like they had anything going on that required commentary. But that eyebrow was getting to her, trying to coerce a confession right out of her. "I'm, um, working on site. Casual. Everybody's casual." So she broke under the pressure and explained. What of it?

"You're going on site this late?" he asked, flat-voiced. "Is that unusual?"

Well, at least the eyebrow went back into place. "Nope. It happens a lot. Besides like I told you, late night's my thing. Works out with my, um, clients." Switch listeners with clients, and it wasn't too far from the truth. "And right now I'm late." Durn it. "Gotta run." Double durn it.

"Before you go, you didn't happen to mis-squirt superglue on the windowsill, did you? The glazier did a measurement earlier. He said it looked like a superglue sabotage."

Busted! And, oh, no! His eyebrow was up again. "Can't recall ever mis-squirting anything." Which wasn't a lie since she'd done it on purpose.

The other eyebrow was raised now, forming a very doubting arch. Time to go on the defensive with some good offense. Arching her eyebrows right back at him, Roxy looked him straight in his mistrustful eyes. "Sounds more like something an inept handyman might do to get himself back into my apartment, wouldn't you say? Especially since he can't exploit his poor pussycat again." Good strategy, turning the tables on him like that. Doctor Val had taught her well. "And as much as I'd like to hang around and wait for your answer, *or your excuse,* I'm afraid I've got to get on out of here. I have a really mean boss who expects me to be punctual." Finally, the whole truth. She did have to get going, though. But he was so darned adorable tonight, his hair mussed, bare feet again, a tiny rip in the neck of his T-shirt. And those jeans… Wow!

"*Except,*" he said, not yielding an eyebrow, "the superglue was applied before the alleged cat incident."

"Alleged superglue, and it could have been a simultaneous cat drop, superglue gluing. I'm betting your fingerprints can be found on both the glue and the cat." Geez, she had to stop this right now, or she wouldn't be going anywhere tonight except wherever Ned wanted to take her. And, boy, was her temperature rising. In another ten seconds she was either going to have to strip, or hit a cold, cold shower. At the risk of Astrid's wrath, it was definitely time to get the heck out of there. "Look, I'll be home around two-thirty, if you want to come over and defend yourself."

"I'll bring the Twinkies."

She nodded. "The old Twinkie defense." More like Twinkie seduction. She hoped.

"Don't forget your hard hat."

"My what?"

"Hard hat. You know, job site requirement." He turned and padded back to his apartment.

"Geez," Roxy gasped, leaning against the wall to steady her wobbly legs. And her wobbly heart. A little chat in the hall and she needed a cigarette, even though she didn't smoke.

Moments later, when the elevator doors opened onto the first floor hall, Roxy was confronted by Georgette—Georgette with an umbrella bigger than its owner hanging on her arm. Sharp, shrew eyes, twisted little weasel smile, smoke rolling out the top of her head.

"You're messing with the wrong woman, missy," Georgette hissed, stepping squarely into the elevator doorway, barring its closure as well as Roxy's escape.

She was about to be bested here. Since the woman banged on walls, she'd probably welcome a head to bang every now and then. "If you'll excuse me…"

"Oh, no, missy. I'll not be excusing what you do. And you think you're getting away with it, trying to keep it a secret, but I know. I know everything. And if I have to, I'll be telling it all to Mr. Proctor."

She wanted to snatch that umbrella right off Georgette's arm and break it, but instead Roxy tucked her hands in the pockets of her jeans and tried stepping around her. Georgette matched her move for move, though. Wouldn't let her out. "If you'll excuse me, I have an appointment...." She waltzed to the left, so did Georgette. "And I'm late." Back to the right, followed by Georgette. "So if you'd kindly—" She stopped in midsentence, her eyes still fixed on the umbrella. Georgette was raising it slowly off her arm, in an implied threat. Her tiny little hand squeezed it as she shoved it closer and closer to Roxy's face. A mere twelve inches from Roxy's nose, she stopped and simply let the umbrella hang there, like a snake suspended from a gnarly tree branch, contemplating its next strike.

Roxy stepped to the side, trying to squeeze herself between the umbrella witch and the door. No way Astrid was buying this story. Held captive by an eighty-two-year-old with a lethal umbrella.

"Not so fast, missy!" Georgette growled, hitting the *hold* button as the alarm started shrieking the warning of an impending elevator Armageddon. "I've already complained to him about the hours you keep. Coming in so late like you do every night *always* wakes me up, then I can't go back to sleep. And Mr. Proctor assures me he's going to do something about it very soon."

A sly grin crossed Roxy's face. "Then I suppose I'll have to take my punishment from Mr. Proctor, won't I?" Maybe a spanking?

"You just keep it quiet over on your side, you hear, or you'll get a lot more than some knocking on your wall. And that's a promise." She shook her umbrella at Roxy one last time, then finally stepped aside to let her pass. "I'll tell Mr. Proctor what I know about you—your secret—and see what he has to say about *that*," Georgette hissed. "Moral turpitude, missy. Moral turpitude." She gave her umbrella a parting shake.

Moral turpitude? That one caught Roxy's attention, and she stopped and spun around to Georgette, who was getting ready to punch the fifth floor button. "And just what do you mean by that?" she asked, out-hissing Georgette's last hiss. "By my *secret*? Moral turpitude?"

The only answer was the ding of the elevator doors sliding shut.

"WELL, I JUST WISH she'd move out," Roxy said, sliding into her chair. It was burgundy leather, big, comfy, with a footrest that slid out from underneath like a recliner, but it was still a desk chair. Just one that pampered her. Her only overindulgence. The rest was standard-issue old and worn, and once she got her house done she intended to redo the studio. No, it wasn't hers in the sense that she owned it. But it was hers in the sense that she made the station a whole bunch of money. Which meant she could, and would, do what she wanted—give Astrid and Doyle better working digs. They deserved it and it was the least she could do for her team since they were as much a part of the show as she was.

"So take your own advice from last night." Doyle laughed. "You know. Fix her up with a stud and let her pound on him for awhile." He was propped haphazardly on the edge of Roxy's desk, eating a sloppy, six-meat submarine sandwich.

"So, are you volunteering, Doyle? Can I pencil you in for the two-thirty assignation?"

"The only thing Doyle's going to be penciled in for is getting those promos ready to air," Astrid said. Stepping into the booth, she gestured Doyle back into his own cubbyhole. "We've got thirty minutes to get ten of them done, and for heaven's sake, Rox, no screwing up this time.

Okay? Management wants to go with them starting tomorrow afternoon, rush hour, and we don't have time to mess around. And while we're on the subject of promos, I've scheduled you to do *Seattle SunUp* next week. Five-minute segment to promote your show."

"That would be TV," Doyle commented dryly. "Real early TV. 6:00 a.m. Bet they'll want you there even earlier than *real* early, Rox. So maybe I should stay with you the night before and make like a rooster in the morning, 'cause I'm betting you'll oversleep."

"You know what? I may already have an interesting way of keeping myself up all night without you." Add some Twinkies to her grocery list, stock up on coffee, buy some kibbles for the cat. "I won't oversleep, but with any luck I'll be late."

"Oh gosh," Astrid sighed. "All roads lead to the handyman. Again! You're getting soft, Rox. What happened to that iron resolve you're always bragging about?"

"Still there. Just taking a break."

"Handyman break," Astrid quipped.

"Actually make that a handyman *who* breaks," Doyle tossed in. Cramming the last of his sandwich into his mouth, he slid off Roxy's desk and headed into his own booth.

"Low, Doyle," Roxy called. "Real low."

"Hey, if the broken faucet fits…"

"Okay guys, back on track here. Promos. Remember?" Astrid slid the copy in front of Roxy. "Short, sweet, simple. Be a good girl, Rox, and I'll buy you a bag of cookies for those gulls."

"Ten bags." Roxy laughed. "Plain, no icing."

Sighing, Astrid headed back into her booth. "Ten bags, but I'm not gonna be the one to feed them to the gulls."

"Deal. Hey, Doyle…whatcha doing in the morning?"

"*Not* going out to your property for starters."

Smiling, Roxy imagined her and Ned and a couple hundred gulls on the beach. "He has a cat. I wonder if he likes birds?"

"Back to the handyman?" Astrid asked.

"Actually, I never got away from him."

"Well, you've got to now. Doyle, you ready?"

Doyle nodded. "But I'm not betting on Rox, right now."

"Rox is ready," Roxy sighed wistfully. For way more than drive-time promos.

No WILD CATS TONIGHT. She'd checked twice already. No kitty, no Ned. So she had plenty of time for house plans, except she wasn't in the mood for house plans. She was in the mood for Twinkies, and not Twinkies for one.

"Well, Rox. If you don't ask, you'll never get." Roxy glanced at the printout of her plans spread out all over her kitchen table.... Nope, her mind just wasn't on architecture, except in the manly physique sense. "So I guess I'll go ask."

After she tucked away the plans, Roxy darted out her door and across the hall. "I was wondering if I could borrow a Twinkie," she said even before his door was fully open. "Since your light was on…"

"My light?"

He didn't step outside. Instead, he leaned casually against the door frame. Bare-chested, barefoot, those low-riding jeans. Like he'd known exactly how she wanted to find him. "Saw it from the street, before I came in."

"My windows are in the back of the building. On the alley. Opposite side of the building from the garage entrance."

Knees, don't fail me now. They were getting ready to wobble right out from underneath her. "Wrong turn, missed the street."

"It's a one-way alley, off a one-way street. Can't get to the garage from that direction, so you must have been…"

Looking to see if you were still up. "Looking for stray alley cats," she purred.

"Find any?"

"Not yet. But maybe you should come over and have a look for yourself."

Ned glanced down at his bare chest. "Think I'd better put on a shirt, first. Had a complaint from your next-door neighbor."

"About my secret?" Sure, she was curious. Also nervous.

"Big secret. Moral turpitude."

So far he wasn't stressing over it. That was good.

"The terrible things you do."

Glint in the eyes. She was already feeling relieved.

"Half-naked men coming and going all hours of the night. She wants me to do something about it."

Big relief! "And what would you suggest?"

"How about I nail a board over her peephole." Smiling, he took a step backwards. "Give me ten minutes, okay?"

Five would have been better.

6

Tuesday Night Temptations, Tussles & Twinkie Seductions

NED DELETED the page he'd been hopelessly stalled on all evening, then retrieved it in case anything on it might be salvageable. He took one final look at four hours of wasted effort and shut down his computer for the night. Man, oh, man, what Roxy was doing to him. Between her and her Twinkies, and his day job with a tool belt, he was seriously in danger of blowing his deadline. Couldn't be helped. Roxy was infinitely more interesting than yet another pop psychology book on relationships. It was getting old; he'd already made enough money for this lifetime, so the lure of another big payoff sure didn't do it for him. He needed something to get the old creative juices flowing again. Something new, like Roxy. And it wasn't just his creative juices she was getting flowing. "Maybe the relationship dude's actually getting a relationship," he said to Hep, on his way out the door.

Twinkies in hand, Ned wandered across the hall, shirt on this time, knocked on Roxy's door, and several minutes later was settled in across from her. No, not in bed like he'd hoped for, thought about, dreamed about all evening. Not even in the living room on a nice cozy couch.

"So, did you listen to that Doctor Val again tonight?" Roxy asked casually, pulling the Twinkie box across the kitchen table to her.

"Some. It's good background noise." Twinkies and root beer. Kind of odd, but nice. Something he'd expect from Roxy, though. "Keeps me awake."

"And you wanted to stay awake, why?"

"Business. I had something to take care of." *Which you totally distracted me from doing.* But he wasn't going to tell her what it was. Not yet. All things would be revealed in due time, and for now he wanted to keep it simple, keep his lives separate.

"So are you a closet fan? The one who always listens, but will never admit it?"

He chuckled. "Anything but. I mean…that advice tonight, where the woman wanted more than just sex from her relationship…"

"Yeah. Where it's always straight to bed and she wants to find out if there's anything more to it than that? I mean geez, imagine that." She laughed. "She wants a little civil conversation with the guy she's sleeping with. Who would have ever figured that a woman would actually want to talk with a man, and have a man talk with her?"

"And Valentine told her to wear him out with sex before they talk about it." Ned paused, shaking his head incredulously. "They should have talked at the beginning, found out if there was enough between them to get them to that next level before they stripped and went at it."

"Point is, they didn't, and now they're stuck," Roxy countered."And getting unstuck's going to be pretty hard to do. So she wears the guy out with sex. What's the big deal? It's not like I'm telling…um, Val's telling her to hold out on him. Just wear him out then go for the conversation. I mean, that Edward stick-up-his-butt Craig who called in said the caller's guy needs to zip and converse before he unzips again. Like that's gonna happen! Once the zipper's down, that's it. Over. Bye-bye. Talking goes right out the window. He actually said she should ask the guy where he wants to go with the relationship, which is really dumb, because he's getting what he wants already, and he's happy with where he's going. I'm not saying that talking's not good, because it is. But if you do the deed before you do the chat, chances are you'll never get back to the chat. So you might as well get everything you can from the deed." She took a deep breath, then added, "That's what Val was saying, anyway."

So Roxy's not an Edward Craig fan. Figures. Thank you very much Valentine McCarthy for that one! "And you agree with her?"

"Personally, I think a couple should get to know each other before jumping right to that next level. But that's the kind of advice you'd expect from Eddie Craig...."

"Edward," he corrected.

"From Edward Craig, not Valentine. But that's not what Val fans want to hear."

Well, so much for *his* plans. A little Twinkie, a little root beer, then maybe some jumping to *any* level. Too bad Roxy didn't have a little bit of Val in her. "Could I have another root beer?"

Roxy split the next bottle with him, although he noticed she took more than half. He liked that. Showed how independent she was, how she didn't exist solely for a man's approval. Actually, he'd figured that out the first time he'd talked to her. She was happy with herself, comfortable with who she was—no changes necessary, not to suit anyone. Yep, he liked that. Liked it a lot.

"So what's your perfect relationship, Ned? One you've had, or one you haven't had and wish you could?"

"Other than with my cat?" He took a second Twinkie, unwrapped it, split it equally with her.

"You like your relationships on equal footing, don't you?" she asked.

"You could tell that from the Twinkie?"

"Equal halves both times we've shared. Doesn't take a shrink to figure it out. If you'd given me the bigger half that means you were trying to get on my good side. Small half means you're trying to dominate me."

"Suppose I'd given you the whole thing?"

"I'm guessing it would have something to do with getting me into bed. If I wasn't full already, we might try it and find out. But I've had my Twinkie limit for the night, so we'll never know."

"I think a gal with a bigger appetite than yours would top my list for the perfect relationship."

"Appetite for what?"

"Nope. I told you mine, now you have to you tell me yours."

"One thing. You told me one lousy thing and it wasn't even a good thing."

"Then maybe I'll tell you something good after you tell me what your perfect relationship would be like." He took a swig of his root beer and settled back in the kitchen chair. "My list is pretty good, by the way." And becoming more and more defined the better he got to know Roxy.

"It had better be good, Proctor, because I don't spill my guts for just anyone. But you owe me a real one, first. Not some pitiful, lame, off-the-top-of-your-head…"

"My perfect relationship would be with someone I respect. Now you."

"Someone I can laugh with."

"Someone who shares the same core values."

"Someone who shares the same core Twinkies," she said, cramming her whole half in her mouth.

So what's that all about? he wondered. Off to a good start, then she pulled up lame.

SOMEONE HE RESPECTS? Someone with his core values? He was beginning to sound an awful lot like Eddie Craig. "So you don't think opposites can attract? Haven't you ever wanted to go to bed with someone who *doesn't* share your core values? I mean, don't you find that a little bit exciting, a variation on the same old theme? You can always go back to the same old theme, you know."

"I thought we were talking relationship?"

"And sex isn't a real relationship?" Roxy asked, heading to the sink for a glass of water to chase the last of her Twinkie. All the sugar was giving her a headache. Or maybe it was from thinking about what was going to happen once Ned met Val. Either way, her head was slamming.

"Sure, it's a relationship. Just not my perfect relationship."

"So what's perfect?" she asked. "Besides equal Twinkies?"

"Maybe unequal root beer."

"Maybe I'm not good at measuring."

"Roxy, if ever there was anybody who was good at measuring *everything*, it's you." He laughed out loud. "You're the most calculating, controlling person I've ever met."

Well, gee, like she hadn't heard that before. At a meeting just last week, the CEO of one syndication outfit she was considering told her he liked that sharky little attribute in her because it would go a long way in stomping out her competition once she got to the national airwaves. A couple of the architects she canned had some choice words on the subject too, which was why she canned them. Then Astrid and Doyle, they *always* accused her of being a control freak. *Et tu, Ned?* "Meaning you hate it." So much for that almost-relationship going any further. Her head throbbed even harder.

"Actually, just the opposite. I think it's kind of cute. Some people might be threatened, but I'm not. I mean, you look like you're always playing the angles. Something's always churning inside. Even right now. It's you and me and a bottle of root beer, but there's a whole lot more going on, isn't there?"

Besides the headache? "Maybe." Damn, he was insightful. And definitely as good as her at playing those angles. "But weren't you playing an angle tonight, when you didn't come over after I got home? You wanted me knocking on your door for a change, didn't you? *You* were controlling *me?*"

"Maybe." He grinned. "But my perfect relationship wouldn't have waited half an hour. Ten minutes tops, then she'd have been banging on my door. So since you waited thirty, was that you controlling me?"

Gosh, a while ago all she'd wanted to do was go to bed with the guy. But this little back-and-forth was almost as good as sex. *Almost.*

"Look, as much as I'd like to stay and finish this, I've got an early morning." He glanced at his watch. "It starts in about four hours with some dirty furnace vents. And God knows, with my track record, I've got to be clear-headed for it."

"So that means even if I break something right now you can't stay?" Durn it. This was just getting to the good part, and miraculously, her head was thumping less.

"Sorry, no tools."

"Meaning you'll come back tomorrow night…with tools?" She licked her lips. *"All your tools?"*

"I suppose you have another late-night *architecture* appointment?"

"Whatever pays the bills, and before you succumb to Georgette Selby's deep-seated suspicions, which I'm sure she'll be telling you shortly, if she hasn't already…no, I'm not a hooker. I may keep hooker hours, occasionally dress like a hooker, but cross my heart, my clothes never come off in the execution of my work." Roxy laughed. "And I'm not an exotic dancer, either. No sense of rhythm."

"Now I'm disappointed. I've always preferred a girl with good rhythm. Part of my perfect relationship list.

Number eight, I think. Just after good sense of direction, as in one-way alleys."

"Okay, so I was spying. A *little*. I didn't want to wake you up if you were sleeping, so I looked." Actually, circled three times, looking, hoping, praying… "So save me the extra miles tomorrow night, okay? Just be here. Bring popcorn. I'm in the mood for something salty."

"You're assuming I like salty?"

"Don't you, Ned?"

"I suppose I do get a little taste for it every now and again." Ned stood, stretched and headed to the door. Once there, he turned back to face her. "Last few days I've really had a craving for it."

Roxy followed him to the door, stopping short of pressing herself into him, then did a slow once-over, head to toe. It wasn't like she hadn't already memorized the route, because she had. But a little refresher course gave her something to tide her over until tomorrow. "Then salty it is, *sugar.*"

"Sugar?"

"Huh?" Geez!

"Oh, nothing. Just hearing things."

ROXY CLOSED HER DOOR quickly.

She'd almost caught it before it slipped out, but it had passed through her lips right into the annals of their history—well, she hoped there would be a *their history*—before she could swallow it. Sugar…just a spoon full of sugar and she sounded dangerously close to Valentine. A mistake Roxy never, ever wanted to make with Ned. At least not until they were in the oohs and aahs of passion and it didn't make a durn bit of difference what she was babbling. *Oh, yes, yes, Ned. Oh, yes! I'm Valentine!* She thought about it for a minute, shook her head. Bad, real bad. With the feelings she was beginning to have about the guy, she was going to have to work on a good way to break it to him, and pretty darn soon.

"So LISTEN TO IT, then tell me what you think," Astrid said, plopping down on Roxy's sofa Wednesday afternoon. "First promo's going to be the tame one you did, and we'll stay tame for several days before we start letting the better ones run. Although for Val, they're pretty tame, too. We don't want to shock the listeners right at the beginning. They'll turn off the radio, or turn it down when you come on, which *isn't* what we want them to do. And besides, Valentine is an acquired taste according to the latest industry surveys. Like Limburger cheese." She wrinkled her nose. "And I've heard from Spartus Syndication, by the way. They're upping the offer since Taber's is in now. Going ten percent over, but I think we can get that to at least fifteen."

"Twenty. Then go back to Taber and get ten over that." Ping pong. And she always won.

"So it's down to those two?"

"Unless someone else can ante up. I'm open, but we're kind of reaching the top now, and I'm not sure any of the smaller players can afford us, not since Spartus *and* Taber threw their hats in the ring. But I'm certainly willing to listen to any reasonable offer, because believe me, I'm not set on this deal yet."

"You know you're going to have to do some writing, don't you? A column, maybe a book. They all do it once they're in syndication."

"Yeah, yeah. Maybe I'll hire Eddie Craig to ghostwrite me something."

"Have you ever read any of those books he's sent you? They might give you some ideas."

"They're still in the box, in my trunk, all taped up. I thought I'd use them as fire starters in the fireplace in my new house."

"At least think about it, Rox. Think about writing something, anything. Okay?"

Astrid was right, of course. She had to play all the angles to get her name out there once the syndication deal went through. *Angles*...that word again. Suddenly, the hard-boiled business Roxy melted into a puddle of sentimental Roxy. She'd seen Ned in the hall a couple times today, he heading one way, she another. And even though there was no time for anything more than a few casual words, that promise of tonight was electric between them. "So how long do I have until the great Valentine invades drive-time?" she asked Astrid.

"Probably about fifteen minutes."

"Fifteen." She nodded, grabbing a handful of house plans off the end table. "Just enough time to eliminate a couple of these." Roxy found the one she wanted to work with, and threw the others away. She pulled out the pencil that had been tucked behind her left ear, crossed one leg over the other, and studied the sheet of paper with her master bedroom plan on it. Not a bad plan. Might have been nicer if it was a master suite for two instead of one. She scribbled some larger dimensions on the corner of the plan.

"Getting better?" Astrid asked casually.

"Yeah, better. A big old box of a house for one."

"Handyman melancholia again?"

"Don't know. It could be, maybe. But there's this one really big thing between us, and believe me, the better I get to know him, the more I realize that Valentine could be a huge problem. So I'm still thinking casual."

"But you're not sounding casual. He's the one I saw on the way in, isn't he? Dark hair, nice tool belt?"

"*Really nice* tool belt."

"Hey, you gotta tell him, Rox. I know you always want to control the situation, over-control it if you can get away with it." She grinned. "But if you're not honest with him, pretty soon you're going to control yourself right out of anything you might have with him. And from what I saw, you really don't want to be doing that."

Roxy threw herself back into the sofa cushions and pulled her feet up. "So what did you think?"

"About our meeting with Aphrodite Chocolates this morning?" Astrid teased. "I think they'll be a great sponsor for the show. You can do a lot of things with chocolate in our kind of format."

"I mean about Ned. What did you think about him?"

"Well, it wasn't like we sat down and did a Q and A. But I did catch a glimpse from the backside. Figured it was him because of the tool belt. And I must say what a spectacular backside it was." She shook her hand like she'd touched something hot.

"It is spectacular, isn't it?" Roxy agreed, matter-of-factly.

"Magnificent."

"Fabulous."

"Extraordinary."

"A butt among butts." Roxy sighed wistfully.

"So?"

"So, what?"

"You know what."

"Nothing to tell." Not that Astrid would believe she'd spent the whole night talking to him. Some things were meant to be kept private though, even from best girlfriends.

"And you really expect me to believe that, Rox?"

Instead of answering, Roxy lobbed a pillow at her. "Turn on the radio. it's time for my promos."

"Captain Casey, KIJI's rush-hour guy in the sky. It's 5:05 and traffic's still backed up on Aurora near 130th Street. Fender-bender involving five cars, looks like no serious injuries, although an ambulance is still en route, about five minutes out. Police have all the cars but one pulled over into the center lane, and one lane's passable each way now.

Passable, and very, very slow—jammed up coming and going for blocks. Lots of broken glass too, so be careful if you decide to go on through. Looks like either 1st or 3rd Avenues are pretty clear, beginning to take a little of the overflow, but so far not too bad. So you might want to detour on over there and take a look. Your best bets are to exit at 115th or 145th Streets to avoid all the congestion."

"I hate rush hour," Roxy muttered, staring up at the ceiling. "Too many people thinking they have to go someplace."

"You mean like home?" Astrid was already investigating the Aphrodites, going for all the chewy centers. *Her box.* Roxy's was tucked away someplace safe.

"Okay, so they have a reason to be there, but I'm running out of reasons to listen to all this drive-time blather." After the traffic report, sports was up. Something about football...big game coming up. "But aren't they all big games? And what makes this big game any different from the last big game or the next one? Sheesh! Just get to the promos, already. Spare me the quarterback hiking something between his legs to the guy behind him." Actually, that part didn't sound bad—substitute Ned for the quarterback, make her the one behind him. Or vice versa.

Astrid glanced at her watch. "About three more minutes. They told me it would be on at the hard break at bottom of the hour, hard break at the next top, and the hard break at the next bottom. Lead-in to the news spot, not the lead-out."

"One," Roxy said, holding up one finger. "That's all I'm listening to."

"All three," countered Astrid. "And there's always the Aphrodites to keep us going in-between."

"Who's the boss here?" Roxy grumbled.

Astrid held up a strawberry-cream filled. "Well, someone's in a big snit, isn't she? Sounds to me like someone needs some handyman sex to calm her down. But since you're not getting it, try an Aphrodite."

"He's really stirring something up in me," Roxy said, taking the chocolate. Admitting it out loud for the first time was not so bad. The roof hadn't fallen in or anything. She glanced up just to make sure.

"Like I haven't noticed. Is it the *L* word?"

"Whoa! We're casual here. Career first, remember? Are there any caramel centers left?"

"I'll give you a caramel if you tell me if he makes you tingle all over, and we're not talking in an orgasmic sense. Just the kind of tingling that happens when you look at him, maybe even think about him."

Not fair! One admission per customer. Astrid was way over her quota. "Maybe in my toes," she conceded, snatching the caramel right out of Astrid's fingers. "Maybe my shoes don't fit right. Too tight." Well, not quite a full admission.

"You've always said that when you meet the guy who makes you tingle…"

"*I know what I've always said.* If he makes me tingle all over, I'll know he's the right one." She popped the caramel in her mouth.

"Does he, Rox?"

Chewing, Roxy shrugged.

"Come on. Be honest, okay? Does he make you tingle?" She shrugged again, still chewing.

"Coward!"

Finally she swallowed. "I don't have a clue what a real tingle feels like. I mean, do you know how long it's been since I even dated anyone, let alone…" Reaching for cream-filled this time, she sighed wistfully. "I'm practically a virgin again. And he's so gorgeous, Astrid. You saw him. Wouldn't you like to jump into bed with him?"

"Sure. *Hello, my name is Astrid. I'm Roxy's friend, and while she's figuring out what she wants to do with you, I get to sleep with you.*" She laughed. "I think you should let it happen, then figure it out later. You're overthinking it, which means you're sure no good to me the way you are."

"The way I am?"

"Yeah, the way you are…horny!"

Roxy grabbed the box of chocolates away from her. "You're demoted."

"Hello out there in rush-hour traffic…" Hearing the promo starting, Roxy took in a deep breath. Sure she'd protested the promos. But now that they were starting, maybe they weren't such a bad idea after all. "This is Doctor Valentine McCarthy with two pieces of advice for you. One is listen to my program. You'll be amazed what you'll hear in grown-up time when we can talk about the good things, the sexy things you'll never hear on your way home from work."

"Damn it, Rox!" Astrid squealed, pounding the sofa cushion. "I told him to get rid of that one."

"And the other piece of advice is drive naked. Makes the whole experience much more fun, especially if everybody else commuting right along with you is driving naked, too. So try it, then call me at midnight and let me know if it was good for you, 'cause if I'm the one commuting next to you, I'll be watching, and it'll sure be good for me. *Midnight Special* every night at…midnight."

"Pretty good," Roxy said, looking down at Astrid, who'd slid all the way to the floor and was curled into a semifetal heap. "And you were right about that driving naked part. It could cause…" She laughed. "A whole lot of rush-hour people to start listening to my program."

"You did that?" Astrid moaned. "On purpose?"

"Actually, no. I didn't do it. I guess that was Doyle. But I think it worked out really well. Bet they'll stay tuned for my next promo."

"We are *so* screwed." Astrid rolled over and sat up. "Management wanted it tame."

"Won't matter if it ups the ratings." No, it wasn't the way Roxy wanted to make her first splash in drive-time, but there was no doubt now that a few of the listeners would stay up past the eleven o'clock news tonight. "And I'm betting it will."

"Well, I'm betting it's *upping* something right now, a lot of somethings all over the place, and I don't have a clue if that will translate into ratings points or not." Moaning again, Astrid returned to the semifetal position.

THAT NIGHT Roxy signed on with her traditional greeting, then went immediately into a break instead of a call because of a phone logjam—every line was blinking. Astrid needed a couple of minutes to get it all organized, so Roxy used the time to prepare herself for the chaotic two hours ahead. Busy night, and her truffle was close at hand for her Eddie encounter. "They're really lighting up all over the place," Astrid exclaimed, as Roxy took a drink of water, a couple of deep breaths, and a quick perusal of the first caller's problem. Not a problem, according to the two-sentence blurb Astrid wrote up for each caller. A thank you. *Interesting.*

"We're backed up on e-mails, too," Astrid said. "Mailbox has shut down, we've had so many."

"So we'll get one of the station interns to sort through them, weed out the ones that need answering, and send an automated response to the rest." Roxy settled back in her chair and gave Doyle a friendly nod. "Ready whenever you are. Oh, and we'll discuss that little mix-up later."

He tossed his hands into the air in mock surrender. "Oops. I'm bad. Thought I'd taped over it. Guess I was wrong. But look how it turned out. You just became the talk of Seattle."

"It ran all three times during rush hour," Astrid snapped. "You were supposed to send them three *different* spots."

Doyle shrugged. "Mistakes happen. And besides, I already heard management wants Rox to retape tomorrow's promos with something a little spicier. So looks like my little mistake worked out pretty well, doesn't it?"

"Pretty well, maybe, but for starters I'm cutting off your pizza supply."

He smiled. "Harsh, Rox. Real harsh. But I don't need pizza gratification after what I saw naked on I-90. She was really *hot*, but I couldn't see much. Guess I'll have to get me a four-wheel drive so I'm sitting higher. Or maybe you could tell them, Rox, to sit up straighter, or on a couple of pillows." He laughed. "Or tell all the really hot chicks to go out and buy convertibles. Thirty seconds…"

"No one was naked," Roxy retorted. "People have better sense than to do something stupid like that."

"Twenty…then you didn't listen to the news, did you? Cops stopped people all over the place. Seattle was a veritable sea of *au naturel* this afternoon. Fifteen…"

"Yeah, well, cops stop people all the time. So what's the big deal?"

"Ten… Naked? I saw them line up some big, ugly, naked bowser down the street from my apartment, then wonder how the hell they were going to frisk him. Really nasty stuff. Guess you underestimated the power of *your* spoken word."

Roxy didn't respond. She merely shook her head and prayed for the segment to start quickly.

"Five, four, three…"

"Doctor Val back with you. And I understand the fine police officers all over the greater Seattle area were kept pretty busy today during rush hour. Getting naked, were you?" She chuckled her deliciously wicked Valentine chuckle. "Guess I'd better get right to the calls, since they're coming in faster than we can handle them tonight. Oh, and before we begin, I'd like to say hello to all my new sugars out there. Doctor Val was hoping for a few more friends to spend her nights with. "She glanced up at the board. Sure enough, one naked rush hour motorist coming up. Fifty-three—*good for her*—divorced, and Astrid had underlined the word *elated*.

"So tell me all about it," Roxy prompted. "What made it so spectacular that you had to call me?"

"It wasn't so much the deed as it was going through with it. You know, doing something to get me out of my rut. I still wear a one-piece on the beach, dress in my closet even though there's nobody else here. But when I heard what you said, I said *what the heck*. And the cop who pulled me over…he was mighty surprised. Said a woman my age should know better. But you know what, Val? Why *should* a woman my age know better? What's that got to do with anything? You get to a certain place in your life and you're supposed to do what—automatically switch your dial over to slow down?

"Well, I've been slowing down for a while now, two years divorced and that's all I've been doing. Then after I listened to your advice, something just clicked in me. There's no reason to slow down, no reason to stay in any rut. So I took off my clothes, and even though I've got to pay a pretty hefty fine for public indecency, I'm glad I did. So thanks, Doctor Val, for kicking me in my settled butt and getting me back out where I belong. Life is too short for the slow lane, isn't it?"

For once, Roxy was speechless. Life certainly *was* too short for the slow lane, and it took a naked, fifty-three-year-old divorcee to drive it home to her. "Good for you," she murmured. "Good for you."

Two hours and twenty-two calls later, Roxy hung up her headphones and stuffed her truffle in the drawer. *Strange*, she thought, signaling Doyle into her booth for a little chat.

If ever there was a topic to draw out Edward Craig, driving naked was it. But she hadn't heard a peep from him tonight. Where was the good doctor and what was he up to?

7

Flooring It On Wednesday Night—Finally!

ROXY REACHED INTO THE BOWL for a handful of popcorn.
Perfect. They were sitting shoulder to shoulder on her
couch, not quite touching, but close enough that she could
feel his body heat, smell his aftershave. Clean and masculine. Not sweet and perfumery. Maybe that was his natural scent. She wanted to find out, but decided any more
encroachment into his space would land her on his lap.
And tonight Ned wasn't giving out any kind of signal that
that was where he wanted her. In fact, if not for some quiet
jazz music in the background, there would have been no
sound at all in her apartment.

"You didn't happen to go out and drive naked today?"
she finally ventured, hoping to break the ice. "I heard a lot
of people did." Nice and light. Maybe it would get him out
of his bad mood so she could broach the Val subject.

"She should be arrested," he muttered. "*Valentine Mc-
Carthy.* That was irresponsible of her, as a counselor, as a
broadcaster."

Nope, no Val broaching tonight. Not when Ned was
practically snarling. "I sure didn't think that so many people would actually take her advice…no, not advice. That
wasn't advice. Just some kidding around, I think."

"The hell it wasn't advice," he exploded. "She's in the
business of giving advice, and when she gives them noth-

ing but yap, like drive naked, that's what people think she's doing. Giving advice."

"Yap?" As good as it was, Roxy pushed away the popcorn. "Did you say yap?" Damn, her hackles were rising. She didn't want them to, but…

"Yap. Trash. Reckless slabber."

And rising and rising…"Slabber?"

"Slabber. Drivel. Complete, total bull. She should have her license yanked."

Okay, it was getting personal now. Her hackles were all the way up. "Her *yap* is popular. So popular it's going to be syndicated. And if you can't accept her for what she is, turn her off."

"I would except her *yap* caused twenty-nine wrecks in rush hour today. Would have been twenty-eight if a couple of kids in the car behind me hadn't taken her yap to heart and stripped naked. While they were doing it, the driver in the car behind them was watching, of course, and somehow, at the intersection, I was the only one who remembered to come to a stop, which means I got slammed from behind, first by the car full of naked hot doggers, then by the hot doggers again when they got slammed from the rear by the gawkers. So if I want to call Doctor Valentine McCarthy's advice *yap*, I'll call it *yap*."

He was right. That promo should have never made it to air once, let alone three times, and she'd straightened it out with Doyle. Even if his little stunt had boosted ratings already, she didn't want to boost them that way. "Was it damaged much…your car? Totaled? Oh, my gosh. You didn't get hurt, did you?"

"Not hurt, except a stiff neck. And my car was dinged, but that's not the point."

Roxy could feel the point coming, and it had a really sharp end on it. "I'm sorry," she said in advance. "Really sorry, Ned." Time to get off the subject altogether, and she knew just how to do it. Reaching over to him, Roxy laid her hand on the back of his neck, then began a gentle massage. Nothing big, just a little light finger stroking on some very stiff tendons.

"That's good," he murmured. "A little higher..." He twisted around until his back was to her. "Perfect," he said, sighing. "But she has a responsibility..."

"If you want to lie down on the floor, maybe I could...' Before all her words were out, he was already on the floor face down. Not bad for starters. Now all she had to do was keep Doctor Val out of the room from here on out, and maybe, just maybe...

"Okay if I straddle you?" she asked. Wow, had she really said that?

"If it works best for you, straddle away."

Of course it would work best for her, and if it didn't she'd make it. Cautiously, Roxy climbed over him, keeping her knees at his hip level. Nice view from the top, she thought. Nice place to ride. Nice place to ride *naked.* Now all she needed was some nice, aromatic massage oil... No, not that kind of massage. He had whiplash, thanks to her. She owed him therapeutic.

But there were all kinds of therapeutic.

"It's mostly in my shoulders and neck," he said. "And the burn on my jaw from the air bag deploying."

"Shhh," she said, applying her fingers to his shoulders. "You want Roxy to work out the kinks, you've got to work with her." Damn, too much Val. Why was she trying to slip out here? Was it some subconscious effort to sabotage this relationship? She'd have to consult the shrink in her later, but right now... "Tell Roxy...er, me what feels good."

"It all feels good," he murmured. Then for the next ten minutes he merely groaned as she let her fingers do the talking.

"OH, THAT FEELS GOOD." Better than good, and Ned didn't want his sour mood to get in the way of it. The day had started out bad. Computer fritzing-out, Hep hacking up a hairball for an hour, getting hit—*this* sure made it all disappear, even if he'd hadn't been able to get through to that damned Valentine tonight to give her a good, solid piece of his mind. Roxy's hands washed it all away—the pain, the stress, the need to pummel one reckless radio shrink.

"You're getting tighter, Ned," Roxy said, probing deeper into his shoulder muscles. "I can feel it. Am I hurting you?"

"Uh-uh," he murmured, enjoying the sensation too much to interrupt it with words. Thinking about Valentine was causing the stress that was tightening him up, though. And frankly, he was surprised Roxy appeared to be so taken in by her. Of course, Valentine knew what it took to reel in the fans. She was the queen of it. So in the interest of keeping his relationship with Roxy on the steadily improving course, maybe he'd just better keep quiet—for now. See how things were going to work out before he spilled his guts. After all, if she knew that her hands were giving so much pleasure to Doctor McCarthy's number one opponent, Doctor Edward Craig, those wonderful fingers of hers might start doing something to him other than working out the soreness. And with Roxy, he did want to take one of Valentine's rare pieces of good advice and explore all the possibilities…of which, Roxy Rose had so many that fascinated him. Thank God for that misadventure with a broken faucet.

"WOULD YOU MIND taking a look at the air bag burn on my face?" Ned asked, twisting over.

Roxy moved forward slightly, just until she was straddling his chest. Then she saw it. A tidy, reddish abrasion about the size of a couple of quarters tucked a little under the edge of his chin. It was hidden in his stubble, and wow, how she loved him in stubble. That was the only way she ever saw him, maybe the only way she ever wanted to see him. "Well, Doctor Roxy diagnoses a special little potion to fix it right up." She traced the burn with the tips of her fingers, a light touch that caused him to shiver.

"Then potion away," he growled.

Leaning down to his face, Roxy brushed the red area with a light kiss. "Does your boo-boo feel better now?" she asked, her cheek pressed to his.

"Not yet."

So she kissed him again, this time a little longer, then traced the abrasion with her tongue. So much restraint...both of them. She could already feel his erection pushing at her, and her erect nipples doing the same against him. Thank heavens she hadn't worn a bra tonight, just in case. "Better yet?"

"I think I may need a complete physical, Doctor. And I may have need of a few of your *other* therapies." Reaching up, he slipped his hands under her shirt and cupped her breasts. "Nice therapy," he murmured. "Think I'm feeling better already."

The first sensation of his hands on her was everything she expected, and more. "And I definitely have need of your therapies too," she gasped. Just that one little caress made her tingle. Tingle everywhere—in her toes, in her ears, between her legs. She was practically exploding with tingle. "So, *this* doctor likes to do her examinations on the floor, if that's okay with the patient." Or the bed, or the shower, or the kitchen table. Didn't matter, as long as the patient was Ned.

"*This* patient would love to be examined anywhere the good doctor wants to examine him. Anywhere..." He grinned up at her. "And everywhere."

That's all he had to say. Within two seconds Roxy's T-shirt was off and she was working on removing his

"Also, the doctor likes to stay on top," she said, her voice so hoarse from pure, passionate excitement she almost sounded like Valentine. Durn that Valentine, always sneaking in like that.

Ned blinked at her for a moment, then laughed. "And will the patient get a sucker if he's a good boy and does what the doctor tells him to?"

"No good boys here, Ned. Only *bad* boys." His eyes were full of such fire—the whiskey hues in them glowing with embers she didn't recognize, that almost frightened her. She couldn't turn away—they pulled her in, made her want to stay longer than she'd ever stayed anywhere.

It seemed this was going to turn into more than what she'd intended—great sex on a hardwood floor. Something fast, satisfying, reckless. Roxy found herself caught up in dreamy thoughts of the next time and the time after that. But that wasn't the way she ordered her life. So she forced herself back into the moment before her little fantasy spoiled the mood. Moment to moment... "And if you're very bad, I just might have something extra-specially..." Oops. Val trying to get out again. "Extra bad for you, too. If you like bad."

"I love bad," he murmured. "Can't wait for it."

"I'll just bet you can't," she chuckled, inching down the length of him until she was straddling his legs. "Now, let me do one little thing here...." She retrieved her T-shirt from the floor and dangled it over his face, tickling his nose and lips with it. "No bra under it," she teased.

"You think I didn't notice?"

"I didn't see you staring."

"I didn't want you to." He took a deep breath. "It smells just like you."

"You already know how I smell?"

"The first time I passed you in the hall." His lips curled into a licentious smile. "You linger."

She pulled the cotton knit across his eyes. "In a good way, I hope."

"The very best way. The way a man can't forget. So are you going to tie me up with it?" Ned asked, his voice edgy with anticipation.

Yanking the shirt away from his eyes, Roxy leaned forward and brushed a flirty little kiss across his lips. "Nope. But I am going to blindfold you." She raised up slightly and caressed his face with the shirt one more time before dropping it over his eyes. In doing so, her breasts passed across his lips, and she took care to make sure her nipples visited his mouth long enough to allow him a little nibble. But just a little. Then she pulled away before he had a chance to do anything more than sigh with pleasure, and reached around his head to tie the knot.

"So I don't get to see *anything?*" he asked.

"In your mind, Ned. You'll see it all in your mind. That's the real turn-on. Of course, I've got to admit I'm sure enjoying looking at you. Have been, since, well, the first time I saw you in the hall. I've enjoyed all kinds of glimpses of you walking away this past month."

"And I've enjoyed you looking." He chuckled—low, throaty, sexy. A chuckle that raised her need to a level she'd never before felt—a chuckle that told her she wanted to race to the finish before she shattered into a million shameless pieces, and yet hold back to enjoy the journey.

"You looked good, so I stared." She leaned forward and whispered in his ear, "I stared a lot."

"So what are you staring at now?"

She whispered into his other ear, "Bad boy, Ned. Very bad boy. That's what your imagination is for. What do you think I'm staring at?" Then she kissed him, on the ear, on the jaw, on the lips. A hard kiss, so potent she could have parted happy if that was all there was to be between them. But that was just the start, as the kiss cheated Roxy of breath, of sense, of everything but the want of him. And she was so dizzy from it all....

"So when did blindfolding me come to you?" he asked, as she pulled back away from him to stop the spinning in her head.

Advice to caller number three, a week ago last Tuesday. "Just now." A part of her wanted to strip him completely naked and indulge herself in the full view of him, the total feel, the entire taste. His jeans were already riding dangerously low, exposing the glorious white band of briefs above the waist, plus a whole lot more—thank heavens he wasn't a boxers man, she hated boxers—but she wasn't ready for that yet. What she'd thought would be speedy and unconnected wasn't anymore, and for that she'd be forever grateful.

Bending over Ned, close to his face, Roxy whispered, "You don't mind being blindfolded, do you? If you do, I can think of other fun places to tie my T-shirt." With that, she twisted sideways and slid her hand along the band of his jeans, first from hip to hip, then just barely inside the fabric, skimming her fingers lightly over his belly until she elicited a gasp from him. Then she withdrew them and picked up his T-shirt.

"Take a good *hard* look, Roxy," he growled. "Does *anything* about me look like I'm minding anything you've done so far?"

She didn't look. She would have liked to, but what was good for Ned was good for Roxy. Meaning his T-shirt, her blindfold. "No advantages," she said to Ned, tying the knot securely behind her head.

"So now we begin?" he asked.

"I think we began about a month ago, didn't we?" she purred, reaching down to feel his chest. Whoa, that sure was the gorgeous chest she remembered. Bare, and so smooth. She ran her fingers lightly from nipple to nipple.

Nipples—so understated on a man, yet with so much promise. She rubbed them with her thumbs, trying to remember the exact color. Brown? No, umber…a raw, earthy color that suited his dark cast.

"That tickles," he choked, shrugging his arms up across his chest protectively.

"Good," she replied, pushing his arms back down. "It's supposed to." Then she moved to flick her tongue over first the left, then the right—what she'd wanted to do the first time she'd seen him shirtless. "Does that?"

"When it's my turn you'll get to see for yourself."

"Feel for myself," she corrected, giving him a light nip with her teeth before she pushed away. Then as a prelude, she slipped her hand down his chest and farther into his jeans than she'd gone before, brushing her fingers lightly over his erection. "And it's feeling pretty good."

"I thought you preferred bad," he said raggedly.

"Good is bad, and bad is good. And what I'm feeling right now is…" Roxy twisted to place a kiss just above his belt line as she withdrew her hand "…is huge."

His response to that was a throaty moan, followed by a shudder so intense she was surprised by it. Surprised, and aroused even more than she already was, learning that something so simple as a touch held such power.

Pushing herself back up toward his chest, Roxy continued her journey, her fingers tracing all the way to his shoulders. That's where she stopped again to explore—the muscles in his upper arms…strong, gentle. His lower arms…sinewy. His hands, fingers…all so soft…so soft she could almost feel them on her, stroking her the way she stroked him.

In good time, she thought, shivering as the goose bumps rose on her arms. "Your hands are soft," and she wanted them all over her, "like a man who's never done a day's worth of hard work."

"Like fixing a faucet?" he growled.

"I rest my case."

"Would you mind resting your case just a little lower?"

Moving back down the length of him to his stomach, she sketched the contours of its musculature with her fingertips, then followed with her tongue. The fingertips elicited a gasp of excitement from him, the tongue a hearty moan. She liked both.

Something so sexy about feeling and hearing, but not seeing. But she wouldn't see, wouldn't allow herself that pleasure...not until she knew him in every intimate detail.

"Is the floor getting too hard yet?" she whispered, unstraddling him for a moment. Time for the jeans to go, and in a way she hated for them to come off because they'd been the source of several good fantasies. But as good as he was in them, she knew he'd be even better out of them. Judging from all she'd been feeling below his waist as she straddled him, *extra-specially* good.

"Everything's getting too hard, and the floor's the least of it."

"Well, can't fix the floor but maybe I can do something for *everything* else." And off came the jeans. Her hands pulling, his pushing until they were a heap scattered who-knows-where, since neither of them could see. At least she couldn't, and she sure hoped he was staying true to his blindfold.

Of course, the visual image of him watching her when she couldn't watch him was almost as exciting as watching him. Almost...

Before Ned's briefs met the same fate as his jeans, Roxy straddled him once more, exploring his legs the same way she'd explored his chest...slowly, one sense at a time—feel, taste—until he was moaning so vigorously she feared Georgette Selby's banging might start up any minute, even though they were nowhere near the kitchen wall. "Can I be on the bottom now?" she asked.

"I thought you'd never ask." Pushing himself up, he pulled Roxy into his arms and pulled her under him almost at the same time, until he was the one doing the straddling. Then he explored her belly, her breasts with his fingertips, and traced the same path with his tongue as she'd done to him. Only his journey was much more urgent than hers, and by the time he was removing her jeans, she was responding with the same frantic urgency, arching her hips to him, writhing, throbbing, moaning.

"Ned," she gasped, reaching out blindly and frantically to pull him to her. "Please..." She needed him in her, now. The pure, aching want of him was taking over, and in the seconds it took him to find his pants and search his wallet for a condom—blindfolded—she thought she would explode. Then the unwrapping...would he ever get it unwrapped? "Let me do that," she cried, sitting up, and reaching out for the foil packet.

"My pleasure. But make sure you do that with the blindfold still on."

It was, but now she wanted it off. "You've got to be kidding."

"You weren't when you started this. I'm not as I finish it."

By the time she'd taken it out of the packet, her fingers were trembling. Then by the time she'd ripped off his briefs—*literally* ripped—her hands were shaking. "I...um...haven't..." She'd never done it before, blindfolded or not, and as she found him, and discovered the obstacle of getting that little tiny thing slipped over his great big...and in a blindfold no less, she suddenly decided on a little detour before the grand finale.

"Roxy," he moaned, the muscles on his thighs stiffening as her lips met his erection. "I can't..."

She laughed, deep and throaty. "I'll just bet you can." Moments later, just as he was about to explode, she slipped on the condom, and slipped herself over him, immodestly positioning herself to reap all the intense pleasure he could give to her. Then she began the rhythm she needed, he needed, rocking slowly at first, uttering wispy little moans that were intimate and hushed. Hers, his…theirs. Nice, unhurried…but not for very long. Because within seconds, Ned matched the rhythm, pushing up at her as she drove herself down on him. Harder, faster, their urgency unchecked. And as their moans grew louder, their thrusting more vigorous, Roxy went on ahead, exploding into an orgasm that shook the walls, the ceiling, the windows on the next floor up. "Ned," she screamed. "Yes! Yes!" And as she exploded, so did he, with the same intensity. "Ned," she screamed again as the last shudder cascaded through her.

"Roxy," he whispered in response.

Eventually, after the blindfolds were finally tossed aside, and just before the ceiling plaster started to crumble from the shaking, Roxy collapsed on top of Ned, panting and sweating, contented and quenched, and, for once in her life, without a single, solitary word to utter.

Well, without a word until Georgette Selby started banging on the wall. "What do you know." Roxy laughed. "I never knew I was a screamer. Guess you and Georgette are the first ones to find out."

No, HE HADN'T SPENT the night with her. It sure would have been nice if he had, but unfortunately, nice came with all sorts of complications Roxy simply didn't want to mess around with right now. So after they'd managed to find some very *imaginative* ways to work out the crimps and charley horses that came after all that spirited commotion on the hardwood floor—*Note to self, buy a nice, cushy rug*—they'd parted amicably. In fact, much better than an unadorned amicably. Their friendly parting at the front door, the clumsy handshake, the anti-climatic peck on the cheek had turned into a zealous bye-bye demanding another five minutes, afterwards making Roxy an unwavering believer in his fine command of the quickie.

Then after *it* was over and he was really gone, she was so weak in the knees she'd slid down the door to the floor and stayed there ten minutes to collect her wits. Even then she'd nearly had to crawl to bed.

And yes, in spite of all that bliss, and the greatest orgasms she'd ever had, Roxy was glad she was alone for the rest of the night. Waking up with Ned next to her would have been so nice, but the thought of actually sleeping in his arms and sharing the intimacies of the morning after, petrified her. Two doors and a hallway separating them was for the best. *Her best*, anyway, since career first and Ned…well, she wasn't so sure about that anymore.

Guarded and casual was okay, Roxy reasoned, as she looked out over her little piece of heaven on earth—the only thing in her crazy life that made complete and perfect sense to her. This morning she was alone there, still sort of afterglowing—not a full-fledged afterglow like immediately after the sex, but just a tinge of warm and fuzzy around the edges, hanging on more like a revered memory than an actual feeling. All she wanted to go with that were a few of the gull cookies she'd brought and a Starbucks, along with the glorious Puget Sound stretching out eternally before her. A perfect moment, and she was glad for the respite. Alone. To think.

"Okay, I give up. You win," she called to the squawking gulls, lining up fifty yards away waiting for their cookies. Grabbing a grocery bag containing the ten bags of cookies Astrid had so generously donated to the seagulls, actually the payoff for doing the promo spots correctly, Roxy wandered out to the sandy area that stretched between the grasses and the water, scattered them all over the ground, then ran as fast as she could for cover before the birds decided she looked like creamy white filling and swooped in on her for dessert.

"You keep doing that and you'll end up with thousands of them flocking out here, then you'll never get rid of them." William Parker, Shorecroft's manager, stepped over the knoll, stopping shoulder to shoulder with her. "They can be a real messy nuisance. Villagers hate them when they swarm in masses, like this. And they don't normally go away once they've been attracted by something. *Like your cookies.*"

"I like them," Roxy said. "Don't mind feeding them either, even if it's by the thousands. And I'm guessing they were here long before we were, so I think we owe them a little something for messing up their habitat. A cookie's not that high a price to pay, is it?" She crammed the empty cookie wrappers into a paper bag, then dropped it on the ground along with her shoes and the remains of her Starbucks. "So what brings you out here this morning, Mr. Parker?" Like she didn't already know. "Another stipulation on my building plans, even though I don't really have any building plans yet?"

"I'm going to cut straight to the chase here," he said, his voice cool. "And I think you need to take this seriously."

"Oh, I take it seriously, Mr. Parker. I've taken every one of your straighten-up-and-build-right letters seriously. I've taken your phone calls seriously. I've taken every bit of harassment over nonexistent house plans seriously, because I've made a huge investment in this land, and I'm not talking about the money. So it's very serious to me, Mr. Parker." She braced herself for the sharp edge, almost felt it sticking between her shoulder blades already.

"We're going to annex your property. I thought I should be the one to tell you. It's been in the works for a while, then for one reason or another never came to a vote. But at an emergency meeting last night we decided that, in the best interest of Shorecroft, we need to proceed with annexation for a lot of reasons. One being taxes. Building out here means you, and a few others who've bought property in the area, will be taking advantage of our village services, but not paying a rightful amount of the burden."

Roxy looked over at him staring into the dirt. He was a nervous man. Soft and Jello-y, balding, fortyish. No devil horns that she could see, no forked tongue either. Never looked anybody straight in the eye, not because he was shifty, but because he always looked at the ground. "You can call it a tax issue if you want, and I don't have a problem paying taxes. But that's not really it, is it, Mr. Parker?" She wasn't surprised about this. She'd known from the day she'd written the check for the property this would probably happen. This, or some other form of protest. The real estate agent had warned her that changing the status quo in places like Shorecroft wasn't an easy thing to do.

"I'm not going to lie to you, Miss Rose. It's true, there have been some concerns expressed about your plans not fitting in with the community. Frank Thomas brought it to our attention, after you fired him, that you intend to go far beyond anything we have around here. But that's not entirely it." Frank Thomas, the Shorecroft architect who'd insisted on a quaint seaside cottage. At the point she'd canned him, he was getting awfully close to a thatched roof.

"I can fight you, you know. I bought the property with stated intentions to build on it long before you lowered the annexation boom on me." Brave words, and they sounded good. But she wasn't especially convinced by them. Government bodies got away with hokey things all the time.

"Oh, you can fight us, Miss Rose. We're aware of your options, but we're also aware of ours."

"And if I build the perfect little seaside cottage? Something more in keeping with the village's image." Not that she necessarily would. But she needed some options, and compromise wasn't out of the question. Her land was certainly worth compromise. "Would that make a difference?"

He turned his head away, looking out across the water, not at her, not at the dirt. "It only just came to my attention who you are, Miss Rose. Or should I say, Doctor Valentine McCarthy. And your notoriety is…well, to be blunt, bothersome to me. We're just a quiet little community of people who want to get away from what you talk about on your radio show." Clearing his throat, he turned back, looking directly at her, maybe for the first time in all the weeks she'd known him. "Out here we don't want to drive naked, or fix up our mothers with handsome studs for the purpose of hot mamma sex." He cleared his throat again. "You use the word p-p-penis in your advice quite liberally. People in Shorecroft don't say it in polite company, and they certainly don't want to hear it. Or have their children hear it. They blush at such things, Miss Rose. And I know that may be a throwback by your standards, but we don't want your kind of influence so close by."

"Because I use the word *penis* without blushing?" Roxy laughed bitterly. 'I'm beginning to take this personally, Mr. Parker."

"I have nothing against you personally, Miss Rose. But like I told you, there were concerns voiced over your house to begin with, then when this latest information surfaced…" He shrugged nervously, looked back down at the dirt. "All I can say is, as village manager, it's my duty to address those concerns and take care of the village the best way I know how."

"Which is by annexing my property and not allowing me to build what I want to build, and hoping I'll give up and sell? I think I should be the one with concerns, Mr. Parker. Sounds like a pretty shaky way to run village business to me. But I'm not going to hold your *duty* to Shorecroft against you, like you're holding my job against me." She gave way to a disenchanted smile. "All I ever wanted was a place to watch the comings and goings of the days, a place to listen to the gulls, watch the waves, a place that would be all the things a home should be...the home that everyone in Shorecroft wants."

"I'm sorry, Miss Rose."

"So am I, Mr. Parker. I expected better from you. So who squealed on me? Can you tell me that much?" She was curious, not that it mattered now.

"E-mail. No source." That was all he said before he left.

Roxy didn't watch him walk away. Instead, she dropped back down into the grassy spot on her knoll, wondering *why now*? Why, after all this time, after all her dreams had finally started to come true, had they only now dug deep enough to find Valentine?

8

"No, I STILL DON'T KNOW what to do about it." Sipping root beer with Astrid in the break room an hour before the show was supposed to start, Roxy was still numb from William Parker's decree earlier that afternoon, and not quite worked up to the emotional level she'd need to see this house fight through. "I went out there, fed the gulls...it started out so good, then it ended up like..."

"Bird crap," Doyle supplied, strolling in, carrying a pizza.

"Do you ever *not* listen?" Roxy snapped.

"Do you ever not turn off your mic?" he retorted, plopping the box down on Roxy's desk. "Extra cheese, double pepperoni, thin crust. Your favorite."

"Sorry. Bad day."

"So I've heard." He tossed out three paper plates and a handful of napkins.

Roxy shot him a wry look. "Yeah, apparently. And that drive naked stunt sure didn't help me any."

"Maybe not on the home front, but the front office is thrilled. They've got new advertisers lining up, advertisers that want to wrap around your promos. How awesome is that? People paying good money to put their commercials on the air next to your commercial. Price went up this afternoon, in case you hadn't heard. And there's already a waiting list. It's all about business, Rox. Your credo." Pulling up a chair, Doyle scooted in between Roxy and Astrid, then opened the box. "So have some pizza, and in case you didn't notice, I haven't even touched it yet, so you can't yell at me about that."

"I didn't yell at you about driving naked," Roxy snapped.

"Depends on what you call yelling. And like I told you before, I know I shouldn't have done it, but it seemed like such a good opportunity to give everyone a taste of the real Val. It worked out great, but I'm sorry. So are we good yet or do I need to buy you another pizza?"

Roxy relented with a forced smile. "It is working out pretty well for the program, isn't it? And yes, you do owe me another pizza. They're giving me grief on building on my property because they found out who I am and they sure didn't like my driving naked spots. And on top of that, my handyman got rear-ended by a car full of naked drivers. Nothing serious, just a fender-bender, but he was sure doing a lot of trash talking about Valentine." Of course, the fender-bender had worked out rather well. Something she wasn't about to mention to Doyle.

"Yeah, I heard you telling some of that to Astrid. The part about your property."

"They're trying to pull out the big guns to keep her from building," Astrid answered. "Hoping she'll give up and go away because they don't like Valentine."

"Like I've been telling you all along. You're city, Rox." Doyle shook his head before he bit into his first piece of pizza—actually, two pieces still joined at the crust. He swallowed almost without chewing.

"That's what you think. Just watch me." She wasn't sure what there was to watch since she didn't have a plan. Not yet. But she would. Roxy Valentine Rose didn't back down in either of her personas.

"Well, don't say I didn't warn you. They probably do secret rituals at night, incantations to cast out the evil radio-woman demons." Doyle wrestled with a string of cheese still attached to the pizza.

"Actually, they're casting out the evil radio-woman demon by annexation, not incantation, not that it matters. However they go for it, it's still going to be one great big pain in the…" Anguish causing a visible crinkle between Roxy's eyes, she grabbed for a piece of pizza while the grabbing was good, since Doyle had already staked his dibs in the way of one fleshy thumb ground squarely into the middle of pieces number three and four. "I still can't believe it," she muttered. "I own that property. They don't have the right to…" She shrugged. "I just don't know."

"So what happens next, Rox?" Astrid asked, snatching her piece.

"Maybe I can throw myself on their mercy at the next town meeting. I mean, it's not like I've done anything wrong. I bought that property in good faith, and maybe once they see that I'm not what they think I am…"

"A slut," Doyle said helpfully.

"Gee, thanks," Roxy snapped, scowling at him. "Always trust Doyle to reduce it to the bottom line."

He fingered the brim of his baseball cap in a salute.

"So maybe once they see that I'm not a…slut, they won't mind having me for a neighbor. And if they won't mind having me for a neighbor, maybe they won't mind the kind of house I want to build. But right now that's jumping way ahead of myself. So I suppose I should go to their next meeting, grovel, beg, plead, sing a chorus of 'Why Can't We Be Friends?' and tell them all I want is to get along since I intend on spending a lot of my life out there."

"Big waste of time," Doyle said, his claiming thumb heading for yet another piece. "If the seagulls don't get ya, the villagers will. They'll rise up from their graves at night…."

"And stick their thumbs in your pizza," Astrid muttered, reaching for her second piece before Doyle's thumb descended upon it.

"Got your point," Roxy said, going after *her* second piece, even though she wasn't hungry enough to finish off her first. Holding it up in the air, she said, "Peace offering for the Shorecroft annex zombies…I come in peace, bringing pizza." Fat lot of good that would do, though. The handwriting was already in the sand, the ink long since pooped upon by the gulls. "Tuesday night, Astrid. Their next town board meeting and I'm going to be there. So let's do reruns then, okay? I have a feeling I won't be in the mood to do a live show after I've been brutalized." She chuckled. "I'm afraid I'd tell the listeners to strip naked and go run through the streets of Shorecroft."

"The annex zombies versus Doctor Valentine's naked motorists. Sort of makes you wish we did television instead of radio, doesn't it?" Doyle finished his pizza then headed into his booth. "Better ratings seeing them naked than just talking about it."

"So, anything new with the handyman other than his little fender-bender?" Astrid asked, once Doyle was out of the booth. "Did he *fix* anything for you last night?"

Roxy glanced at the microphone, turned it off, then leaned over and whispered to Astrid, "Oh, he fixed, all right. In fact, he put a new spin on the word *fix*. And that's another problem."

"Oh, my God! You tingled, didn't you?" Astrid squealed so loud Doyle tapped on the glass, giving them a big, over-exaggerated shrug, meaning he didn't know what was going on, and he wanted to. Both women shooed him off with a swatting motion. "You're falling for him," Astrid continued, making sure her back was to Doyle so he wouldn't read her lips—which they both suspected that he could do. This was a strictly-between-girlfriends talk, not meant for him. "You two finally slept together and it was great. Better than great, and you're falling in love with him, but now that someone's finally rocked your world you don't know what to do about it. Right?"

"Will you keep it down!" Roxy snapped. "And yes, we did, and yes, it was, and that's as far as it goes, except I'm scared to death because it *was* nice, Astrid. Really nice. Nicer than anything I could have ever imagined *with anyone,* and I'm not just talking about the sex here. I'm talking about the two of us together. Before the sex, after the sex. Talking, laughing, whatever. It's all so good I'm totally afraid of it."

"And *sooo good* scares you, why? Because he's only a handyman and you're a famous soon-to-be millionaire radio shrink?"

"Way off. He owns the building. Several others, too, I think. But that wouldn't matter, and you know that."

"So you're afraid he won't fit into your plans? Career first, the rest later. *Sorry, Mr. Handyman, you're okay for bed but don't you get yourself involved in my life.* Come on, that's so lame, Rox. We crossed over the twentieth *and* twenty-first century marks. Women have been master jugglers for a long time now. Having it all is what it's about."

"Yeah, well lately, my juggling isn't very good," Roxy moaned. "Everything I'm tossing up is coming right back down and hitting me on the head. Like my Rose Palace...the one that's gonna have to be converted into a Rose Pup Tent if I want to live on my property any time soon."

"Hey, don't knock it until you've tried it. I've heard about some pretty neat things two people can do in a pup tent."

Roxy laughed. "I'm getting too old for hard surfaces." She rubbed her stiff lower back, remembering everything she and Ned had done on the floor. Definitely worth the pain. "Of course, working out the kinks comes with its own set of interesting possibilities."

"Not even going to ask about it," Astrid said, scooting out the door. "We'll talk later, after we're off. Unless you've got other kinks to explore."

"Later," Roxy promised, turning around and putting on her headphones. Then she wrinkled her nose at Doyle. "And in case you're reading my lips, you're not invited."

He arched his eyebrows innocently, giving her the one-minute-until-air signal. Then Astrid gave her the high sign. *It's him!* she mouthed.

After her normal sign on, Roxy went straight to the call. "Well, Edward. I thought maybe you'd forsaken us. We didn't hear from you last night." She opened her drawer and pulled out her truffle.

"And you missed me?"

"Well, of course I did, because I knew you'd have so many interesting things to say. You know, driving naked." He seemed awfully mellow. He should have snapped right to the argument, but she wasn't sure she could even drag him into it. "You didn't try it, did you? Let me guess, you tried it and you liked it."

"Did you try it, Val? Did you take off your clothes and drive around like you told everybody else to do?"

"I never get out in rush-hour traffic."

"It was irresponsible, but you know that."

"I'd prefer to think of it as liberating. Haven't you ever wanted to liberate yourself, Edward? Chuck the conventional standards and just go right out there to the end of the limb to see what it feels like?"

"Out on a limb? I've seen your face on billboards, Val. Dark glasses, long bangs, scarf around your neck, wide-brimmed hat, lots of makeup. Not much of you showing. Certainly nothing close to naked. A long, *long* way back from the end of the limb. Makes me wonder why, since *you're* so liberated. So here's the offer. When you decide you want to drive naked, give me a call. I'll pick you up and we'll do it together. And the moral of this lesson, Valentine, is if you're going to preach it, practice it. I'm betting a lot of your listeners would love to see you do what you tell them to do." Then he hung up, leaving Roxy speechless, and totally out of the mood for her truffle. Score a big one for Eddie.

IT WAS A LITTLE AFTER FOUR when Roxy finally slipped her key in the lock and crept into her apartment, trying not to invoke the wrath of the wall-banging she-devil sitting on the other side. They'd gone for coffee—her and Astrid. It was one of those tacky little all-night diners; the kind where greasy fare and awesome pie was served twenty-four seven, and one letter on the flashing neon sign was always burned out. Tonight it was an *iner,* and they'd both had a heavenly slice of cherry pie, à la mode of course, to go with the coffee. And they'd talked and speculated and what-iffed on the state of Roxy's dizzy emotions until Roxy had a dizzy headache. Then they'd said their good-nights with nothing firm figured out, except that if Roxy kept eating truffles after Eddie and Twinkies with Ned she was going to get fat—funny how they both had that sugary effect on her—and that Roxy more than liked Ned and she was getting a great big case of the guilts over hiding Val. That's why Val was always trying to sneak up on her. But Roxy already knew that going in.

Still, it was good to talk to a girlfriend...something she and Astrid didn't get to do too much these days. Work always managed to butt in. Like it would manage to butt in if she did anything more than let Ned slip in and out of her bed.

Pushing the door open, Roxy had only taken one step inside when the familiar voice greeted her from behind. "Another late-night client?" Ned asked from his door across the hall. His voice was friendly, not suspicious or accusatory. Not even proprietary, and maybe she would have liked a little proprietary...someone to watch over Roxy. *That* sure was a thought she'd never had before.

"Out with a girlfriend. Best friend." She didn't bother

turning around. "We don't get to see much of each other any more." Not a lie. She was the queen of letting assumptions ride, cloaking them in half truths, but she didn't lie.

"Georgette Selby called about an hour ago. She thought you might be sprawled out dead somewhere in your apartment since you weren't making your usual racket. She said she was concerned."

"And you? Were you concerned? Or are you checking in an official capacity, as owner of the building?" She wanted concerned. But she didn't want it.

"Well, I was a little concerned, I'll admit. But you're a big girl. You know what you're doing."

Yeah right. More like girl without a clue lately. "But you stayed up, anyway?" Promising.

"Maybe. Unless that offends your liberated sensibilities. If it does, I was catching up on some paperwork."

Liberated? Uh-oh. He'd been listening to Val, again. Thin line time, here, and she had to make sure Val didn't sneak over it. "Believe me, my sensibilities are pretty tough. Though after the day I've had, I'm not sure I have any left."

Still standing behind her, Ned raised his hands to her neck and began a gentle massage. "Anything I can do to make it better?"

"Believe me, you're already making it a whole lot better." She hadn't realized how much tension she was carrying in her body until now, and what he was doing was pure heaven. Maybe even better than sex. *Maybe.*

"Want to talk about it?"

"Nothing to talk about, except everywhere I turned something went wrong. Absolutely nothing went according to plan." He was sans shirt again, just the way she liked him. Barefooted, too. And Roxy could see the two of them on her beach, him without the shirt and shoes, his face shadowed by late-night stubble, his hair mussed. Just like he was now—the irresistible image she wanted to invite in and make love to until daylight.

"And you plan everything?"

"Everything?"

"Everything."

"Did you plan this?"

She waited for the kiss, expected it on her neck, her shoulders, anywhere. Even shut her eyes to enjoy it. But nothing...no kiss. And he even stopped the massage. "Ned?" she said, opening her eyes to make sure he hadn't gone home. He hadn't. He was in front of her now, sitting in the middle of a rug that hadn't been there when she'd left home.

"So did you?" he prompted, patting the rug, inviting her to come sit with him.

"Well, I'll admit, you got me." First Edward got her, now Ned. So big deal. Maybe a little bit of her control was slipping. For Ned, it was worth it.

"Actually, what I'd like to do is get you on the rug."

Nice rug, she thought, dropping down onto it next to him. Plush, soft, its nap deep and snugly. And it was ecru, with a gentle wave pattern throughout, woven like ocean waves...the waves she could see from her shoreline. Like he'd known. "My thoughts exactly," she said, dropping to her knees and opening her arms to him.

ROXY WAS SLEEPING SOUNDLY when Ned kissed her lightly on the forehead and went back across the hall. Not quite seven in the morning. He had about two hours in which to grab a nap, strap on his tool belt and go see about Mr. Starsiak's running toilet. Come tomorrow—Saturday—Oswald would be back to take over the building management and handyman duties, thank the divine being of building husbandry, and *he'd* be back to normal life—writing by day, doing an occasional book signing when he could fit it in, and sleeping normal hours. Well, maybe not *that* anymore since Roxy sure didn't like keeping normal hours, and he intended on keeping Roxy in his schedule— if she wanted to be kept. Good thing he'd given up his practice. It was a tough decision, but private practice and media psychology just didn't mix. And truth be told, he really liked the media psychology better. Thanks to his call-ins to Doctor Val, he actually had a couple of deals possibly in the works for himself. His own call-in radio show, maybe. Or even a TV show à la Doctor Phil. *Eat your heart out, Valentine!* Plus his books, of course. They were his bread and butter.

"So it's getting damned complicated," he said to Hep. "And I'm counting on you for some support here." Dropping down into bed without bothering to take off his jeans, Ned punched a dent in the pillow for his head then switched off the bedside lamp. "I've never known anyone like her," he murmured, as Hep kneaded a spot alongside him. "And I don't have time to get involved with her, which is a problem, because I'm going to get involved with her, anyway." He laughed, glancing at the clock. It was time to get up. "*Am* involved with her and her damn odd hours." Looking to get even more involved. Maybe even spend the whole night sometime. "And it's a damned nice rug," he said, lazily stroking Hep as both man and cat drifted off.

GOOD THING SHE DIDN'T NEED much sleep because Roxy was up three hours after her eyes closed. Still on the rug, alone, she ran her hand over the dent he'd made, and basked there for about a minute before she remembered her appointment. Two prospective sponsors before noon, sponsors she hoped to carry over into syndication. Then she was going to knock out some of the nitty-gritty with one of the syndicators. Pin them to some figures. Get them to commit to some offers—how many stations initially, if there were going to be any censorship issues. Things she had to know before she sealed the deal.

Her leisurely shower lasted about five minutes, then she dashed into her bedroom to slip into Valentine. Whoops! Big mistake. No way to explain Val if he caught her. "Geez, I've got to tell him," she said, stuffing her wig into a bag, along with her Val makeup and a very tight, slinky Val kind of dress—one that showed the cleavage she'd have to hoist up and over. Hey, it's what they expected. The package sold the show. But she sure hated the damn stilettoes.

"Look, I'll have to make a quick change somewhere else," she told Astrid, as she plodded to her door, cell phone to her ear, Valentine in the bag she was carrying.

"You haven't told him yet?" Astrid screeched in her ear.

Out in the hall now, she was fumbling through her jeans pocket for her key. "No, I haven't told him yet."

"Told who what?" Ned asked, taking the bag full of Val from her hands.

She clicked off the phone without even saying goodbye. "Told someone I, um, have an arrangement with about my credentials." Good. She spun around and looked at him. His face was pretty noncommittal. *Guess he's buying it.*

"You don't think he has a right to know?"

Talk about being in a tight spot. Right about now somewhere between that rock and that hard place looked pretty darn good. "It's complicated. He knows my, um, work. Likes it really well." Judging from the way he moaned last night, really, really well. "And pretty much he's been judging me by those merits."

"So what's the problem?"

"My, um, school." Good, good. "He hates it. Some of the core ideals between our, um, school philosophies differ, I suppose you could say. And if he knew I was, um, from that particular school, I think he'd end our arrangement based purely on that fact. You know, forget about my work and hold my school against me, even though I'm nothing like my school, and my school is...was solely for educational purposes."

"But he's seen what you do, and likes it?"

"Uh-huh." She was beginning to sweat. Face turning red. Hyperventilation coming right up. "Haven't had a complaint so far."

"And you get along well with him?"

Boy, do we! "Yes."

"Then don't tell him. Why risk a good thing when you don't have to? If he's happy with what you're doing for him, and you're happy with him, I'd say leave well enough alone. People really overcomplicate their lives sometimes, don't you think?"

Yep, he'd hit that nail on the head. And without a hammer. "But don't you think that's being dishonest, not telling him?"

"You're not lying to him, are you?"

"No, I wouldn't do that."

"Not hurting him in any way?"

She shook her head.

"Then like I said, don't overcomplicate it. Just give him what he wants, what he expects from you, and if your school ever should come up, maybe by that time he'll be so happy with what you're doing it won't matter."

Well, they were sure the words she wanted to hear. But they didn't make her feel any better. "I, um, I've got to run," she said, snatching Val from his hands. "And about tonight...I've got to work. *All night.* Sorry." She really needed some solitary thinking time.

Ned bent down and gave her a quick kiss. "Don't understand the hours, but I certainly understand the drive. I'll miss you, though."

Not as much as she'd miss him.

"BEFORE YOU SAY ANYTHING, I know. I've got to tell him."
Climbing into the car next to Astrid, Roxy tossed the Val
accoutrements into the backseat. "And I came really close
just now. Wanted to, should have, couldn't. I'm weak, I'm
a chicken."

"A chicken who's falling in love."

"It's not like that between us."

"The lips say casual, the eyes say head over heels. I'm
believing the eyes."

"You need glasses," Roxy quipped.

"Apparently, so do you. Now, the salesman's name is
Curtis Keltner. He's a little glib, and he's going to go for
the moon *and* the stars, so we've got to be firm. Keep up
the attitude that we're doing him a favor by letting him
buy time on our program."

"I know you haven't met him, but do you think he
might love me? I mean, I know I have some issues, but that
doesn't make me totally a bitch, does it? Someone like him
could love me."

"He's gay."

"Ned?"

"Curtis Keltner. The man I was trying to talk to you
about. Remember? He wants to buy time from us for his
bistro. Our first appointment this morning. Don't go soft
on me now, Roxy. He's going to wine us and dine us and
try to screw us for more minutes and less money, and with
the mood you're in right now, it's going to be pretty easy."

"But he did say I shouldn't tell him. Not if things were
going great the way they were. And they *are* going great."

"I'm not feeling good about this, Rox. You're scaring me."

"I haven't been feeling too good about it either, and it
scares *me*. But I'm afraid if I do tell him, that'll be the end
of it. And I don't want it to end."

"You're about to blow a big deal for us here."

Roxy snapped her head toward Astrid. "I've got to tell

him. I've decided. Right time, right place, and I've got to go through with it. And if you think I'm going to blow a deal with Keltner over this, ain't gonna happen, girlfriend. Roxy Rose on the personal side might be a mess right now, but when it comes to business, I'm going to have my way with Keltner, glib, gay, or otherwise."

9

A Really Beachin' Saturday Afternoon

NO NED AFTER Friday night's show. She'd asked him to stay away and he had, but she would have made room on the rug if he'd come over, anyway. She wants him, she wants him not, she wants him… Twice with Ned could still be considered a little bit of spontaneous whoopee, but three times would make it an item. While she was all for the whoopee, the item was way out there on the limb for her. The limb Edward Craig said she wouldn't go out on. *Wonder what he'd say if he could see me climbing my way out there, inch by shaky inch?* And it was definitely shaky.

Sleep was a good thing though. At least that's how she'd consoled herself as she dropped down onto the rug— *their rug*—alone and spent the night. Then by Saturday, late morning, she actually felt up to her little weekend jaunt to the beach. Brand-new day, and things weren't quite so bleak as they'd been two days ago, when Mr. Parker started leading his full frontal annexation attack. That was her property out there, durn his prudish hide. And nobody but nobody was going to railroad her into selling, submitting or otherwise compromising her dream just because she could say *penis* without blushing. Not Roxy Rose.

"Going on a trip?" Ned asked, stepping into the hall just as Roxy came out with her second armload of getaway essentials—cooler, flashlight, Twinkies…

"To the shore," she said, trying not to sound too hoity-toity. Or in her case, to an empty patch of land swooping with a bunch of seagulls. Struggling with her gear, she managed to pull shut her door. "Just carrying a few things down to my car." The rest was already there—cabana chairs, radio, change of clothes, toothpaste in case she turned it into an overnighter, which she was hoping to do, *depending on who took the hint*. She intended on taking a full weekend off—no radio promos, sponsor appointments or syndication talk, no house plans, no nothing except enjoying it. Even if her shore didn't come with shelter yet. But hey, the weather forecast was good, the air was clean, so who needed a roof? "Trying to get away."

"Looks like you're getting away for a week. Saw you taking the first load down a few minutes ago. Except for the rug, that pretty much wipes out your apartment, doesn't it?"

"I might spend the night."

"Roughing it?"

"Depends on the definition." She turned, heading to the elevator, giving Georgette Selby's door a wave as she whooshed by, even though Georgette wasn't visible. But it had become her paranoid habit, waving at the peephole. "And I love the rug, by the way. Couldn't be any better if I'd picked it out myself."

"And you're not threatened because that could be my way of trying to control you?"

She turned back around to face him. "Is it?"

"Maybe, or maybe it's just a gift."

"So maybe this is the place where we explore the ulterior motives of certain gifts."

"Like wanting to keep my bare butt off the cold floor?" He grinned. "Or wanting to keep your bare butt off the cold floor if you ever get into that position? You know, your bottom on the bottom."

"So it is a control thing?"

"You tell me."

"Most people want a little piece of control, Ned, and if you're like everybody else, you'll be stepping over that line momentarily. Prefaced by a rug, maybe."

"And what if I don't want control, Roxy? Maybe I don't buy into that kind of manipulative relationship. What if a rug is a rug is a rug, and if I'm happy to let you hang on to all the control you want?"

Then he'd be a keeper—*the* keeper. Except she didn't want a keeper. "What if I'm not wrong?" she countered, marching onto the elevator. "I'm not sure I want to risk letting in yet one more person."

"Meaning me?"

Roxy shrugged, punching the door shut button. "I'm just having a bad morning, which is why I'm running away for a little while. Leave my stuff there and I'll be back up to get it in a minute. "The door was beginning to shut. Should she? Shouldn't she? What was the matter with her? Since when had Roxy Rose gone so indecisive? "Ned," she said, stepping between the doors before they shut. "In my apartment. On the kitchen table. There's a map." Then she stepped back and let the door close. A few minutes later, when she returned for the rest of her things, they were lying on the floor just outside the elevator. And Ned was nowhere in sight.

Probably for the best.

But a kiss goodbye would have been nice.

Or an elevator quickie! *Guess we'll see, won't we?*

IT WAS A BEAUTIFUL, WARM AFTERNOON when Roxy pulled her Toyota almost all the way back to her knoll, the one she was now affectionately calling Rose Hill. First thing she did when she got out was plant her flag on Rose Hill. Well, not exactly a flag so much as a red bandana on a broomstick. But it was symbolic. She'd captured her hill, and she owned it. And no matter what anybody did, that wasn't going to change.

It took her a few minutes to haul everything out of the car—everything *except* the box of Edward Craig books. She was saving those for kindling in case she needed to make a bonfire to keep herself warm. With any luck, there'd be a much better way to keep herself toasty coming her way really soon. She sure hoped so, anyway.

A couple of trips back and forth and Roxy was finally plodding back to the Rose Hill for her last time, carrying the second cabana chair, when she noticed a bright yellow monster rolling its way over her property, coming straight at her. A Hummer! It was like one she'd seen in the parking garage. Since she and Ned didn't date in the traditional sense though—dinner, movie, anything that involved transportation—she didn't know if the Hummer was his. Looked promising, anyway.

Chair still in hand, Roxy scurried back to her little camping spot, planted the second chair next to hers, and was stretched out, sunglasses on, book in hand, when the Hummer rolled to a stop right next to her Toyota. She thought about standing up for a better look, but decided the composed approach was better, just in case it was...well, someone she really wanted to spend the day *and night* with. Totally not cool to go running over there, squawking around like a seagull after a cookie.

So Roxy remained seated and tried for unaffected, going for that day-at-the-beach kind of look by slipping on a pink, wide-brimmed straw hat. Then she listened to the padded footfalls in the grass get closer and closer, discovering with every single goose bump rising on her skin that her reaction could only mean one person. And that wasn't good, reacting to him that way. Not good at all. Even though having him there was all good.

"We could have just come together, you know," he said.

"But I didn't know if you'd be the kind who could rough it. You know, spend the whole night."

"That's what you want?"

"Believe me Ned, I don't have a clue what I want. I always thought I did. Sometimes I still think I do, but things get complicated. Which is why I come out here, to uncomplicate them."

"You own the place?"

"Every blade of grass and grain of sand." She pushed up her hat and looked up at him. "Care to share some of it with me?" She pointed to the empty cabana chair next to her, then watched Ned drop down into his lounger, kick off his shoes and begin unbuttoning his shirt.

White shirt, blue jeans, sandals... She couldn't take her eyes off him. Every button opened, even inch of flesh revealed, added more goose bumps to her already growing collection. So what if she did have this little fantasy about the two of them on the beach? And what if she had facilitated it a little? Or maybe it was her evil twin Valentine who facilitated it. And what if this is the way she'd dreamed it would start—something totally impulsive, where she snapped her fingers and he appeared out of thin air? Or in this case, rolled in, in a yellow Hummer. Same thing. Hopefully same outcome.

"You've got lots of facets, Roxy," he said, settling in.

"And you don't know the half of them." But when she got up the courage he would. Just not today. She didn't want it to end out here, if that's what happened. She didn't want those memories lingering over her land like heavy Washington humidity.

He pulled his shirt open all the way but didn't take it off. "Why didn't you just ask me? So maybe you didn't want to come out here in only one vehicle. I can understand that. You lose your control that way, and you won't put yourself in the position. But why leave the map instead of just asking me, *Hey Ned, want to cozy up on the beach with me for the weekend?*"

"I guess so it could be your decision. So I wouldn't be putting you on the spot."

"Or so I wouldn't be rejecting you on the spot? Is that it? You weren't sure you could control the situation?"

"I know how I am, Ned. Believe me, I know. But sometimes I like to take it all off. Just be simple. No agendas, no control. Only the moment." She was laying herself bare here, something she'd never done with anybody before. "I'm thirty, all alone. And I live that life just fine. I'm happy with it, in fact. Arranged it to be just what I want. Then one day you just slid in there from nowhere and for the first time I was beginning to see that no matter how I ordered my life, there will always be things that change it. Things out of my control. And I didn't ask you because, well, you were right—I didn't want to be rejected. Sure goes to the heart of my control issues, doesn't it? Where's a good shrink when you need one?"

"There's nothing wrong with wanting control. Everybody does, some more than others." He chuckled. "And you more than most. But that's okay, and I think somewhere along the way you've convinced yourself that it's not, that you've got to justify who you are. But you don't have to do that, Roxy. Your friends are your friends because of, *and* in spite of it. I'm here with you right now because I want to be, not because you maneuvered me into doing it. And I really think you should reframe the way you look at it. Think of it as determination, not control."

Roxy laughed. "You sound like a shrink."

Ned opened up the cooler sitting on the ground between them, pulled out a root beer and handed it to her, then pulled out another one for himself. "I sound like a man who's looking forward to spending the day, and maybe the night, with a great-looking chick. And I've gotta tell you, I like your choice in beaches. Couldn't have picked better myself. And I brought the rug, by the way."

"*The* rug?" Roxy finally gave in to a grin. "No promises, Ned."

"I'm not asking for promises, Miz Rose. Just a piece of chicken. You did bring chicken, didn't you?"

"What's a good picnic without chicken?" And a nice, cozy rug for two.

An hour later, after the chicken was eaten, Roxy kicked off her shoes and headed for the water. In September, there was still enough warmth left for wading, and while her property ended at the shoreline, she still considered the first few inches Rose water, and wanted to do a little toe-wiggling in it.

"Are you coming?" she asked. They'd talked about inconsequential things so far—weather, sports, how happy he was to have Oswald back on the job. And he'd never once asked her how she afforded this piece of property, which, quite honestly, surprised her. He owned real estate, so he knew the value. But so far he didn't seem the least curious. So, maybe she was wrong about him after all. Maybe he wasn't lining up to control her. Which was good…and bad. Good because she really liked him. Bad because she really liked him.

"Just wading?" he asked, catching up to her. "Nothing a little more outgoing from Roxy Rose?"

Ned was already barefoot and Roxy expected him to roll up the bottoms of his jeans, but instead he unzipped, took them off and stood there in his briefs. "Too cold for these to go, I'm afraid. Shrinkage…very embarrassing to a man. We haven't known each other long enough for you to see that kind of humiliation."

"You don't expect *me* to take off my clothes, do you?" It was still daylight, the light just barely beginning to fade.

And she'd never, ever been naked out here. Never, ever been naked outside anywhere.

"On your own property, I'd expect you have that right."

"That's what you think," she snorted. "I don't even have the right to build my house…." Oops, too much. He didn't need all the nitty-gritty details. "I'm betting that right now someone from Shorecroft is watching through binoculars."

He laughed. "Then I'm the lucky one since I get to watch up close."

"It's cold," she argued.

"Not that cold. And once you get in you'll adjust."

"I didn't bring a towel to dry off with."

"Yes you did. I saw it."

"We just ate. Don't we have to wait an hour before we go in the water?"

"Old wives' tale. And as far as I can tell, there are no old wives around here to catch us. You're not an old wife, are you?"

She shook her head, on the verge of defeat. "Once. But I got cured of that real fast."

"So then what's stopping you?"

"Propriety, for starters."

"And I thought you listened to Valentine McCarthy. Right about now I think she'd be telling you to go for it. I mean, skinny-dipping is far safer than driving naked."

Roxy laughed. He was using *her* against *her*, and *she* was winning. Only Roxy wasn't sure which she. "Except for the shrinkage. And I'm not taking off my panties."

She didn't either. Not for the ten minutes they romped like children in the water. It was a little too brisk for a good swim, not brisk enough to make them run for blankets once they dipped in their toes. So they played, splashed, pushed, shoved and after ten minutes when her nipples were so puckered and cold they were practically blue, she headed back to find her blanket, and Ned followed, showing his own signs of a good, hard chill.

"I only brought one blanket," she said, dropping down onto the rug, then crawling under the blanket to strip off her wet panties. And that was the truth. But there was no way she was telling him she had a change of clothing. That would take all the fun out of the naked-under-the-blanket fantasies she'd been having since the moment they waded into her few inches of Puget Sound.

"And…"

"And it's gonna cost ya."

"What?" he asked, pulling the waistband of his briefs away from his skin.

"For starters, my toes are cold."

"That I can take care of."

"And my knees are cold."

"That, too."

"And something else is *really* cold." She opened the blanket to him, and he practically dove in, then wrapped it around them like a cocoon. Thank heavens they had the rug.

"No shrinkage now," she murmured, giving his wet briefs a toss.

"Imagine that. So do you want me to start with your toes?"

HIS WORDS WERE BARELY OUT when they were answered with a hard, swift kiss from her. It came with such a demand he was totally surprised by it. Roxy had been exuberant and passionate before, but now there was another dimension, one he couldn't quite define. But it set his toes to tingling unlike anything he'd ever had tingle before, and he met her kiss with the same intensity she was giving him, holding nothing back, not any last scrap of him.

"I'm all wet," she finally whispered, her voice so throaty, so familiar, he felt its heat tear right through him.

"In a good way, I hope," he growled into her ear.

"In a very good way if you'd warm me up by getting on top of me." Side by side, they were wrapped so tightly in the blanket that he could feel her heart beating against his chest, feel the rush of air into her lungs as she breathed in, feel the tickle of exhalation against his neck as she let it back out.

"The lady wants me on top?" He chuckled. "Are you sure about that? Because I don't mind…."

"The lady definitely wants you on top. If you want to be on top," she added, almost shyly.

"Oh, I want," he replied, rolling off his side. "Anything to please the lady."

She nibbled his ear. "But I have other places I want you, too." Then she ran her tongue down the side of his neck and stopped at his jaw. "Good places, if you're interested."

"Want to feel how interested I am?" he asked, still sliding until he was on top of her.

She wiggled against him. "Oh, I can feel it, all right."

"You ain't felt the half of it," he growled, nestling himself all the way in between her legs.

"There's more? Bad, bad boy hiding it from me. I guess I'll have to punish you." Instead of wiggling, she ground her hips hard into his, so hard he groaned out loud. "Take that," she laughed, grinding again. "And that."

"Do you know what you're doing to me?" he gasped. Other than driving him so close to the brink he'd lost the capacity to put together cohesive thoughts.

"Making you throb, I hope?"

"Hmmm…" was all he could manage. And barely that.

"No hands," she said. "Not this time. And I want it fast. You're ready, I'm ready. I don't want to wait 'cause I've got something extra-specially fun to show you."

"Extra-specially?"

"Especially," she said. "*Es*-specially fun."

That was all it took to push his need to a raging edge,

here he wanted so much more—all the texture of her, all
he taste. Underneath him Roxy was already finding her
osition, once again grinding her pelvis into his, only this
me not to tease him but to pull him over the edge with
er. She was moving so wildly against his erection now, he
new she would have her way, and very soon. And did he
ver want to give Roxy her way.

"The condom?" he asked raggedly.

"I have a brand-new trick," she said. "Learned it the
ther night listening to *Midnight Special*. No hands."

"No hands? Then what's left?"

"Want me to tell you or want me to show you?" Roxy
ormed her lips into a circle and kissed him on the throat, elic-
ing a groan so guttural he didn't even know he had it in him.

"Oh, my…" he gasped. "You're not going to…"

"You're going to owe Valentine a big apology when I'm
hrough with you, Mr. Proctor." Then she cheated just a lit-
e. She tore open the foil packet with her fingers. "A real
ig apology." And placed the condom in her mouth.

It was like nothing he'd ever felt before…. "You're kill-
ng me," he moaned as the tiny little sensations before or-
asm shot through him. "Roxy…" he begged, "I can't…
…oh, thank you, Valentine!"

In the end, before his climax, Roxy found her place un-
erneath him again, and he dove hard into her, just in the
ick of time for both of them. "Ned!" she screamed, grab-
ing hold of his back, digging in her fingers. "Oh my…yes!
es!" He was used to her screams by now. And if any-
hing, they drove him closer, faster, so that his climax
tarted shortly after hers, and they ended together. And as
he last gasps came, and she went limp under him, and he
vent limp on top of her, Ned rolled off to the side, took
.oxy into his arms, and pulled the blanket up over them,
eady to snuggle. Maybe this time ready to stay there for
 long time…even for the night.

The words he wanted to say, but wasn't sure she wanted
to hear, were so close to the edge. Because yes, he did love
her. Loved her like crazy, and that was crazy because everything he prescribed for others didn't allow for something like this to happen. Not to him, anyway. Everything
he counseled was about weighing and measuring a relationship. Everything he felt for Roxy was about experiencing it. And dear God, he was experiencing it in ways he'd
never come close to writing about, or lecturing about, or
even believing could happen. "Roxy, I…" Before his words
slipped out, a raucous cacophony of screeches and screams
and shrieks split right through the mood, and he pulled her
even closer to protect her as he looked out from under the
blanket to see what was going on. "Don't look now, but
we're not alone."

"Cookies." Roxy laughed, poking her head out from
under the blanket. "Over there, in the bag. And Ned, once
you dump them, run like hell."

"AM I ALLOWED to ask about him?" Ned asked, stoking the
fire in the hibachi. It was past sunset now, the gulls were
long gone, the air was cooling down, and dinner would be
hot dogs, chips, maybe some s'mores.

"Who?" she asked, trying to sound casual, even though
she knew exactly who he was talking about. It wasn't like
that part of her life was a well-kept secret or anything.
More like the memory less traveled. And she really had-
n't intended on letting him into it. Not yet, anyway. She'd
been the one to open that door, though, so maybe it was
time to start cluing him in on the finer details of one Roxy
Rose. Roxy first, then eventually Valentine, because that
need was getting more and more urgent. He needed to
know, deserved to know, *after* she let him know Roxy.

"The man who never succeeded in making you an old
wife. Your ex…I'm assuming he's an ex."

"Oh, he's an ex, all right. A long, long time ago." She pitched him the package of hot dogs and rifled through the picnic basket for the buns. "It was a fling," she said from its depths. "We were young. He wanted...pretty much nothing. I wanted everything." Shutting the basket, she tossed the bag of buns on the rug. "It didn't work out. We were too different, different ambitions, different perceptions of life in general." She smiled wistfully. "Bruce was a nice man, and I was a lot worse for him than he was for me."

"And you didn't try anything to save your marriage? You know, counseling?"

She drew in a sharp breath. *Shades of Edward Craig.* "We didn't have the money for counseling, which was okay because we didn't have enough invested in the marriage to waste the money, anyway, and there really wasn't any sense in trying to put pieces back together because there were never any pieces to begin with. So we walked away, the textbook amicable parting, end of story. Didn't look back, never saw each other again. No Eddie Craig happily-ever-after."

"Edward," he corrected, his voice surprisingly abrupt. "Counseling's been known to work, you know. If you're open-minded enough to allow it."

"If you want to save the marriage, which we didn't. And I was open-minded enough for the both of us when I married him, but believe me, the door shut fast on that one. Staying together would only have prolonged the fiasco. It wasn't like we walked away hating each other though, because we didn't. We simply walked away untouched. He was a man with a strong vision of what he wanted out of life, but it wasn't my vision, and we knew, almost from the start, it couldn't work between us. But for some crazy reason, and I don't even remember what it was, we said *what the heck, let's give it a try, anyway.* But nothing clicked. Not even the sex. And I know Eddie... er, Edward Craig extols the virtues of making love over merely having sex, but we never even came close to the place where we were making love." Never came close to the place where she had feelings for him like she was having for Ned.

"Virgin, I'm guessing?"

She laughed. "More ways than one. But yes, that was when I was a chaste, young thing who wanted to wear white."

"And did you?"

"Nope. Jeans. We ran down to Vegas." And she still wanted to wear white. But she'd never admit it out loud, not even to Astrid.

"So you married the guy, pretty much wrote it off as a bust right away, but you stayed with him for a while, gave it a try, anyway?"

Roxy nodded. "Sounds pretty crazy when you put it that way, doesn't it? But yes, we gave it a try, limited edition. I mean, who goes into a marriage thinking divorce. As dumb as we were, we didn't. Of course, no one could really accuse us of thinking about anything when we got married. But since we had the piece of paper, we decided to hang out together and see what came of it. Which was nothing." Not even sex after their first couple of times. "My life changes, expands, contracts. I'm not a linear person, Ned, in case you haven't guessed. I don't walk this straight and narrow line, where I come to all the right stops at the right times—graduate from college, get married, have children. My life fans out all over the place, and maybe that's the only true vision I've ever had for myself—to keep fanning. And he was linear. I was looking for something he couldn't be."

"Are you still looking?"

"There are so many *somethings* to find, and I think life would get really boring if you set your sight on one, went after it, got it, then stopped. Like I said, I'm not linear.

don't want to miss anything. So I don't necessarily include, or exclude anything. Mostly I just wait and see, and occasionally try it out to see if it works." Roxy paused, looking up at the sky. Almost dark now. And still so many possibilities. "Now it's my turn to ask a question."

"Shoot."

"Did you ever take the plunge?"

"Nope."

She waited, but that's as far as he went. "That's it? I spill my guts all over the place and all I get from you is a simple *nope?*"

"Yep."

"So I get another question." Reaching into the cooler, she pulled out the condiments—mustard, ketchup, *no* onion. "And if all I get is a one-word answer, it doesn't count, either."

"Do you always get to make the rules, Roxy?" Ned interrupted as he opened the dogs. "How many do you want?"

She held up three fingers, then changed it to four. "Most of the time." She laughed. "Since I spend most of my life playing in my own arena, it only seems fair."

"Why your arena? Why not somebody else's?"

"Remember, I tried that? Dismal failure, and I'm not sure anybody in their right mind would want me in their arena. Not on a permanent basis, anyway. I have a tendency to bust balls."

"You haven't busted mine. Haven't even tried."

"That's because you're different. You're not...bustable. And I don't know how to explain that except..." She shrugged. "I don't know." Not so much didn't know as wouldn't admit.

"So let's say somebody who's not in his right mind comes along, invites you into his arena. Would you take a stab at it again...permanent relationship, marriage, whatever you want to call it?"

"Are you a closet shrink, Ned? Because this is beginning to sound an awful lot like some kind of analysis, when all I want is a hot dog."

He held up four fingers and waved them at her. "Analysis, which you don't believe in." He tossed the dogs on the grill, then sat down on the ground next to the hibachi. "Do you?"

"For some people...a lot of people, it works. For me?" She shrugged. There was nothing left to say except that for her, it wasn't necessary. She didn't need it, didn't want it, and her life had worked out without it. "For me, I prefer mustard on my hot dog. How about you?"

"Is that my question? Because if it is, I'm afraid my answer's only one word...ketchup."

"Figures," she muttered.

10

Things That Go Bump in Her Night

"Roxy!"

Oh no! She knew that voice, and it certainly wasn't Ned's. He was wandering around out there someplace in the dark, heeding the call of nature or something, and the last thing she expected her fire to attract in his absence was Doyle Hopps.

"Rox, are you out there?"

Maybe she could douse the fire before he saw it… Quickly, Roxy scooped up a handful of dirt and threw it on the flame, and it died down to an ember immediately.

"Come on Rox, I know you're over there!"

Damn, it didn't work.

"Rox…you-hoo!"

Not Astrid, too! Good grief, she couldn't escape them even on her day off. Hadn't they seen his Hummer parked with her Toyota and figured out that Hummer and Toyota added up to hanky-panky? "Go away," she yelled. "This is private property. Trespassers will be tossed to the seagulls."

She was stretched out in her cabana chair, trying to finish her last s'more before Doyle saw it, and thank goodness she was fully clothed when they rounded the knoll. "Didn't you bring a flashlight?" Astrid snapped, tripping her way over to the area she and Ned had set up for spending the night. Rug, blanket, a couple of pillows, some citronella candles to keep away the pests. Well, most of the pests.

"It's so dark out here, Rox. Don't you have a lantern or something?"

"It's supposed to be dark out here," Roxy grumbled. "That's the way I like it at night. Dark, quiet...*alone!*"

"We thought you might like some company," Doyle said, plopping down on the rug. "You brought a carpet?" He had a pizza box and a two-liter bottle of root beer. "Cool."

"I brought a *rug*, and get off my rug! I don't want anything spilled on it." More than that she didn't want anybody on it but her and Ned. Sentimental about a rug, maybe. Silly, probably. But it was her rug, and once upon a rug... "Get up," she snapped, impatiently. "Right now. Get up...get up!"

"Okay, okay," Doyle said, sliding off the rug onto the ground. "But you're being real bitchy about a piece of shag, Rox. Not too cool."

"It's not shag, and even if it was, it's *my* shag and I can do anything with it"—or on it—"I like, including kicking you off it." So his butt had made contact with it for what? Two seconds. That didn't count for anything more than a trial sitting which meant her rug was still, technically, unsullied by any and all unacceptable rug discommoders. And everyone but she and Ned *were* unacceptable rug discommoders, which she intended on keeping that way.

"Being out here alone's already making you nuts, Rox. You're not gonna make it through the night all by yourself. And once they start rising from their graves, it's gonna get real ugly." Automatically, Doyle handed a piece of extra pepperoni, extra cheese over to Roxy, but she declined it. She'd eaten three dogs with mustard, skipped the fourth to save room for the s'mores, along with slaw and chips, and she was already in her baggy jeans and barely zipping them at that.

"It's your favorite," Doyle coaxed, leaning over, waving it under her nose.

"Already ate."

"Are we interrupting something?" Astrid asked cautiously. "Because when you told me you were coming out here, and I asked if you were coming alone, you said yes. And when I asked if you were sure…"

"I know, I said yes, which is what I meant at the time. But I was wrong. I mean, didn't you see that yellow Hummer out there by my Toyota?"

Astrid slapped Doyle on the shoulder. "I told you we shouldn't come in the back way, like we were sneaking in or something." She turned to Roxy. "He got lost, and we ended up on the other side, over near the road to town. So he decided we should just park there and walk on in instead of backtracking out to the main road and risk ending up in the Sound or in somebody's back yard." She grabbed the pizza box away from Doyle. "I told you I should drive, but no. You said you knew the way. Now look what you've done! And I told you this was a bad idea didn't I? That we shouldn't come out here without calling first."

He grabbed the box back. "So there's enough pizza for four. What's the big deal? It's not like we walked up on them while they were still boinking."

"Boinking?" Roxy sputtered.

"Didn't I heard Doctor Val use that term the other night?" he snorted, laughing.

"You know what, Doyle…Astrid… It's a long way back and it's getting late. There's a nice little inn in town. Why don't you two go spend the night there *on me*. Okay? I appreciate your coming out here checking on me, but I promise, I don't need to be checked on." And the last thing she needed was getting her Valentine cohorts near her Roxy lover. Bad mix. Things would slip out, which was all right, but she wanted to be the one letting them slip. And at the right time, which still wasn't now.

"Okay?" she repeated. "Order room service, anything you like." She grabbed her purse, pulled out her credit card and tossed it to Doyle. "Anything. Filet mignon, two of them if you want."

"Meaning she doesn't want us here," Astrid said, kicking Doyle's foot. "So let's get out of here before she fires us."

"Want me to leave the pizza?" Doyle asked, clutching it to his chest.

"No!"

IMMEDIATELY AFTER THEY had gone, Ned returned to the fire. "You're their boss?" he asked.

"You were listening?"

"Didn't want to interrupt. Didn't want to put you in a position of having to explain anything to them…or me, if that's what you want."

"Yes, they work for me."

"Then you own your own company? Guess I missed that somewhere."

"You missed it because I never told you." Suddenly her mood for the evening, and the night, was over. She was owing him explanations now. He was expecting details. And that's where it became complicated…complicated because she was falling in love with a man who didn't have a clue who she was, and would probably dump her when he found out.

"NO, WE DIDN'T DO ANYTHING ELSE. We left right after you did," Roxy groused to Astrid. "I came home and spent the rest of the weekend doing nothing but house plans and sleeping, and I don't know what he did because he didn't call, didn't come over. Nothing. And why should he after the way I acted? Kicking him off my beach the way I kicked Doyle off my rug. I mean, it was crazy. All of a sudden the two parts of my life are together in the wrong place, and I can't handle it. So I faked a stomachache from the hot dogs and told him I had to go home."

Then she hadn't gone out, hadn't invited anybody in except the pizza delivery boy, the Chinese food delivery boy and the pizza delivery boy again. Drowning her problems in junk food hadn't been the fix she needed, though, because she'd missed him. And it wasn't just about the sex. She'd missed *him.* And she'd wanted to call him, thought about calling him, picked up the phone and put it down a hundred times, but she wouldn't do it because missing him scared her to death. Having those kinds of strong, getting-stronger-every-day feelings scared her even *more* to death. "And I know what you're going to say before you say it. I'm running away. I'll admit it. Running like a marathoner. But I can't help it. This is all so new to me, and every bit of resolve I put up so it won't happen just keeps failing me. Yeah, I want him. No, I don't. Yes, I do. And that's *so* not like me, Astrid. I'm not in control here."

"So who says you have to be in control all the time? Sometimes a nice, uncontrolled detour is just what we need to spice up our lives. And I think, right now, that's exactly what you need. Spice!"

Astrid handed Roxy the blush. A nice rosy color to go with the bluish eyeliner. Good camera appeal, even though her eyes would hide behind dark glasses for the whole five-minute shoot. Even so, the makeup enhanced her attitude. Without it she was just plain Roxy, with it she was anything but plain Valentine. Makeup to Valentine was like spinach to Popeye. "So maybe it's not about total control. I did give in to some things."

Astrid chuckled. "Dare I ask?"

"No, you *daren't.* But even on an uncontrolled detour, there's got to be some control, doesn't there? I mean, this guy drags a rug out to the beach, for heaven's sake, and I just throw myself down on it and wait for him to come take me. Which is so totally about losing control. *All* control, Astrid. And when I'm with him I don't even care. It's almost like I'm waiting for him to come take it away."

"But if you love him…"

"Who said anything about love?" Roxy snapped.

"Like I was saying, *if you love him,* control shouldn't be an issue. And like it or not, Rox, your giving it up willingly pretty much tells me how you love the guy. For a relationship counselor you're not too sharp about your own relationship, but let me give you a little piece of advice. Figure it out before he gets tired of you waffling all over the place and walks away. If he does that, girlfriend, I'm gonna kill you because beautiful butts like that don't come along every day. Neither do people who make you all gushy, and you're not too bad in a little gush. Kinda makes you seem like the rest of us peons."

Laughing, Roxy gave her Val wig a good shake then stuck it on her head. "I'm *not* gushy. Just…cautious." She considered the wild, sexy look of her uncombed wig, then decided to go with her usual, sleek and sophisticated. That's what people knew, what they expected from Val. The same—like pretty much everything else in her life.

"I love you, Rox, but you're not easy. Not for me, not for Doyle, and I imagine not for your handyman. You've got to have it your way all the time or you take your toys and go home, like Saturday night. We interrupted you for, like, three minutes tops, and you pack up your rug and hike fanny all the way home." She shook her head. "And I'm betting you didn't even think about what your handyman wanted, did you? You were angry, at us for showing up, at him for asking personal questions you weren't ready to answer, so you left. Right?"

"Someone needs to slap me," Roxy said, slipping the wires to some flamboyant two-inch chandeliers earrings through her ears.

"Believe me, another time or two with you and he probably will. For heaven's sake, Rox. Get a clue. The man loves you, or he wouldn't keep coming back for more. So all I can say is, if you don't admit it to yourself first, that *you* love him, then get yourself out on some rooftop and shout it, you're going to get everything you've always wanted, *except* him. And sweetie, a rug for one can get awfully lonely."

"It was, all weekend," she admitted sadly. That's where she'd spent most of her time. Even slept there. On a bright note, if it could be called a bright note, the house plans were done now. All the toilets were in the bathrooms, the appliances in the kitchen, the bannisters on the stairs, it was exactly what she wanted. Steel, cement and glass—no fuss, no muss. Not like her feelings, though. All fuss, all muss. She sighed the melancholy sigh of a woman who would have rather spent the weekend doing something other than a do-it-yourself CAD program. "Do you think maybe Doctor Craig might have some advice for me? Because Valentine's advice sure isn't working out, is it?"

"I'm so sorry, Rox. I really didn't mean to walk in on anything out there," Astrid said, handing Roxy her glasses. "But Doyle's in the big-brother mode with you and he really didn't think you should be staying out there alone, especially with all the trouble you're having with the locals. And since it was Saturday night and God knows I never have a date, I thought it sounded like a good idea…at the time. But I did want to call first. Cross my heart."

"Doesn't matter. Like I said, I panicked. If I were going about this the right way I wouldn't have. But I'm not, and I got myself in such a knot over how to fix the mess I'd have managed to wreck the weekend, anyway." Roxy took one final appraisal in the mirror, added another four inches to her height with some killer spikes and Valentine was good to go. "So tell me, what do I need to do out there?"

Ten minutes until air, then she'd be the sunrise sensation on *Seattle SunUp*. Another of the mandatory promos that went along with her career.

"Just promote the hell out of the show. Interviewer's name is Brianna Dean, by the way. She said the time is yours to do with as you see fit. That she'll lead you in with a couple of general questions, then it's up to Val to do what Val does best. Except no sex, Rox. Not this audience, and I'm warning you..."

"Yeah, yeah, no sex. Did you give this Brianna the regular prelim sheet of Valentine questions, or is she just winging it?" Winging it was always dangerous. Some of these interviewers went way out there in an attempt to grab a few ratings points. She chuckled. Yeah, like she hadn't done that herself.

"Sent her the sheet last week, along with your bio. She should be all set."

"And it's live, right? You did tell me that, didn't you?"

"Absolutely live, which is why you've got to behave yourself. Where's your other bra, Rox? You're too flat."

Roxy glanced down. "Way too early for cleavage. They'll just have to accept me flat." One more quick glance in the mirror showed nothing out of place. Wig okay, makeup caked on like she'd fallen in a mud puddle, extra-large shades to make up for the lack of a hat. And she did so love hiding under that hat! Yep, she was ready. "Okay, well, any time Brianna's ready to go."

Roxy tugged her Valentine-standard barely-below-the-buns skirt into place and headed down the hall to the studio. As she wiggled into her seat across from Brianna on the set, crossing her legs so that everything showing on TV was appropriate for the 6:00 a.m. crowd to see, she smiled over at the interviewer who was gulping coffee by the bucket and not making eye contact. Not a morning person, Roxy decided. "Thanks so much for inviting me," Roxy said, adjusting her Valentine voice.

Brianna blinked, then forced a tight smile. "Welcome. And I'll just ask some simple questions, if that's okay with you. You've done television before, haven't you?"

"It's the same as radio, sugar, only they get to have a look at me." Finally, Valentine had arrived.

Brianna nodded curtly, then stared at her program notes until she was prompted to go. "I'd like to welcome a special guest to *SunUp* this morning...one who's been keeping some of you up very late at night, listening to her number-one-rated radio program, *Midnight Special*. Valentine McCarthy. Or should I say, Doctor Valentine McCarthy? You are a doctor, aren't you? Because from some of the advice I've heard, well, let's just say it doesn't sound much like what someone who's earned a doctorate would give."

The camera switched to Roxy. "Ph.D. in psychology does make me a doctor," she responded, forcing a smile. Someone should have told her Brianna was a twit. "And thanks for inviting me to your little segment of *Seattle SunUp*, Bri."

"Brianna," she corrected. "And it's my pleasure. So tell me, Valentine..."

"Just call me Val, Bri. Everybody does."

"Brianna," she corrected again. "So tell me, Val, why radio junk psychology is more rewarding for you than being in a private practice, since you're obviously qualified to be in private practice, although I couldn't find any record of it."

That's because my practice was in my real name, you twit. "Well, Bri, I'm not really sure how to answer you. I suppose I could debate you on the merits of what's considered junk radio or even junk television, for that matter. Or talk to you about *Midnight Special's* tremendous ratings thanks to its extra-specially supportive listeners. Or even ask you why you're doing a tiny little five-minute segment on the early-morning news for people to watch while gargling.

But instead, let me just say that I do what I love to do. And *Midnight Special* is what I love to do, have loved doing since the first time I went on air. And I don't have to make excuses, Bri." Roxy tilted her shades down just enough to glare over the tops of them at Bri. "Or defend my choice." Her message delivered quite clearly, the shades went back up. "*Midnight Special* has a wonderful audience and I look forward to chatting with them each and every night."

"Well, Val, you do have quite the reputation for what you do *each and every night*," Brianna continued, undaunted. "Good and bad, according to some critics. Speaking of which, we have one of those critics with us this morning. A name you might recognize…Doctor Edward Craig, in person."

Doctor Edward… His name took a second to sink in, then Roxy's heart jumped all the way up into her throat and almost choked her. "Craig?" she sputtered. He was here? No way! She searched frantically for Astrid, who was standing off to the side of the set looking dumbstruck. "M-my Doctor Craig?" Roxy stammered, her Valentine voice coming out like a goose with a sore throat.

"That's right, Val. *Your* Doctor Craig. We listen to the two of you go at each other every night, and I thought it might be nice for your listeners to see you debate face-to-face for a change."

"How interesting, Bri," she managed. "Only thing is, *my* listeners are still sound asleep. But I'm sure the couple of people who are tuning in right now might find it interesting." *Okay, Rox. You can do this.* It was inevitable. There had to be a meeting. But she wanted one where she had the…control. Yikes, Ned was right about her. Astrid was right. The whole freakin' universe was right. *Doesn't matter. You can still do this.* So since they were all right about her, where was the control when she needed it? Needed it, like right now! *You have to do this.* Val could for sure, but what about Roxy? And right now Roxy was front and center, wishing she was home under her rug.

Brianna tossed her a wry look, then turned to the camera. "I'm pleased to welcome Doctor Edward Craig this morning. He's author of twelve riveting *relationship* bestsellers, including his latest book, *Looking Beyond the Bedroom*. Doctor Craig…"

"Riveting?" Roxy muttered, almost under her breath. "Guess you haven't read them, have you?" Not that she had either. But nothing about Craig could be riveting.

"Hello, Brianna. Hello, Valentine…at last we meet." The voice was behind her, getting closer and closer. "Face to face."

He stepped around the little grouping of chairs, extending his hand first to Roxy. She saw the hand, looked up, saw the chest…then the throat…the face. No, uh-uh. Couldn't be. Dreaming…this was a dream. Or she was hallucinating?

"Edward," she said, taking his hand, trying to make sure hers was rock-steady. "So nice to meet you in person, after all this time." Same hand. She knew that hand. Boy, did she know that hand. *Please let the coma come and take me now!*

"So please sit down, Doctor Craig." Brianna pointed to the chair across from Roxy. "And tell us what you think about Doctor Val as a relationship counselor."

"Not a relationship counselor, Bri," Roxy snapped, her eyes still on Ned. Did he recognize her? No signs of it if he did. "A radio talk-show host. There's a big difference. And yes, Edward, please tell us what you think about me. I'm sure the two people out there listening to this show probably haven't heard it all before." He was smiling, but it wasn't a smile she knew. It was too reserved, not sexy at all like she was used to. No humor in it, no spark, no real challenge, not like she got from Ned. So maybe it was his professional smile, and he didn't look nearly so good in it. He didn't look nearly so good in his gray wool suit as he did his jeans, either...without his shirt. Hard to imagine that gorgeous chest under that stuffed shirt and noose of a silk neck tie. Although she had to admit, now that she was getting used to it, he did look pretty good all starched up.

But this was Ned, for heaven's sake. Ned and Edward...Craig and Proctor. Ned Proctor, Edward Craig... Ned a nickname for Edward. So Edward Craig...Proctor. Doctor Edward Craig Proctor. Suddenly, Roxy laughed out loud. No wonder he'd changed his name. Doctor Proctor!

"Excuse me?" Ned quipped, raising his eyebrows stiffly. "I don't see where that's funny."

"What?" she asked, realizing she hadn't been listening to him.

"About the problems associated with establishing the sexual relationship before the emotional one. People are always eager to jump into bed right away, but not so eager to talk. Sex is easy, talk's not. And the talking needs to come first. If that's good, the rest will take care of itself later on. But you, Valentine, send out the clear-cut message every night that as long as it's good in the bedroom, the rest will work out. It's putting the cart before the horse, which is irresponsible, don't you think? Especially since every other marriage ends in divorce?"

"And you don't believe both parts of the relationship can be worked out simultaneously, Edward? Haven't you ever met someone you've been so hot for you can't sustain all that chitchat past, say, the second date? Maybe not even a full-fledged date. Maybe it's a casual encounter, and you know, say when you brush past each other in the hallway, that this is going to work out and the order it falls into doesn't matter. Then you sleep together, have sex, maybe even make love, and as that element of your relationship continues to develop over time you discover that other aspects are growing right along with it, too? That putting the cart before the horse, as you call it, really did work out?" Hard to imagine those smug words coming out of Ned, but there had been a few times when he did sound dangerously close to Edward.

"So what you're saying, Val, is that you actually believe in love at first sight? True love, the kind that won't end up as a bad divorce statistic. Just one look's all it takes and you know it's forever?"

"It happens," she admitted, not that she wanted to. Not too long ago she would have debated him on the subject, laughed at him, told him love at first sight was a load of romantic drivel. That it was really only sex at first sight. But *he'd* been the one to show her just how wrong she was about it. And yes, all it took was just one look. Which was causing her some great big problems. Bigger than she'd known just five minutes ago, when he was *only* Ned. "For some people. For the lucky ones. But it's rare, Ne…Edward. And most of the time that first look produces a hormonal drive—one that can lead to bigger, better things…things you call a real relationship. And I'm all for that. Happily-ever-after is nice." Waxing too romantic here. Val falling under the Edward charm. Bad for ratings. *Roxy* falling under the Edward charm. Bad for the heart. "So is some good, hot sex. Skip the emotions, go with the urge. Urges can be really fun, Eddie." She wrinkled her nose at him. "You ought to act on one sometime instead of always pontificating."

He smiled at her. Almost a Ned smile—the one he always used when they got into a little Valentine-Edward skirmish. "I think you're a gifted broadcaster, Val. And a good entertainer. But a deluded counselor, if you believe that starting in the bedroom makes for a solid relationship. It never does. And I'm not saying that the sexual relationship isn't important. I'm just cautioning you that if that's where it goes after a couple of dates, and there isn't a solid basis for anything else already established, the relationship may already be in trouble. Maybe even doomed to failure."

Like theirs? she wondered. Is that what he really believed? Twice together for Twinkies and nonessential handyman duties, then hot and sweaty on the hardwood floor, meant they were doomed? So maybe she'd been reading a whole lot more into it than he had. Especially if he really believed what he was saying, and from the square set of his jaw right now, he did. Meaning what *she* thought was real between them was just sex? The rug was just about sex?

Another wall for Roxy Rose. A very hard wall, judging from the size of the lump in her throat. "My radio program is offering people something they're missing in their lives, Edward. Someone to listen to them, a shoulder to cry on, someone ready with a little friendly advice. As far as my being a deluded counselor, I suppose I'd have to hear your definition of *real* counseling before I could respond to that. Because in my book, it's all relative, relative to what a person needs or wants from his or her experience. I know what my callers need and want, and I give it to them for two hours a night, Monday through Friday. No pretenses, no hypocrisy. Simple as that, Eddie. So, see ya around, sugar." Standing, Roxy unclipped her microphone and strutted off the set.

11

Close Encounters of the Catastrophic Kind

"DAMN," ROXY MUTTERED, banging her head against the dressing room wall. "Damn, damn, damn," she repeated with each bang. "Of all the rotten luck, can you believe it? Can you actually believe it?'

"I'll swear Rox, I didn't know about this," Astrid cried, once she got to Roxy. "They didn't tell me they were going to do this, or I would have…"

Roxy stopped banging and lifted her hand to rub the sore spot on her forehead. "Don't you recognize him, Astrid?" she hissed, her knees suddenly so weak she had to grab on to Astrid to stay upright. "*Him!* Edward Craig. Take a good look at him. Don't you recognize him?"

Astrid glanced up at the overhead television monitor mounted to the wall. "No," she said tentatively. "I mean he does look familiar, and he's a whole lot cuter than I thought he'd be. Actually, he's drop-dead, but I don't know him. Am I supposed to?"

"Of course he's a lot cuter. Drop-dead. Especially his backside," Roxy hissed. "*His backside, Astrid!* You know, the best-looking butt you've ever seen."

"That would be your handyman," Astrid replied.

Astrid and Roxy both looked up at the television monitor in time to catch Edward AKA Ned holding up his book, promoting the heck out of it. Brianna, the dit, was swooning all over him. She was practically unbuttoning on camera. A reaction to Ned Roxy knew oh, so well. Roxy rooted for him to hit her with the durn book—probably the only thing it was good for. "Exactly. That would be my handyman. *He* is my handyman, Astrid!"

It took a second for it to sink in, then Astrid squealed, "No way! That's him? The guy you're sleeping with? The one you're falling in—"

"Don't say it, Astrid. I'm warning you—"

"Well, I never did get a good look at his face. And judging from what I'm seeing on TV, Brianna's not exactly concentrating on his face, either." She scooted closer to the TV monitor, took another look. "No way! Valentine and Edward doing the horizontal, in the literal sense? How ironic is that?"

"Yes, way! Valerie and Edward. Talk about sleeping with the enemy."

"Whoa. Not just sleeping, but…and I'm not saying the words, but I'm thinking them and you know what they are." She laughed. "Sorry, can't help myself. Gotta say them just once. Valentine McCarthy in love with Edward Craig. Wow! Bet I can get us some ratings points out of that." She took another look at Ned. "You've done some crazy things, Rox, but this sure wasn't one I would have seen coming."

"It's not funny," Roxy snapped.

"Sure it is. And romantic. And…"

"Shut up! Just shut up."

Astrid shook her head, the laughter still bubbling in her eyes and shaking her shoulders. "So do you think he recognized you?"

"Don't think so. Bright lights, all my makeup. That stupid wig. And he didn't react to me. Of course, I didn't react to him, either, so who knows?" She glanced at the monitor again, then dropped her head back to the wall for another couple of bangs. "So what am I going to do now?" she moaned. "After I kill Brianna."

"You could march right out there on camera, take off the wig, throw yourself in his arms and confess how much you love him. And if you want to go for the big time, ask him to marry you."

"You're fired!"

Undaunted, Astrid continued, "Or Plan B, get the heck outta here before he nabs you. After that…darned if I know." Astrid started tossing all of Roxy's makeup, clothes and other paraphernalia into a tote bag for a hasty getaway. "Maybe you could read one of his books and see if he has an answer for a problem like this. You know, she love-hates him, he love-hates her." She singsonged it to the melody of the familiar Barney tune. "They're a love-hate family."

Roxy didn't wait around to take off the Valentine exterior and put Roxy back on. Instead, she grabbed her tote bag and street clothes and ran out the door. Half an hour later, still stunned, she dropped the carton of Doctor Edward Craig's books, the ones she'd been carrying around in the back of her car forever, onto her living room floor, locked every one of the four locks on her front door so *he* couldn't get in, and threw herself down onto the rug…*his rug*…to think.

"How could something like this have happened?" she asked, picking up his first book, turning it over to see his photo. Sure enough, there he was, Mister One and the Same. Make that Doctor One and the Same. Handsome and sexy and all Ned grinning for the camera. "He's living right here under my nose all the time, and I don't even know who he is. I'm falling in love with him, sleeping with him, having these fantasies about spending my life with him, and he turns out to be none other than…" She threw the book across the room and it hit the wall with a thud. Ten seconds later someone knocked on the door, and Roxy sat straight up. Georgette Selby come to cuss her out, she hoped. Better her than Ned, because right now, she didn't have a clue what to do about him...or with him. Or without him.

"Rox?"

No, not Ned's voice, thank heavens.

"I heard your door slam. Can I come in?"

Doyle?

"I know you're in there."

Roxy zipped over to the door, opened it, grabbed hold of his arm and practically dragged him inside, then shut the door and locked it again. "What are you doing here and what do you want?" she hissed, almost out of breath. She ran back over to the rug and plopped down in relief. "You saw the show this morning, didn't you? And that's why you're here. Because I walked off."

Doyle picked up Ned's book, took a look, dropped it back on the floor, then wandered over to the sofa, careful not to tread upon the rug, and sat down. "Actually, I just came over to say hello to my new neighbor." He was dressed in baggy gray sweatpants and a black T-shirt with the words *Kiss My*...and the image of a donkey beneath them. So typically Doyle.

"What do you mean, new neighbor?"

"I'm moving in, right next door." He pointed in the direction of Georgette Selby's apartment. "Your neighbor got herself into a real nice seniors' complex closer to some of the services she needs, and I was next on the waiting list for the building."

"Waiting list? When you recommended this place, you didn't tell me there was a waiting list. So how did I get in right away?" In, like, two days.

He gave her a sheepish grin. "I let you have my slot. I was next up, this one came open and I knew you needed a place right away, so I slipped Oswald a little cash to let you in ahead of me."

"You did that for me?" She tried smiling, even though she wasn't in the mood. Maybe would never be in the mood to smile again. But Doyle deserved the best she could manage. "Really?"

He nodded, almost shyly. "No big deal."

"Yes it is, Doyle, and I don't know what to say, except thanks." Roxy grabbed another of Ned's books out of the carton, glanced at the photo on the back cover, then lobbed it at the wall. "I wish you would have said something, though." Seemed like within the last hour, her life had started crowding in all around her in a gigantic way. Too much too close. Her two lives were colliding. "I think I owe you a pizza," she said. For Doyle, saying it with pizza always worked, and she did, after all, owe him a thank-you. If things somehow worked out with Ned, maybe a whole year's supply. Yeah, right. Like things *could* work out now.

"So you don't mind me living right next door?"

"No, you're fine. And I'm not going to be here much longer, anyway." *Maybe Georgette Selby can find me an apartment somewhere closer to the services I need.* Like stupidity-repair services. She grabbed a third book from the carton, and didn't even bother looking at the photo before she chucked it at the wall.

"Astrid called," he said cautiously.

"And?"

"And she told me what happened. That they sprang Edward Craig on you this morning."

"And?"

"And that you handled yourself pretty good, all things considered."

"All things considered," she mumbled. Doyle didn't know the half of it, and she intended to keep it that way. "I walked off the set, if that's what you want to call pretty good." Book four in the Craig series came out of the carton, and went flying into the heap with the rest of them. "So did Astrid say anything else?" Like the syndication was off, her advertisers were dropping like flies, the radio station had fired her?

"That's all, except you're pretty upset over it, and to leave you alone for a while."

"Astrid was right. I am, and I do want to be alone for a while, if you don't mind. So, I'll see you at work later, okay? And tonight, after the show, we'll have that pizza. Extra meat, *your* favorite this time."

Doyle shrugged. "Well, you know where I am. If you need anything before then, just pound on the wall. I'll be moving in all day."

SHE WAS AT THE PEEPHOLE when *he* came home. Her hundredth time at the peephole in the last couple of hours. And sure enough, there was no evil twin scenario like she'd been praying for. *He* was decked in the same gray suit, his hair combed in the same manner. And *he* didn't even look over at her apartment when he went inside his own. The door was shut—not even slammed in an angry, incensed, hostile or otherwise churlish manner—and that was it. He never came out, at least not that she heard, anyway, and she did spend most of the day with her aural faculties finetuned to the comings and going in the hallway. Unfortunately, they were all Doyle's, moving in some pretty clunky furniture every time she looked out.

"I'm still numb," she said to Astrid, hours later, as she was getting ready to go on air—*her air*, and she was sure going to have to fake it tonight because she didn't feel like talking to one person let alone thousands of them. "I mean, I know I've been hiding Val from him, so I really can't say anything about his hiding Edward from me. I'm not even angry about that because after everything we've talked about—he hates Val, I hate Eddie—I totally understand it. He's basically the same chicken that I am. But what are the odds? Seattle's like a billion people, and *he* lives right across the hall from me. Not only that, *he* owns my building and I'm sleeping with him.

"I want some Chardonnay for real tonight," Roxy said. "Skip the root beer."

"Fruit punch. You don't need to go on the air all liquored up."

"Spiked? Just a little. I deserve a good buzz, at least."

Astrid laughed. "You're sounding like someone who might agree with what Doctor Edward Craig's been saying about relationships, that the good ones are about a whole lot more than sex."

"I *wanted* to keep it simple," Roxy moaned. "That's what I kept telling myself. No matter how I was feeling about him, I didn't want complications. And now I've got them all over the place." She glanced over at Doyle who was just entering his booth, then waved. "Am still feeling about him," she corrected. "Not *was*. And that's another thing. How can I feel one way about him professionally, and another personally? Is that weird, or what?"

Astrid scooted away the microphone and Roxy's mug of fruit punch, then sat down on the corner of the desk. "If he comes knocking on your door tonight, will you sleep with him?"

"You mean ignore my professional feelings? Because no matter how it turns out, one thing I won't do is put my professional judgment aside. I need him on this program."

"I mean exactly that. All professional feelings aside. He comes knocking, you let him in. Will that happen?"

Roxy laughed bitterly. "Truthfully, I don't know. So much of me wants to. But now, with the way things have changed, so much of me doesn't. And I'm afraid that it's just sex for him, Astrid. Which is the way Val would like it, but I'm not Val, and I was hoping…" She shrugged. "I was, and I guess I still am hoping it's more. And I don't know what I'll do if it's not." She glanced over at Doyle, who was giving her the two-minute warning, then automatically put on her headphones. "I spent all morning listening at my door. Every time I heard a noise…I mean, I wanted him to come in, but I didn't. And I was scared that he would, and now I'm scared that he won't. Silly, isn't it?"

Astrid threw her arms around Roxy. "It's never silly, being in love." Astrid and Roxy both looked over at Doyle, who was waving one finger at them and grinning.

Nodding, Roxy pulled her mic over and braced herself for the onslaught. And tonight it was an onslaught to which she wasn't looking forward. "Welcome to *Midnight Special*, sugars. Are you ready for something special? Because if you are, you've certainly come to the right place. Doctor Val has something *extra-specially* special for you tonight."

Roxy glanced up at the board for her first caller, then slashed her throat at Doyle, then at Astrid. No way was she going to take Edward Craig's call right out of the starting gate. Not tonight, anyway! But Astrid shook her head, and Doyle was giving her the speed-it-up sign. "So it looks like we have Doctor Craig to start us off this evening," she said, not even bothering to take out a chocolate truffle. "And how are you tonight, Edward?" Her voice was noticeably stiff. No usual Val flirting.

"Much better, now that we've finally met face-to-face, Valentine."

"Unfortunate little incident," Roxy said. "Having them slip you into my interview without even warning me. Not very good broadcast ethics, but I trust you made the most of the opportunity once I left. Promoted your next book, I assume?"

"I'm surprised you didn't listen," he replied, his voice totally calm and, as usual, in command. And not at all like

Ned's, she noticed. Oh, there were some similarities, now that she knew. The same deep richness, that smooth-as-silk flow, but it was different, like Roxy's voice was different from Val's. "After you left we talked about you, Valentine."

"Only good things, I'm sure." Not!

"Actually, yes. We discussed your role as a radio call-in psychologist, and how you fulfill it."

"My role?"

"As in entertainment. You *are* quite entertaining, Valentine. Frustrating, sometimes dangerous, but always entertaining."

Roxy drew in a deep breath. This could go either way. Might be fun. Might break her heart even more than it already was. "Entertaining, Edward? Well, why don't you tell me how I entertain you? In your fantasies, perhaps? Or in your dreams?" The edge in her voice was finally disappearing, being replaced by a little of the Valentine flirt. Not much! Just a little, *with caution.*

"Is that how you want to entertain me, Valentine? Is that *your* fantasy…*your* dream? To entertain me in mine?"

Damn, if it didn't sound like he was trying to seduce her right there on the radio. Nah. Wishful thinking. This was his brand of on-air foreplay. Whatever he had lined up for the main event would pack a mighty punch, one that intrigued her just a little. "My dream, Edward, or my fantasy, if you will, is not about entertaining someone in *their* dreams or fantasies. That's lonely, depressing. When I choose to entertain someone, it's on a secluded beach somewhere, just the two of us under the stars, all naked and sweaty. So hot the sex turns the sand into glass and the glass shatters into a million shards." The way it had done with them.

"Are you making love, Valentine, or merely having sex?"

"It's whatever you want to call it, Edward. I don't want to argue the details with you, since we don't ever agree."

"But it's a very important detail, Valentine. Anybody can have hot, sweaty sex in the sand. But not everybody can make love there. In fact, very few can. And there's a difference, one you've deprived yourself of if you haven't experienced it personally."

"Choices, Doctor. We all have them to make, and we all choose differently. If you've ever had sex for the sake of sex, you'd know what I was talking about. It can be good, so good it actually deludes you into thinking it might be love. But then when you step back and analyze it, or have the truth revealed to you, you see it for what it is. Sex for sex. But that doesn't change the fact that it rocked your world for a few minutes. And maybe in those few minutes you were actually a little in love." Or completely and forever.

"But I have, Valentine. And what I know, without a doubt, is that making love is so much better than sex for sex. There's nothing to compare. One is about hormones, the other is about genuine emotions. If you've ever made love, because you were in love, you'd know what I was talking about."

"But I have," Roxy said, not intending that to go out over the air. "And believe it or not, I truly admire the people who are in love. But I'm a pragmatist about those who aren't. And I don't believe they should deny themselves one of the finer *entertainments* in life just because they haven't found a soul mate to share their genuine emotions with. And that entertainment, Edward, doesn't have to be in a fantasy or a dream. It can be on a hardwood floor and be just as good as…" As what? Making love with somebody you love? Even Valentine wasn't buying into that one this evening. Nothing was better than being with the person you love, no matter what you were doing. "…As good as you can imagine it to be." Well, maybe that didn't prove her point exactly, but it did carry her over into the first commercial break, and that's all she wanted. After that, the real callers would call in and she'd be off the hook for a couple of hours. At least until she got home.

Then, dear lord, what was she going to do about Ned?

2:46 A.M.

A phone call in the night and it wasn't Ned. Not that she wanted it to be because she still didn't know what to say to him. Not yet. She'd been too numb to figure it out. "No Astrid, I haven't even seen him tonight. Haven't heard him, haven't heard from him, haven't even caught a whiff of his after-shave." Musk, masculine. She loved it. Loved smelling it when they were making love, loved smelling it when he simply breezed by her in the hallway, even before they'd first made eye contact. "This isn't exactly how I expected things to work out between us. I mean, I don't know what I was expecting, but this sure wasn't it." *Liar. You wanted a white picket fence. You've got it penciled into your house plans.* "And now, even though I know who he is, I'm not sure I want to end it. Of course I'm not going to have much of a choice in the matter since I did actually sleep with the man on our second date which, according to him, dooms us for anything more. *His words.* We're doomed. And they weren't even real dates," she moaned. "Not like dinner, dancing, movie, monster truck rally."

"So just go over there and tell him it's the real deal for you," Astrid said. "Heart and soul forever, happily-ever-after, morning breath and bed hair don't even matter, that kind of love."

"I've never spent the night with him."

"Rox...you've got to be kidding? You *are* kidding, aren't you? Sex then adios? I'm not surprised the man predicts doom and gloom for you two. That's one of those issues we talked about. Letting the guy launch some Fourth of July fireworks for you, then sending him away. *Thanks for the great orgasm, buddy. See you next time I'm in the mood.* Big-time control issue, Rox. You don't know what to do without it. No wonder he's still on the casual wavelength. You haven't given him enough to make him switch his dial."

"I've never spent the night with *any* man," Roxy confessed, surprised to hear herself doing it. "Never."

"I seem to recall a marriage...."

"A marriage where we had separate bedrooms. We did the deed on our honeymoon, a couple of times, then he immediately checked himself into another room for the duration. It was a snore, Astrid. A big zero, and I sure didn't want to wake up to that the next morning. I always had these dreams about waking up with the man I loved. I've just never been able to..."

"Really? Never?"

"Never. And I wanted to. *With Ned.* Almost did that night at the beach...which didn't work out. It's like sex can be casual if you want to be, but spending the night in his arms can't be. Not ever. And I want to spend the night in his arms. But something stops me from doing it. Maybe the fear of waking up in the morning and finding him gone."

"So what you're telling me is that he's been giving you the kind of casual relationship you've always said you want, probably even said that to him in so many words...or actions. When all the time, deep down, you're really are a hopeless romantic?"

"Well, the hopeless part, anyway. And in all fairness *to me*, I didn't know what I wanted until I met him."

"Deluding yourself, girlfriend?"

"I'd rather think of it as naivete. I mean, how is anyone supposed to know for sure until they see it or almost have it? I always thought I wanted to be a psychologist but I didn't know I wanted to be a radio host until I got the chance." The more she talked, the worse Roxy felt. She wanted him to come over, didn't want him coming over. Did, didn't. Did... Wasn't sure. Geez!

"Bottom line time, Rox. Do you love him enough to do all the fixing yourself? Get down on your knees and crawl across the hall if you have to?"

"Maybe he won't open the door."

"Raising my finger to cut off the connection."

"Do I have to crawl?"

"Finger getting closer."

"Can't I just wait until I see him come out in the hall?"

"Finger resting gently on the button."

"Okay."

"Okay, what?"

"Maybe I do."

"Finger beginning to apply pressure."

"Knock it off, Astrid. I love him, okay. Are you happy? Love him! As in totally in love, want to have his babies and a white picket fence kind of love. And sure, I'll crawl if I have to. Is that good enough for you?"

"For now."

"That's all I get?"

"Well, I hate pink and yellow. Green's a good color with my hair. Blue's iffy, depending on the shade. And there's nothing wrong with a bridesmaid wearing a nice off-white. Or black, if it's evening. But not lavender and for heaven's sake no ruffles or bows. I won't be there if you want ruffles and bows."

"Yeah, like I'm getting married," Roxy snorted, crawling on her hands and knees over to the pile of Edward Craig books. Picking one out of the heap, she studied the photo on the back. Not the Ned she knew, but nice. There was some twinkle in his eyes. But his hair was combed and he had on a shirt, damn him! Grabbing a pen from her pocket, she did a little facial rearranging, then chucked the book at the wall. It hit with a dull thud. The same dull thud as her heart.

"Have you ever wondered if maybe you battle Edward

so vigorously because there's something sexual in *that?* I'm sure not the shrink here, but you two do have a certain chemistry, and I'm betting he knows it, or he wouldn't keep coming back for more. As Edward."

"You're fired," Roxy replied, despondently.

"You mean I'm right. You always light up when Edward's on the line. You get that little spark thing going in your eyes, gear up for battle, and as soon as he's off air, you bask in the afterglow of a truffle."

Carrying another of his books with her, Roxy crawled back over to her rug and sprawled out flat in the middle of it. "You are sooo wrong, I'm not even going to argue with you." Absently, she glanced over at the door, wondering if he knew she was home. She'd rattled her keys when she came in, dropped them, messed with the lock, dropped her briefcase twice, done a quick round of Riverdancing—all that and still no Ned. "Look, I can't think about this any more tonight and I'm tired of throwing his books at the wall. So I'm going to bed. Okay?"

"Sure you don't want to come have a jammie party with me? Unless you're planning on one with him…a jammie party *without* your jammies."

"Good night, Astrid," she said emphatically, clicking off and tossing her cell phone aside. She looked at the jacket cover photo one more time. Each one had been different, and all were good. Nice eyes, nice smile. Damn it again! *This just wasn't fair.* The *she* who promoted sex was in love, and the *he* who promoted love only wanted sex. His book hit the wall, landing in the heap with all the rest. "Like that'll fix things."

Pulling herself up off the rug, Roxy plodded over to the hall mirror. Automatically, she pulled the step out and jumped up on it, then took a good look at…her chin! He'd lowered it. "Damn him," she muttered, stepping back down then kicking the step across the hall. "He just comes and goes…fixes a mirror, buys a rug, makes me love him then, *I think you're a gifted broadcaster, Val. But a deluded counselor, if you believe that starting in the bedroom makes for a solid relationship.*" They hadn't, but it was pretty damned close. And she'd swear on every Twinkie she'd ever eaten, she really had thought it was a solid relationship.

"You hypocrite," she snapped in the direction of his apartment.

I'm just cautioning you that after a couple of dates, if that's where it goes, the relationship may already be in trouble. Or maybe already doomed to failure. And that's exactly where it had gone with them. "Only crazy me…I wasn't seeing doom there at all. But apparently you had, Ned. So I guess a couple of times on the floor is all you wanted out of this thing. So pronounce it doomed." She stomped on the floor. "Be thou doomed!"

Roxy plopped back down on the rug—his *second-time* gift to her—ran her fingers over the soft nap, shut her eyes and thought about that second time. Actually, it was the third time, wasn't it? Which meant, with their little beach frolic, they were already way over their quota. But it was a nice rug, anyway, one she'd apparently read too much into. "So Ned, do you give all your girlfriends a rug on your second date?"

Really pathetic, being so sentimental about a seven-by-nine piece of floor covering. So maybe she'd get rid of it tomorrow. Give it to Doyle as an apartment-warming gift. *It's almost like new, Doyle. Owned by a little old lady who only used it for sex twice on her way to the grocery store.* Even if she did give it the heave-ho, there was still the likelihood she'd spend the rest of her life getting mopey over any old rug on any old floor. God forbid she should go see her mom's brand-new house with wall-to-wall Berber. How would she ever explain all the sobbing?

Instinctively, Roxy glanced at the ticking cat in the

kitchen. Two fifty-four, ho-hum. No use thinking about it any longer. What was done was done. It was over.

And Ned...well, no eulogy for him. Not for the mighty Edward...the mighty hypocritical Edward, who wanted sex, not a relationship, and didn't walk the talk he talked. Yeah, wouldn't that just make a wonderful footnote for his next book. Or one of those rave reviews on the front cover. *The most exceptional book I've ever read!* Or, *I couldn't put it down once I started it.* Right, Edward. *The most deceiving pile of yap since the printing press was invented.*

Purely for spite, she went back over to his book pile, and heaved one at the wall just as someone knocked on her door. "Ned?" Roxy gasped, scrambling to her feet.

Even though she'd been thinking about this moment all day, planning it, unplanning it, chopping him up with an imaginary hatchet, now that he was here she didn't know what to do. Sure, she wanted to let him in and give him a huge chunk of her mind. But she also wanted to let him in and give him a huge chunk of her heart, too. *Them's the facts Roxy, like 'em or not!* Most of all, she wanted to see if he wanted that chunk of her heart. Or not.

"Extra meat, just the way I like it," Doyle said, shoving the pizza box into Roxy's hands. "Double-extra cheese, too. But I left off the onions. Hope that's okay."

"Huh?"

"You said you wanted us to have pizza tonight. You know, on account of my letting you have this apartment. It took me a while to find a pizza place open this late over in this neighborhood. But I did and here it is. Oh, and Rox, it's on your tab. They know you, and since you invited me... Anyway, I bought root beer, too. Actually, it's next door in my fridge. Be right back."

Flabbergasted, Roxy stood in her doorway holding the pizza box while Doyle dashed back to his apartment. Well, at least with Doyle she didn't have to face the obvious.

He'd eat himself into oblivion in about five minutes, and she'd be so exhausted watching him shove it in that when he left her place she'd sleep like a baby, if only to escape the visual reminder. Sleep, hopefully not counting pizzas.

Waiting for Doyle to return, crossing her fingers he wouldn't, but not having the heart to turn him away since it was, after all, her invitation, Roxy didn't notice Ned's door creeping open until it was too late, and he was standing face-to-face with her in the hall. Ned, not Edward. Jeans, no shirt, barefoot. So gorgeous. Grrr!

"Looks like a big one," he said, grinning.

She glanced down. "Super-size," she muttered, for lack of anything brilliant to say. "Extra meat. Double-extra cheese."

"You must be hungry."

"Got company. Old friend stopped by." Maybe telling him that was good, maybe it was bad. She didn't know. Whatever it was, though, it precluded Ned from the rest of her night, gave her more time to think things through. The look of being turned down for something that hadn't quite yet materialized into an invitation was as obvious on his face as was the bare chest she so wanted to dribble pizza sauce over. Then lick it up.

"Well, I've got work to do. Hope you and your friend enjoy it." Without missing a beat, he stepped back inside his apartment, and by the time Doyle reappeared with a two-liter root beer, she was once again standing alone in her doorway, without a trace of anyone else having just been there. Without a trace, except his after-shave. And her goose bumps.

12

Uproars and Assorted Dirty Words

"SO WHO DO YOU THINK the friend is?" Ned asked Hep, resisting the urge to look out his peephole and see. Hep merely ignored him, choosing instead to make a bed in the gray suit Ned hadn't hung up since he'd come home from his early-morning television catastrophe.

They hadn't told him he'd be going face-to-face with Valentine McCarthy. No, they'd given him an invitation to come do the short segment and promote his new book. Then Jerry freakin' Springer almost broke out. That's what Bri would have liked, anyway. But Valentine had been pretty cool about it. Much cooler than he might have expected from her.

Ned smiled. Valentine...Val...Roxy...whatever she wanted to call herself, she hadn't missed a beat with Brianna, and he actually admired her for it. Sure, he was shocked that they were the same person, although it made sense, in a peculiar sort of way. Roxy's late-night hours, some of her opinions. And they both had this over-the-top attitude. But sleeping with her? "Problem is, Hep, I don't want to walk away from Roxy, which would be the smart thing to do right now. Smart for my career, anyway. Get over her, don't look back." But not smart for his heart, and he knew he *would* look back. "So, she knows who I am now, but she's wondering if I know who she is," he said, dropping down onto the bed next to the cat who looked mildly miffed to be sharing it with anybody. "Like I wouldn't recognize the person I'm in love with, even when she's disguised as Valentine." He'd seen Valentine McCarthy's pictures plastered on billboards and buses for months, but those were flat images, and this morning, discovering Roxy in that getup…well, she was anything but a flat image. And she smelled like Roxy—that sweet, fragrant scent he could pull up from memory, even now, when she wasn't around. Knew it the moment he'd stepped out onto the set. Knew her, too, even in that disguise.

Ned chuckled. Of course, Ricky had never recognized Lucy in any of her disguises, had he? Lucy as a foreign princess, Lucy as a cabaret dancer, Lucy as a man with a fake mustache, and poor, dumb Ricky never caught on, never once recognized the woman he loved, the woman who cooked his breakfast, bore his children, made him famous. "So maybe the wise thing to do is pull a Ricky Ricardo and see how far it goes." In other words, leave it up to Roxy, let her have the control.

The more he was with her, the more he wanted what Roxy wanted. He never knew from moment to moment what that was going to be, but hey, it sure spiced up his life when he found out. So since he wanted that spice around for the rest of his life, he knew the next move had to be hers. For one thing, it would prove, beyond a shadow of a doubt, what this relationship was about. Sure, he thought he knew, especially when he was dealing with just Roxy. But now that Valentine was included in it, he had to admit there was some doubt. Not much. But some. And basically, he still trusted her to make the right decision in spite of the fact that she *was* Valentine, who, apparently, wasn't quite as wrong as he'd thought. Which he would admit to Roxy after she confessed to him.

"Lucy always pulled it off in the last few minutes," he

told Hep. Of course, sometimes Ricky just had to go in for the kiss, even when she was still mustachioed. Then he'd end up with the fake mustache on his upper lip, which didn't matter because it always came with a happily-ever-after for them. "So I guess I'll be standing in the wings with that kiss just in case she doesn't get that mustache off in time." But he did hope she'd be the one to remove it.

Pushing himself off the bed, Ned padded to the front door and looked out the peephole again, even though he'd promised himself he wouldn't. Not a creature was stirring out there, so he pulled a chair closer to the door then plopped down in it. "To think, not to spy," he told Hep, who swaggered out to see what he was doing, then swaggered back to bed when it didn't interest her.

So what if he was curious? He had a right. That was his rug over there across the hall. Well, his gift to her. And he sure as heck hadn't planned on anybody else using it…not the way they'd used it. "Just looking out for the moral integrity of the rug in question," he muttered. "Right?" After all, *she* was Val, which was an X-factor he never expected in this relationship. The Val who slept with them for sex but never loved them. But damn it, she still seemed like Roxy to him. And he didn't want Roxy over there with anybody else, on or off the rug. So sue him, he was jealous. Jealous enough he was pounding on her front door before he realized what he was doing.

"Ned?" Roxy said, smiling up at him.

The Roxy smile. *Not* the Val smile.

"Do you need something?"

"You're damned right I need something," he snapped, pushing in past her. First thing he saw was a pile of books on the floor. His books, jackets off, heaped, piled, splayed open. One of his pictures had devil horns inked in. Then he saw the rug, thankfully vacant. No clothes dropped haphazardly around it, no unidentified naked body scrambling for cover.

"What?" she asked, still standing at the door.

He took a quick survey of the rest of the apartment, and unless the unidentified *he* was in the bedroom, or hiding in the hall closet, she was alone. And the *identified* he was making one great big ass of himself. "My hammer. Can't find it with my other tools."

"Haven't seen it. Sorry."

"I lowered your mirror earlier. Thought maybe…"

"Saw the mirror, thanks. Didn't see the hammer, sorry."

"Okay…well…" The awkward moment was swelling like a water balloon hooked to the faucet. And he knew he'd better get out of there before it either exploded or she threw it at him. "I'll be getting on back, then. If you do happen to see it here somewhere…" A quick glance at the rug—no strange indentations. Thank God! So maybe it had been just a pizza date with an old friend after all. *Stupid Ned. This is Roxy, not Val.*

"Thanks again for lowering the mirror. And if I see your hammer, I'll bring it over. So, is there anything else?"

Do *you* want anything else? he wanted desperately to ask. But she was keeping her distance. Which meant he needed to keep his, too. Didn't take a shrink to figure out *this* body language. Arms folded, jaw set, body armor all shined up. "No, nothing. So, um, good night, Roxy," he said, hoping it was not also goodbye.

"Good night, Ned," was all she said before she shut her door. And standing in the hall, he heard the click of all four of her locks.

ROXY SAT BETWEEN Doyle and Astrid, who were there with her for support. The people were trickling into the Shorecroft town meeting at a crawl, driving her nuts. She repressed the urge to run into the outer hall and physically drag them to their seats, one by one, so she could get this…this…inquisition, witch trial, bogus act of occupational narrow-mindedness over with. They didn't appreciate her chosen means of livelihood, therefore, they were going to burn her house plans at the stake. "Well, they may not look like trolls under the bridge, but they're sure not going to let me cross over it without paying a mighty high toll," she whispered to Astrid. "Assuming they'll even take a toll. Maybe they won't let me over, no matter what."

Three people sat at the conference table facing her—William Parker clenching his gavel and obviously shunning eye contact with her; Frank Thomas, one of the many architects she'd fired who was making direct, gloating, eye contact with her, reveling in his power, and an older woman who was crocheting and clearly didn't care about anything going on around her. To think, her fate rested in the hands of these people! "So is the smile working on them?" she asked Astrid, without so much as moving her lips. She'd been sitting there fifteen minutes already, smiling nonstop, forcing her lips to stay curved upward so long they were beginning to go numb.

Astrid glanced over at her, then shook her head. "Nope. You didn't think it would, did you?"

"Think anything will work?"

"Sex? You take Parker, I'll take the guy who looks like he's gonna meet you in the parking lot with a tire iron, and Doyle can have grandma. Two of us should be good enough to get you the majority vote."

Roxy slapped Astrid on the arm then glanced over her shoulder to make sure nobody had overheard her. "You trying to get me thrown in jail?"

"So when are they gonna start this thing, 'cause I'm hungry?" Doyle asked, none too quietly, causing the three board members at the table to finally glance up, in unison, scowl, then return to what they were doing before. In unison.

"When they're ready," Astrid hissed.

Roxy looked over at the three of them sitting there in the

front row—Doyle, Astrid, her—their hands folded neatly in their laps, knees properly together, backs straight—and she had to bite her lower lip to fight back a giggle. Her attire du jour was a prim little blue knee-length skirt and a white button-up blouse. Astrid was in the exact same getup, and poor Doyle pretty much the same thing, substituting slacks for a skirt. They looked like a parochial-school kids' choir. "More like when they're ready to hang me, you mean," Roxy whispered through her smile.

She glanced at William Parker, who'd started sneaking peeks at her from behind a manila file folder. "Not good," she muttered, looking over at the crocheter—a tiny, bespectacled, gray-haired seventy-something who was wrestling with an afghan that was already large enough to cover a football field. Like William Parker, she snatched a quick look at Roxy above the top of her wire rims, then went back to her granny squares.

"Ugly color," Astrid commented. "Her blues clash. She needs to stay in the true shade and get away from the greens altogether."

"She needs to pick up that damned hammer and start this meeting," Doyle snapped, tugging at his clip-on blue tie.

That remark was greeted by a collective throat-clearing from the board, and several of the Shorecrofters sitting around Roxy and crew.

"Before midnight," Doyle continued. "And you know what happens at midnight." He widened his eyes, pulled in his chin, stiffened his shoulder and arms, raising his arms slowly out in front of him like a zombie.

"Stop that," Astrid said, punching him in the arm.

Both actions—Doyle's zombie and Astrid's slap—were acknowledged by an officious throat-clearing from the board, and pretty much from all the Shorecrofters in the room, too.

Roxy slunk down in her seat, resisting the urge to cross

one leg over the other since William Parker might construe it as some sort of sexual advance. *Honestly, I saw her you-know-what.* "So when do we begin," she finally asked, her nerves frayed to a single, moth-eaten thread.

William Parker glanced at the crowd still creeping in behind Roxy, apparently satisfied enough of the fifty seats were filled to begin. "Now, Miss Rose." Flat voice, no intonation whatsoever. He banged his gavel. First bang didn't take since the ladies' recipe klatch in the second row behind Roxy was still going over the ingredients for the best lobster bisque ever. "Heavy cream or will half-and-half work?" were the last words that sailed out over the proceedings as William Parker banged one more time. He covered the microphone sitting on the table in front of him with his hand, then leaned forward. "Cream for flavor, half-and-half for health. Try half of each for a nice compromise."

Several people in the audience murmured agreement, a few disapproval, as William Parker shifted the microphone closer to his mouth. "As you know, we have a proposal before us tonight for the annexation of certain properties adjoining the village into the village proper. We tabled the vote at our last meeting in order to choose the village Christmas decorations—red poinsettias this year—and the meeting before that to discuss switching vendors for our swimming pool chemicals. But Miss Rose, owner of one of the properties in question, is proceeding with house plans, and in all fairness to her we need to address this issue before she goes any farther, since what we do, most likely, will have bearing on what she does out there. And just let me start off by offering my opinion. The properties before us for annexation already make use of our village services, so they might as well be on the tax rolls and pay for them."

The audience muttered a unified agreement, and Roxy already felt the hand of defeat knocking her down. Nothing she hadn't felt before she got here. But this was pretty much the death blow.

"Your comments, Miss Rose?" he continued. "For the record, are you opposed to annexation?"

The little old gray-hair glanced up from her afghan for the answer.

"My objection is not to annexation, per se," Roxy began, deciding to stay seated since this was a moot appearance, anyway. No point getting up and making a spectacle of herself. "If you want my tax money, you can have it. And actually, if I do use your village services, then I should pay for them. But what you can't have is my right to build whatever I want on my property. It's zoned for a residential structure, and I intend on building a residence, Mr. Parker."

"You may *intend* a residence, Miss Rose, but the village has strict building covenants, and after we take a vote, they'll extend to your property. And while you may think that has a certain unfairness to it, since, for all intents and purposes, you purchased that property prior to annexation, the intent to annex has been there for quite some time. And we *intend* on holding you to the same building restrictions everybody in Shorecroft is bound to follow. It's a matter of the research, Miss Rose. Our intent was on file, and if you, or your realtor, failed to find it, I am sorry. That's valuable property...."

"Told you the dotted line was too fast," Astrid muttered under her breath. "And I'm betting your real estate agent wasn't anywhere near retirement like she told you. It was a scheme to get your money PDQ because she knew what these bastards would do to you and she didn't want you finding out."

William Parker cleared his throat as Roxy punched Astrid in the ribs with her elbow. "As I was saying," he continued, "that's valuable property and I'm sure you will have no trouble disposing of it."

"You'd like that, wouldn't you? Me selling out. Is that what this is all about? You don't want me here, and you'll do whatever it takes to get rid of me, including annexing my property, sticking me with those asinine building covenants, then never okaying anything I submit to Frank Thomas, who hates me, anyway because I fired his sorry as...him. All because you don't like my sex talk."

A round of mutterings and tsk-tsks resounded throughout the tiny chamber, and the recipe klatch got up and marched out *en masse*, even before the lobster bisque was completely done.

William Parker watched the exodus and when the last lobster-cooker was gone, turned his attention back to Roxy. "I'm sorry, Miss Rose, but like I told you in earlier discussions, it's not personal. I'm doing what I think is best for the village, and annexing your property is what I think is best. As far as approving your plans," he glanced over at Frank Thomas, "it's a committee decision."

Roxy shook her head. Pure exasperation! Sure, this was exactly what she expected, but the optimist in her had been still holding out some hope when she came in here this evening. False hope, evidently. "It's all about sex, isn't it, Mr. Parker? Sex! It makes me a pretty good living and you don't like that." She stood up, walked across the wooden floor to face him directly at his table. "You've made it pretty clear before that you have an aversion to what I do, at least in the public forum, and you're using your sexual preferences now to run me out of town. Which isn't fair, Mr. Parker. It's only a job. When it's over, I go home just like everybody else, and I really want to go home to a house on my property. A house designed the way I like it. And I'll be damned if I'll let your distaste for my job cheat me out of it. Although I must say, I was quite surprised when you were the one who came to me, because I certainly never had any intention of mixing that part of my life with this. You were the one who wanted it, though. That day out on my beach…"

Collective gasps from the audience. And one, rather boisterous "Wow!"

"So what's the big deal, anyway? What's the big deal with suggesting that someone hook up his meddling mother for sex…"

"*Hot mamma sex*, if I'm not mistaken," William Parker inserted.

The gray-hair at the table dropped her crochet hook, and her scowl was replaced by a smidgen of interest.

"Okay, you're right. I suggest hot mamma sex, then suddenly you don't want me living here in Shorecroft, so you covenant me, hoping I'll give up. Right?"

Chairs started moving. Some people were switching seats to get closer. Others scooted away.

"Miss Rose," William Parker sputtered. "That's not quite—"

"Right?" Roxy interrupted. "Kick me out because I can say the word *penis* in public and not even blush when I do? It's not like we all haven't said the word before. I just happen to say it in public more often than most people do, but that's what I'm paid for. What people expect to hear from me. What you've heard from me before, Mr. Parker, and I'm betting on a whole lot of different occasions."

The gray-hair dropped her afghan.

"And saying it doesn't make me a bad person. If you care to look at my house plans, you won't see one single penis in them anywhere." She hoped.

Doyle raised his fist in a power salute, but Astrid struck it down.

"Sex is what I do for a living, Mr. Parker, not who I am. And I have thousands…hundreds of thousands of people who can't wait for me to go to work every night. It's how I make a pretty darned good living, a living that enabled me to buy that property in the first place, and, hopefully, will enable me to build that house on it in the near future, if you can get past the preconceived notion that what I do is bad. Because it's not. More and more people spend the night with me each and every night, and they know what to expect from me, and I never let them down. And that's what will put some pretty significant tax dollars in your coffers. My saying penis, Mr. Parker, can pay for those freakin' red poinsettias."

"Like out there in Nevada?" the gray-hair asked.

Roxy blinked. "I'm sorry?"

"You know, those ranches out in Nevada."

Roxy drew a blank, and looked back to Astrid for clarification.

"Prostitutes," Doyle supplied, grinning. "Ladies of the evening."

"Oh, no!" Astrid sputtered, catching on while Roxy was still pondering the connection. "They don't have a clue what you're talking about, Rox. None of them, I don't think, except Mr. Parker. You're talking about the show and they think that you're a…"

Flabbergasted, Roxy spun back to William Parker. "You didn't tell them about me? After that day on the beach, I assumed you'd go back and tell them. And you didn't?" she asked, as he tried to slide under the table. "You *really* didn't tell them who I am, what I do?" she screeched, suddenly so weak in the knees she had to stagger back to her chair and sit down.

"No," he squeaked. "I wanted to respect your privacy."

"And everything I've been saying this evening, they really think I'm a…?"

"Now they do, I suppose," he squeaked again.

"Yep, Rox. They think you're a hooker," Doyle piped up, turning to watch the rest of the audience run from the room. "So, now that this thing's over, and I'm assuming they won't even let you build a sand castle here, wanna go grab a pizza?"

NED BARELY MADE IT BACK to his Hummer before Roxy stormed out of the town building. He hadn't gone inside the meeting room. She'd have seen him and her sense of independence might have been offended. And after all, this was still her situation to fix between them. If she wanted anything between them. But he'd heard everything from the hall. Every last word, every last gasp. And he had to hand it to her, she had guts. Guts in a bit of disarray right now, but guts nonetheless. Sticking his key in the ignition, Ned chuckled as his Hummer started. Ricky sure didn't know what he was missing, not loving Roxy.

FACE DOWN ON THE RUG, Roxy hadn't moved in two hours, except to breathe. And even that was an effort. If she were a drinking kind of woman she'd be drunk. But she wasn't and there was no other escape open to her, and man, oh man did she need an escape right now. "Beam me up, somebody. Please."

What a mess! "My life. Yeah, right!" she mumbled into the nap. On top of the world one minute, then climbing into that deep, dark hole she'd dug for herself the next.

She wanted to call him. Didn't want to call him. Too scared to call him. The real Roxy would have marched straight across the hall, squared her shoulders and said *Hey, Ned, you know that Valentine McCarthy you hate? I'm her, but that's okay because you're that Edward Craig I hate. So let's just skip it and get back to the real deal—Roxy and Ned— okay?*

But she was chicken. The rug was holding her down. She was coming down with a case of laryngitis. Choose one excuse. Or all three. Didn't matter, since she couldn't do it. Not right now, anyway. Not until she was ready to face the consequences, because it could go either way.

So for now she was safe not knowing. Safe, sorry and sad. And stupid for thinking that she almost had it all. That she could ever have it all. Didn't happen. No one got it. Poor Roxy Rose. She had expectations, silly her. A career she loved, a piece of property she loved, and yes, the most unpardonable of all expectations—a man she loved. Way too much for any one girl to expect. Silly girl.

"Yeah, yeah," she muttered. "Way too much." But the consolation prize, if she could console herself with it, was that she would walk away with her career unscathed. The home she wanted was probably a goner now. Same with her relationship with Ned. But she had her job, and it was getting bigger and better every day. *Here lies Roxanna Valentine Rose. She had her work.*

"Wow," she muttered, finally turning over on her back, stretching to get a look at the ticking cat. Almost midnight. "Wonder what words of wisdom Valentine has for us tonight."

In three years, this was the first night she'd taken off. No vacation, no substitute, lest he or she do what she had done three years ago when she was the substitute—snatch the show away from the regular host. Sure, his ratings were way down, and hers were way up. But still, it could happen, so she always had a show or two in the can. Old ones cut and pasted to sound like new ones, ready to go just in case she wasn't. But until now, there'd never been a reason to use them. Come midnight, every weeknight, she was always at her desk, ready to utter her sugars into the microphone. Until tonight. Listeners might not like it, might not like the fact that the phone lines were closed down, but they'd get over it tomorrow night, when she was back.

Raising up just enough to grab the remote off the end

table next to the sofa, Roxy turned on her radio, then turned back over on her stomach, wondering why Ned hadn't come over. "Maybe because you rejected him, Roxy. Control freakin' bitch that you are. Doesn't take Valentine to figure it out." A control freakin' bitch without the backbone to lift the phone or crawl across the hall to him.

"Welcome to *Midnight Special*, sugars. Are you ready for something special? Because if you are, you've certainly come to the right place. Doctor Val has something *extra-specially* special for you tonight."

"I sure hope so, Val," Roxy moaned, "because I've done some extra-specially big screwing up this time."

"Doctor Val, I have this problem," the first caller began. "There's this guy I like a lot. Even love."

Me, too, Roxy thought. *Me, too.*

"That's a good start. So tell Doctor Val why you're having a problem with this guy you love."

"For starters, I haven't told him everything about me. At first it didn't matter, because I didn't know where the relationship was headed to. But now, I think we really have something, and I'm afraid if I start telling him things he should have known a long time ago that he'll leave me. I'm just so scared, Doctor Val."

"Look, I know you are. And believe me, Doctor Val is all for keeping a few little secrets in a relationship. Spilling everything can cause quite a mess, especially if you don't know where that relationship's going at the beginning."

"Which is exactly what I did," Roxy said to the rug. "Which was stupid, Val. Tell the lady how stupid it was."

"Well, sugar, there comes a point when the relationship looks like it's going to turn into more than a one or two-night stand, where you've got to fess up if you want to keep him around."

Truer words never spoken, at least by Valentine.

"And Valentine's sensing that you do. Isn't that right, sugar?"

"Maybe I do," the caller responded.

"Maybe I do, too," Roxy responded also. "And I never meant for it to go this far. But it sort of sneaked up on me. And what I thought was going to be casual wasn't. Then suddenly the secrets became important."

"And I didn't know how to tell him, so I just kept avoiding it," the caller added.

"You and me both," Roxy agreed.

"You can do one of two things here, but keep in mind, that at this stage of the game, there's no guarantee. It can go either way. You can walk away, lesson learned and vow not to do that again. Or you can tell him. Then depending on the kind of man he is, he'll either forgive you or leave."

"He's a nice man, Doctor Val. Kind, generous, and he trusts me."

"And he trusts me, too," Roxy added.

"Sounds to me like you need to do better by that man of yours," Val said. "And I think you already knew that when you called in. But you were hoping there was another way around it, is that correct?"

"Maybe," the called answered. "Something I could do without possibly losing him."

"More like probably losing him," Roxy said. "If he fell in love with the person you've been putting forward to him, then suddenly discovers you're not that person at all, there's no guarantee that the feelings he had for her will be the ones he has for you."

"Well, sugar, you could seduce that man of yours like you've never done before. Give him the thrill of his life, let him have everything his little heart desires in the bedroom, then break the news in dribs and drabs between orgasms. That might give you a headstart on keeping him, if he realizes in the middle of your confession what he'll be losing if he leaves."

Roxy flopped over and sat up. "Tell me I didn't say that," she moaned. "Please tell me."

"You go make him so weak he can't walk out that door. Make his head spin, make his eyes cross in his head, and pull out every sexual favor you know, if that's what it takes."

"No!" Roxy yelled. "Bad advice. She's giving you...*I'm* giving you bad advice. You need to sit down with the man and talk to him. Be honest. Be sincere. He might still leave, but if he does, you'll know you gave it your best shot. And sex isn't your best shot here."

"Thanks, Doctor Val. You're right, I do need to tell him. And what you're suggesting—I'm betting in the future, when I keep other secrets from him, he won't mind the confession so much."

Roxy picked up her remote and threw it at the stereo. "So if I take my advice, I'll just go across the hall, sleep with Ned, and that will make it all better." No wonder her life was so screwed up. *She'd been listening to herself.*

And no wonder Edward Craig had been nipping at Valentine's heels. They deserved some nipping.

"Okay, Hep. I get that she's Valentine. That's cool. But what the hell does she think I am?" Ned grunted as he paced the perimeter of his living room. "*Who* the hell does she think I am? She gets me out to the beach, and like an idiot I thought it was more than what she thought it was, because once she got what she wanted, that was it. She went home. Sex on the beach, Hep. That's what it was. And I thought..." Nope. He wasn't even going to think those words. He'd been kidding himself with them long enough. So maybe she was Valentine after all, and Roxy was the character, instead of the other way around. "You know, it makes sense. I just couldn't see it. And even after I found out she was Val, I just kept on kidding myself, kept on thinking she'd finally tell me. Kept telling myself that it was more than sex for her. That we were falling in love, be-cause I sure as hell…" Talk about feeling stupid. "I thought I could read people better than that, Hep."

He'd plodded to the door a thousand times in the past hour, watching for her to come home, wondering if they could make this better between them. But then he'd turned on the radio and there she was, telling her caller to set the lies straight with sex. That's all he heard, all he could listen to. It's what he expected from Val, *not* what he expected from Roxy. So maybe they couldn't be separated.

But he loved her, damn it! In spite of it all, he loved her. And now, he just didn't know what came next.

13

Waking Up Wednesday Morning with the Ned Flu

"I'm CALLING IN SICK for the rest of the week, Astrid. Stick on some reruns for me, will you?"

"We've had a million complaints already because last night was a rerun. Your regulars recognized the cut-and-paste version, and I guarantee if they don't get somebody live on the other end of the wire next time they call, they won't be calling back. Or listening. Since we're so close to setting that syndication deal in motion, we need a warm body in your chair giving out advice."

So she was wrong, it did matter. For business, that was good; for Roxy, she just couldn't handle it right now. "Then get one," she said dismally. Sure, she could stay, go through the motions. Her heart wouldn't be in it, though, and her listeners would hear that. *Okay sugars, not to worry. Doctor Val took her own advice and it sucked.* "Your choice. I know I said I'd never use a sub, but I really do need to get out of here for a few days. So I'm trusting you to find someone adequate, *not good*, because I want a job to come back to."

"I'm guessing this is about getting away from your handyman?"

Roxy nodded. "I really wanted to fix it last night, but I was..."

"Scared," Astrid supplied. "Scared he wouldn't want it fixed?"

Roxy nodded. "You were so right. I haven't been thinking about what he wants. It's always been about me. And
after that night after I kicked him off my beach, I kicked
him out again when he wanted to have pizza with me. I
sent him away because I couldn't face him. Didn't know
how to, and it was easier for me to get rid of him. *For me*,
Astrid. It was easier for me. I haven't seen him since, and
it's got nothing to do with Val. It's me. *All me*. He got tired
of my control issues, even though he said he wouldn't.
And I can't blame him, because I'm pretty damned tired
of them myself. So I just need to go away for a while and
have a heart to heart with myself, figure out how, and if, I
can make this right between us. Figure out how to do it in
a way that's best for both of us, not just me. And I'm not
very good at that." She had to figure out how to start over
with Ned. Or how to live with a broken heart if he
wouldn't.

"I'm so sorry about all this, Rox. Are you sure you're
going to be okay?"

"I'm Roxy Rose. Of course I'm going to be okay." But
there was none of the usual Roxy Rose conviction in her
voice. "So let me tape a lead-in, and get out of here."

NOT EXACTLY WHAT SHE HAD PLANNED when she was pack-
ing to run away from home, but she was tired, and a nice
little B-and-B just outside Tacoma suited her fine. She was
already feeling a little better mentally, not being just two
peepholes away from him.

Mrs. Willoughby's B-and-B was a quaint little place.
Traditional, cozy charm in a nice wooded area. Even had
a white picket fence, and Roxy was amazed at how much
she liked it. It reminded her of Ned.

The fresh muffins and banana bread promised for
breakfast made her think of Twinkies, which made her
think about...well, the obvious. A bookshelf full of classics

downstairs reminded her that he was a writer. No radio or television in her room. Yep, made her think of him too. And the faucet in the bathroom had a slight drip.

There was so much Ned everywhere.

Roxy slept from the moment she arrived, a little after noon, until well after eleven that night, when she finally wandered downstairs hoping somebody might be up who could point her to food. Real food, not Twinkies. Or truffles…

"Go make yourself a sandwich," Mrs. Willoughby said, pointing Roxy to the kitchen. "Then come on back out here and join me. You're my only guest tonight, and it's nice to have someone to keep me company. I'm alone now."

Alone now, like *she* was. Roxy put together a ham sandwich and headed back into the living room where Mrs. Willoughby, sixtyish and plump, snuggled into her couch, listening to her radio. *"Midnight Special,"* she told Roxy. "Ever hear it?"

"Used to," she said, wishing now she hadn't come down. Since she was eating Mrs. Willoughby's food though, she felt obligated to keep the woman company. And that included listening to the show, which she didn't want to do. Didn't want to listen to it, didn't want to think about it.

"Well, make yourself at home, dear. That chair over there's the best seat in the house." She nodded at a flower-covered, overstuffed wingback. "Sit down, get yourself comfortable." Then she giggled, sounding almost like a little girl. "You're not embarrassed about the things they talk about on this show, are you, dear? It can get pretty hot sometimes. Especially when that Edward calls her and they go at it. Talk about chemistry."

"Chemistry? More like bloodthirsty hostility, don't you mean?"

"That's not hostility, dear. I've been listening to the two of them go at it ever since he started calling, and those two, well, I'm betting in the same room they'd blow the roof off the building, and not from bloodthirsty hostility." She picked up a cup of hot tea and nodded toward the chair again. "More like sexual chemistry, dear. The kind that'll knock your socks off. Now, sit down, enjoy that sandwich. I have a chocolate cake in the kitchen if you'd like some later."

Blowing the roof off the building? Knock your socks off sexual chemistry? Is that what her listeners were hearing? "You really think they're hot?"

"Well, dear, I saw them on *SunUp* the other day. And the way that man watched her when she got up and walked away…sure miss having a man looking at me that way."

Sighing, Roxy dropped into the chair. "I think I'll turn in after I finish the sandwich, if you don't mind," she said. Only she wasn't hungry anymore.

"Welcome to *Midnight Special*, sugars. Are you ready for something special? Because if you are, you've certainly come to the right place. Doctor Val has something *extra-specially* special for you tonight. And tonight it's coming to you in the form of one extra-specially special guest host, while Valentine takes a few days off to go practice a little bit of what she's been preaching. So be gentle. I'm leaving you in good hands."

"She really gives me a good laugh sometimes," Mrs. Willoughby commented. "I hope whoever's taking over for her is as good as she is."

Frankly, Roxy didn't care. Astrid wouldn't torpedo the show, and beyond that all Roxy wanted to do was go back to bed and *not* worry about her show…her life…tomorrow—or the day after that.

"Welcome to *Midnight Special*," the dark-chocolate voice whispered across the airwaves.

Roxy dropped her ham sandwich on the floor. "I can't believe it," she sputtered, every one of her senses cracking to attention.

"This is Doctor Edward Craig, filling in for Doctor Mc-Carthy for the rest of the week."

"I'll fire her," Roxy snapped. "For real this time."

"Excuse me, dear?" Mrs. Willoughby said. "I didn't quite catch that."

"And while Valentine is off doing whatever it is Valentine does, I promise she's left you in very good hands," he continued.

"Doesn't he have just the nicest voice?" Mrs. Willoughby asked. "Dreamy. And he's a hunk. The kind you want in bed next to you. I'll tell you, if I were thirty years younger…heck, even if I *weren't* thirty years younger." She chuckled. "That's a topic I haven't heard Valentine talk about yet. Unless you count the one on hot mamma sex, but it didn't ever get around to women my age and men his age."

"She shouldn't have done it," Roxy growled. "*Astrid, how could you do this to me? You're my best friend. You, more than anybody else, know how I feel about him.*" Roxy hissed out an agitated breath. "The minute I leave town, who does she go out and get?"

"So this Astrid went out and got herself a younger man, dear? Is that what you're saying? You seem pretty angry about it. Maybe a nice jigger of scotch will calm you down."

"Getting herself a younger man…it should be that simple," Roxy grumbled, scooping her sandwich up off the floor. "And I *am* angry! Furious!"

"If I were you, dear, I'd call Doctor Craig right up and ask his opinion, but he's pretty traditional, so it might not be anything you'd like to hear. But he's honest." Mrs. Willoughby set her teacup down on the end table, kicked off her shoes, pulled her feet up on the sofa and settled in for the show.

"Ha! You think he's honest? Just ask him about sex on the rug, on the door, on the rug on the beach. Ask him how honest that is," Roxy snapped, pulling her cell phone out of her pocket. She punched in the studio phone number, then drummed her fingers impatiently on the table next to her chair while she waited for Doyle to pick up. "Was that honest, hauling my rug out to the beach just so he could... Hello, Doyle?"

"Rox?" Doyle said.

"Why him?" Roxy screeched. "Of all the people she could have gotten, why him?"

"She thought it would be fun, I guess. And she was right. The lines are really lighting up tonight."

"Well, stick me in the queue for next caller up, then put her on the phone for me."

"You're not going to fire her, are you?" Doyle asked.

"That would be too good for her."

"Now I get it," Mrs. Willoughby chimed in. "Your friend Astrid hooked herself up with *your* younger man? That's why you're so angry. And I would be, too, dear. Since you're so young yourself, though, mind if I ask if he's legal?"

"He's legal, but what I'm thinking about doing isn't." Roxy waited another two minutes before Astrid came on, passing the time listening to Edward's advice to caller number one.

"So I catch him with the baby-sitter, Doctor Craig. And while they're not, like, doing it yet, she's on his lap. And he tells me she's got something in her eye and he's trying to help her get it out. So should I believe him, Doctor?"

"No way in hell you should believe him!" Roxy shouted.

Mrs. Willoughby looked at across her, giving her the thumbs-up sign.

"Sorry," Roxy muttered. "Sometimes I get carried away."

"Does he have a history of being unfaithful?" Edward asked.

"It's cheating, Eddie," Roxy snapped. "Cheating. Unfaithful is what happens when Old Faithful doesn't go off. Cheating is what happens when a hubby does! So call it as it is. Don't soft-pedal it."

"Not that I know of," the caller continued. "But this could be the first time."

"How old is the baby-sitter?" Edward questioned.

"Like that makes a difference?" Roxy shrieked. "For heaven's sake, Eddie, the man's doing the freakin' baby-sitter. Doesn't matter if he's done it before, and unless she's a kid, doesn't matter how old she is."

"Twenty," the caller said. "College student."

Roxy jumped up from the chair and started pacing the room. "Tell her to kick the bum out right now, then ask questions later, cause if daddy's got the sitter on his lap checking out her eye this time, next time it won't be her eye he's checking out."

"Marriage counseling," Edward said. "Immediately. Your marriage has some serious problems that need to be worked through before the situation gets any worse."

"New door locks," Roxy muttered. "Cheaper than counseling."

"I think you might have been a good fill-in for Valentine yourself," Mrs. Willoughby said, pushing herself off the couch and heading over to a concealed wet bar in the bookcase. "Care for a shot of scotch now?"

"I'd rather have a shot at Edward Craig," she replied.

"Rox?" Astrid finally answered the phone.

"I'm listening to it," Roxy said, lowering her voice to almost Valentine proportions. "And I'm not liking what I'm hearing."

"I thought he'd be a natural, since your listeners already know him. Some continuity, you know. And they sure as heck won't want a steady diet of him, which was one of your concerns, wasn't it? Losing your job to your sub. Won't happen with him."

"I don't care! Just kick that continuity out the door and put it on a rerun."

The phone started crackling. "Can't hear you, Rox. You're breaking up."

"Don't you dare..."

"Can't hear you, Rox."

"Astrid, you're fired. So help me, it's for real this time."

"Rox, are you still there...can't...hear..."

"Welcome to *Midnight Special*. This is Doctor Edward Craig, and what can I do for you tonight?"

His words in her ear shocked her, even though she'd told Doyle to put her next in the queue, and she pulled the phone away like it was sizzling hot, then stared for a moment.

"Hello?" he said, both from her phone and the radio across the room.

To prevent feedback, Roxy slipped into the dining room while Mrs. Willoughby slipped back onto the couch with a jigger of scotch.

"Hello," Roxy said quietly. Not her Roxy voice, not her Valentine voice, either.

"So tell me what's bothering you tonight."

"Sex, Doctor Craig. Good sex, the best sex I've ever had."

"Was it good for him?" he asked.

"Better than good. And a woman knows these things. I think it was the best sex he's ever had, too." She shut her eyes, thinking about the quivers, the moans—his, hers.... Yep, as good for him as it was for her.

"So what's the problem, other than the fact that I haven't heard anything about a real relationship mentioned so far."

"Oh, it's a real relationship, and I don't think either one of us would argue that." She chuckled devilishly into the phone. "Not the way he does *it* for me...you know, like four, five times in a row. His mouth, Doc. What he can do with his mouth on my..."

"Your *what*?" Edward sputtered.

"Anything, everything. And his tongue. It drives me wild, like nothing I've ever felt in my whole life. It's like fire on my skin. I'm mean, I'm getting all hot right now just thinking about it." And she was. Shivering, sweating, going weak in the knees. "I want him, Doctor, in ways I've never wanted a man before. And I've had him in ways I've never had a man before. Ways I never want to have any other man, ever again. It's like our sex is on a higher plane. All we have to do is get naked—his body touching mine, mine touching his, his hands all over me, mine all over him—and we surpass what we did together the last time. And the last time was always so good."

"Meaning it gets better every time?" Edward gulped. It was audible on air.

"Better doesn't even describe it, Doc. I mean right now, just thinking about the way he moans when I…well, there are so many things I can do that make him moan. And the way he shudders when I…well, that too. You know what makes a man shudder, don't you? It's like that and more for me, too, when he does it for me."

"It?"

"You know, Doctor. *It.* Starting with my toes and working all the way up to my… The big *it.* And it's so big for both of us it practically blows the roof off the building. That kind of sex, Doc. Do you know what I'm talking about?" Roxy smiled, cutting herself a piece of Mrs. Willoughby's chocolate cake. "Sex so great there aren't even adequate words to describe it?"

Very audible sigh. "I get the picture," he snapped. "So what's the problem?"

"You're sounding a little bothered by what I'm describing, Doctor. Obviously, you've never found yourself in this kind of situation, have you? Or you'd know what the problem is."

He didn't answer.

"Have you, Doctor?" Roxy persisted. "Because what I want to know is what makes the sex so good between us? Is it merely great sex between two people who know how to do it really well with each other—you know, the mechanical aspects. Or do you think there could be more to it? You know, maybe we have deeper feelings for each other…feelings that are driving the sex between us to that higher level? Like, if we didn't have those deeper feelings maybe the sex wouldn't be so good. *Are we actually making love, Doctor? Could we be two people in love making love?*"

Edward cleared his throat, and his voice came back a little shaky. "Have you talked about it?" he asked, clearing his throat once more. "Have you ever told him how you feel? Asked him how he feels? Explored, together, the possibility that you're in love?"

Smiling, Roxy crinkled a cellophane wrapper next to the phone. "Can't hear you, Doctor. You're breaking up."

"Honesty is the best…"

"Can't hear…" Crinkle, crinkle.

"Talk to him…."

Roxy clicked off the phone, picked up two paper plates with huge pieces of cake on them and carried them back into the living room, where Mrs. Willoughby was sprawled flat on the couch, fanning herself with one hand, hugging an empty jigger with the other. "I need cake, dear. Now!"

"Too bad we were cut off," Edward continued, "or I would have told her…"

"Yeah, yeah," Roxy muttered. "Get counseling."

His voice was resolute. "I would have told her that yes, it sounds to me like they're in love. Totally, truly, in love."

Roxy dropped her cake on the floor. "Well, I'll be damned."

"Nice piece of property," Ned said, opening a bag of cookies for the gulls. "Too bad she won't be building out here."

Doyle turned around, startled. "I didn't hear you coming."

"I didn't intend for you to." He walked out past the knoll, scattered the plain vanilla wafers, then turned back to Doyle. "Looking for Roxy out here?"

"Thought she might be here. I'm kind of worried. She's been doing some pretty crazy stuff...crazy even for Roxy." He narrowed his eyes. "*Like falling for you.* Oswald told me who you were a couple of weeks ago. I took him some beer for his recovery one night and he let it slip about you. Of course, by then, she'd already moved in across from you. I let her do that, you know. Take my place on the waiting list. She needed something real bad. Her place was a pit. But if I'd known she'd end up living across the hall from Edward Craig, I sure as hell wouldn't have let it happen. But I kept thinking it would be okay. Rox is real busy, especially lately, looking for syndicators. And she's got this business first, everything else later motto. So I figured she'd stick to it. But hell, was I way off on that one.

"I started hearing her say things about the handyman, and it wasn't Oswald. So I asked, and he told me it was you standing in for him. *You* were the one with the tool belt she was drooling over. *She was falling for Doctor Edward Craig.* Believe me, man, I was sure kicking myself for screwing things up the way I did. I mean, she's not Val. Val's tough. She can give as good as she gets. But Roxy's, well, I guess you could call her vulnerable. She always believes things will work out. She's, you know, optimistic, and naive in a lot of ways.

"Then when I heard she was falling for you, I figured once you knew who she was, with the way you always go after her on the air, you'd dump her. That Edward dude...*you*...sometimes you're a real bastard, you know. Especially since it's just radio entertainment." Doyle paused, shook his head. "And after you dumped Rox, she'd be hurt because she really was falling for you. So since it was my fault she met you in the first place, I wanted to be there to help her through it."

Radio entertainment. Damn! *Radio entertainment just like him.* Score one for the pizza guy. "So you made that arrangement for Georgette Selby?"

Doyle nodded. "She was annoying Rox, anyway, so I just found her an apartment in a seniors' place. Actually the one you own. Oswald helped me get her in. And it's real nice for her. Believe me, man, she was thrilled to get in there. Then after she was gone, I got her apartment."

"You went to a lot of trouble for Roxy, Doyle. Are you in love with her?"

"It's not like you think, man," Doyle exclaimed. "I'm trying to look out for Roxy. That's all. Like a brother. But she doesn't always listen."

"Are you in love with Roxy, Doyle?"

"Sure, I love her," Doyle admitted. "But not the way you do, dude."

"You love her so much you let the Shorecroft manager know she's Valentine, hoping that would kill her plans for building out there?"

"Okay, so I sent an e-mail and ratted her out. But it was for her own good, since she wouldn't listen to me, I swear. You gotta know that, man. I was just trying to save her from herself. I've lived in a small town like that half of my life. I know how they are when it comes to people like Rox. She was investing everything she had without taking a good look at what she'd be getting, and I just couldn't stand by and let her do that. Sure, I warned her. Over and over. But she wouldn't listen to me, didn't believe what I was saying about people like the ones who live in Shorecroft. They didn't like her house, and they wouldn't like her if they ever found out who she was. With the syndication deal getting so close, a lot more of Roxy was about to go public. In fact, if you Google her, it's already out there on the Web—Roxy is Val, Val is Roxy. So I took care of the Shorecroft problem before it went too far. Before she ended up putting more into it than she already had and ended up getting hurt."

Ned squinted up at the sun. It would have been a nice day for a picnic here with Roxy. And he missed her, which was why he'd come out here, to be close to her spirit…and her seagulls. To think—which he'd been doing for hours, sitting on top of her knoll.

Well, thanks to Doyle's moment of insightfulness, now there wasn't as much to think about as he'd thought there would be. He loved Roxy. That was it. Nothing else mattered. Sure, she was complicated as hell, but whoever said life was meant to be simple. And sure, they didn't agree on a lot of things. But the flip side was sparks and sizzle and excitement.

So he'd come prepared to do a lot of soul-searching, but all he needed was one thought of Roxy and the rest was clear. *She wasn't Val.* Just like he wasn't Edward. Roxy was who she was—a little bit of both, which made her the woman he loved. And he prayed she loved the little bit of both in him.

"I don't want her hurt, either, Doyle." Ned studied Doyle for a minute. The man protected Roxy like a pit bull, loved her, defended her. The things *he* should have been doing, instead of analyzing it like Edward would do. Meaning, Edward's advice pretty much sucked. He laughed. Valentine, *and Roxy*, could have told him that!

"I'm not some kind of perv or stalker," Doyle said. "If that's what you're thinking this is all about. And I sure as hell didn't mean for it to turn into this kind of mess for her. All I really ever wanted to do was be there, you know, as her friend. So are you going to tell her it was me? That I did her in on the property deal? Because when she finds out, you know she'll kill me, man."

"Nope. You're her friend. And she's *your* friend, Doyle. She cares about you. You're the one who's got to tell her." He had his own telling to do.

Doyle jammed his hands into the pockets of his baggy jeans and looked at the seagulls squawking over the cookies. "Like I told you, man. She's in love with you. I've seen you two in the hall back at the apartment, saw the way she looked at you, you looked at her. And I've heard the things she whispers to Astrid about the handyman when they forget I'm listening. And the damnedest part of this is, while Roxy's in love with you, Valentine's just as in love with Edward, although she'd rip out her tongue, and mine, before she'd cop to that one." He laughed. "After you two get through fighting on air, the listeners need to go light up a cigarette, the talk between you is so sexy, Doc. Not like in porno, but…"

"Chemistry," Ned said.

Doyle nodded. "We've gotten thousands of calls and e-mails about it, just haven't let Rox see them 'cause they'd have made her mad as hell, thinking she was hating you, when all the time she wasn't. And she *is* a shrink. She'd have figured it out what it was, then that would have wrecked things for the show. Wrecked them for Roxy too, but she's always said the show comes first. Of course, I believed she meant it. Guess I was wrong on a lot of things, and now I've got a lot to patch up with her if she'll let me."

"She'll let you," Ned reassured him. But would she let him?

"You *do* know that was her calling in last night, don't you? She's circling around like those stupid gulls out there, trying to figure out if there's going to be a cookie for her when she lands. So are you going to give her a cookie, man?"

"I sure as hell intend to try, but I've got a few things to patch up myself."

"Wanna go grab a pizza first?"

14

Another Night, Another Piece of Cake

"Better hurry, dear, it's almost time." Mrs. Willoughby was settling in with her jigger of scotch while Roxy was settling in with a piece of carrot cake tonight. "You're going to call him again, aren't you? That was so exciting, knowing you were right there in my kitchen talking on the radio. I'll swear, you almost sounded like that Doctor Val."

"I may sound like Valentine, but I'm sure not like her," she replied, her glum mood not going away in spite of the yummy cake, and this was her third piece already this evening. Tonight she'd know one way or another. She had to, it was time. "Valentine would never find herself in this mess."

"I heard what you said on the radio last night, dear. So, why don't you just tell him you love him? Firecracker sex with the man you love…you'd be nuts if you didn't. Mr. Willoughby was a freight train in the sack, dear, and I was crazy about the man. Until he left me for a younger woman. I can tell you from personal experience, you just can't beat it when it's all good. But you're not going to find out if you just keep sitting here eating cake."

"And Mr. Willoughby never came back?" Roxy asked, suddenly too full to take another bite.

"Oh, he came back, dear. But I was having a hell of a good time with the plumber by then, so I kicked him right back out."

"I had a good thing going with the plumber once," Roxy said wistfully. "Loved that pipe wrench." Loved that plumber.

"Well, I prefer the chain grip pliers myself, dear. But those telescoping inspection mirrors can sure be fun, too." She winked at Roxy, then chugged down her scotch.

"And he's gone now, your plumber?"

"Yes, dear. For a couple more days. Plumbing convention in Vegas. He's checking out some new tools."

"WELCOME BACK to *Midnight Special*. Again, I'd like to thank Doctor McCarthy for allowing me to sit in for her, last night, tonight and tomorrow. And I'd also like to thank each and every one of you for calling in. Now, we have only a few minutes left, so let's make the most of them, shall we?"

So far he'd covered two cheating husbands, one wife who wished her hubby would cheat so she could have a little time off, a sex goddess who couldn't find Mr. Studly, and a Mr. Studly who couldn't find his sex goddess. Too bad this wasn't a dating service. And oh, yes. The one about hot grandpa sex. Seemed that granny had revved it up in the bedroom since she'd been listening to Doctor Val and gramps just called in to say thanks.

Ned glanced at the computer screen. One call left. Relationship down the tubes. Coming in on a mobile. Was it her? "And what's on your mind tonight?" God, he hoped it was.

"Lies, Doctor."

Ned sucked in a sharp breath. "What about lies?"

"They come between people." It was Roxy's voice all the way. "And once the lie starts, it's so hard to take it back, or change it, or set it straight. Something like that can ruin a relationship."

"So tell me about your lie."

"It didn't start out to be a lie. More like a little deception. Which shouldn't have been a big deal. I liked him, he liked me. I thought it would be casual, but it never was. Not for me, anyway. But I kept kidding myself that I'd get over it, move on, so it didn't matter what I was doing."

"And did you get over it?"

"No. And I never will."

"So what was this big lie you told him?"

"Not him. Me. I lied to myself, over and over, that I didn't love him. That all the differences between us meant I couldn't love him, or that he wouldn't love me. But I do love him, Doctor. With all my heart. Like I said, we had all these differences that scared me, all these similarities that scared me, too. So I kept on lying to myself instead of facing them. Telling myself that I couldn't have it all, that nobody can have it all. Easier that way, in case he wasn't feeling what I was feeling. Self-protection. Shielding myself from rejection."

"A little self-doubt?"

"A lot of self-doubt. I've failed before."

"We've all failed."

"I know. But I've set myself up with things I won't fail at, things I can keep under my control. Then I met him and realized what meant the most to me wasn't under my control at all. And I could fail again. So I pushed him away so that wouldn't happen."

"You mentioned you had differences and similarities that scare you. Did you ever think that these differences and similarities might scare him as much as they do you? Especially since he loves you in the same way you talk about loving him. Heart and soul and forever."

"He does?"

"He *absolutely* does."

"Me too. But I was afraid that all he wanted was casual. That's what I thought he was saying. You know, that we went so fast it couldn't be the real thing. Guess maybe I should have taken your advice and talked to him."

"*He* should have taken my advice and talked to you, because if that's what he was saying, he was wrong, and I know he's sorry for making you think that. But I think he was lying to himself, too. Thinking that because the feelings were so strong from the beginning, that it couldn't possibly be the real thing. Maybe looking for ways to make sure it wasn't in case you didn't want him the way he wanted you."

"So maybe we were both scared? Maybe because it was love at first sight?"

"He sounds like the kind of man who didn't believe in it. I think he was probably trying to dispel the romantic notion and look for something more practical. But he was wrong on that one, and you should tell him that."

"You mean tell him that there are some things you simply know without thinking about them or trying to argue yourself out of them or reasoning away the glorious rush that comes with spontaneity. No, Doctor. He's the one who should tell me."

"Sounds to me like you already know."

"What I know is that every story has two sides to it, including mine, and I'm so sorry I didn't tell him both sides to begin with. At first I didn't think it mattered, but when I realized that it did I was…"

"Chicken," he said.

"Yep. And the better it got between us the more I was afraid…"

"That it would end when you finally did let him see the other side?"

"It was killing me, and I'm so sorry."

"It was killing him, too, keeping the other half of his story to himself, and he's sorry too."

"Sounds to me like there were two great big sorry chickens in that pot, Edward."

"Two chickens who should have been talking to each other. But even though you didn't tell him, he knew both sides. A man knows the woman he loves no matter how she's dressed. And he loved you in spite of that other side, and because of it." She'd taken off the mustache herself. Finally! "So caller, he loves you, you love him. Anything else you want to talk about?"

"Well, Edward, I think he needs...deserves more. I think he deserves to know that the differences are a big slice of the relationship, something that adds to attraction. And I also think that if he's a very good boy, those differences can result in the best makeup sex he's ever had. Sex that will pop his eyes right out of their sockets and curl his toes, Doctor. Sex that will make those differences between us an extra-specially exciting part of our relationship." She was slipping back into Valentine's voice now.

"So as usual, Valentine, it's all about sex? You hear this heartfelt discussion about two people who have fallen deeply and forever in love and you take it right back to the bedroom and make it all about sex?"

"Absolutely not. It's all about making love to the person you loved at first sight and who you're going to love for the rest of your life. And I'm talking some red hot granny lovemaking way down the line, Eddie."

Roxy clicked off her phone and stepped into the booth, then took the mic from Ned. "And this is Doctor Val signing off, hoping your midnight tonight is the most extra-specially special one ever, sugars." She opened her drawer, took out two truffles and handed him one.

"You know what I was thinking?" Ned said, pulling her into his arms.

"About a rug?"

"And some Twinkies."

THREE MONTHS LATER...

"I don't want the picket fence anymore," Ned protested, perusing the house plans. "Doesn't work out there on the beach. And it's going to get in the way when I have to go out and feed your gulls." Their gulls now. "I thought you wanted a nice, unobstructed view of the Sound."

"From the bedroom."

He glanced at the prints and shook his head. "Going to be hard to do since you got rid of the windows. And as far as I know, most Victorians came with windows."

So she'd given up the cement, steel and glass. No biggie. Traditional was wonderful when it came with Ned. And once Ned's new CAD program had popped out a reasonable Victorian facsimile, the Shorecroft mob relented. A little. The house was approved, but she was forever banned from Shorecroft public functions.

"Two minutes," Doyle called, immediately pulling off the headphones so he wouldn't overhear any of the newlywed conversation. Not that everybody at the station hadn't been hearing it for the past few days. He'd fessed-up his deeds to Roxy, and to show him there were no hard feelings, she subscribed him to the pizza-of-the-month club as a thank-you for caring, even if in a Doyle-ish clumsy way. Plus she assured him, there was no way she was going syndicated without him.

She'd been honeymooning while Astrid was working out the syndication details, actually. Big details translating into lots of money. Sure, it was hard stepping back and letting Astrid take control of the deal. But she'd been caught up with a VP at Taber Syndicators lately, his butt not quite as good as Ned's, even though Astrid would never admit it, and it seemed the natural thing to do. Besides, there'd been this awesome Rose-Proctor, make that Proctor-Rose, honeymoon in the works...pup tenting out on a beach... and there was no amount of control anybody could have offered Roxy that could have compared with what was going on out on Rose Hill, in Rose Water, Rose Beach...

And there was an upside waiting for her after the honeymoon. With the pizza, Doyle got the pizza delivery girl, which looked exceptionally promising, according to Doctor Val and her new on-air partner, Doctor Edward. Collaboration—probably the only thing they'd agreed on professionally, so far. Amazing how the syndication deal exploded when that announcement hit the airwaves. Eddie and Val together... Sure, Ned was still writing by day. With lots of vigor now that he and Roxy were on the same schedule. Roxy was even thinking about picking up a pen and doing a little of that herself. Something called *An Opposite's Guide to Making Sex Even Better*. Nothing like the book Ned was writing, of course.

"So stick in a window someplace," Roxy said, looking over the program notes. Same ol', same ol', with one exception. And having *him* sitting right here in the booth with her every night, she was beginning to anticipate the fun things she might do to him during the breaks. Or during the broadcast, on the rug they'd bought for the booth. Just thinking about it made her tingle! Sliding one truffle over to him, and placing one next to her microphone, she continued, "And while you're at it, we might need some stairs to get us from the first floor to the second." Leaning into him, she whispered, "Unless you'd prefer to use a pole. And there are some extra-specially fun things I can do for you on a pole, sugar."

"I heard that," Astrid said from her booth.

"Think maybe I'll put that pole in the bedroom," Ned growled, leaning to give Roxy a quick kiss as Doyle gave them the countdown.

"Five, four, three, two..."

As the one count came down on them, Roxy took hold of Ned's hand and gave it a squeeze. "Welcome to *Midnight*

Special, sugars. Are you ready for something special? Because if you are, you've certainly come to the right place. Doctors Valentine and Edward *both* have something *extra-specially* special for you tonight."

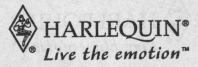

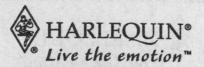

Harlequin Romance®

*Every month, sample the fresh new talent in
Harlequin Romance®!
For sparkling, emotional, feel-good romance, try:*

January 2005
Marriage Make-Over, #3830
by *Ally Blake*

February 2005
Hired by Mr. Right, #3834
by *Nicola Marsh*

March 2005
For Our Children's Sake, #3838
by *Natasha Oakley*

April 2005
The Bridal Bet, #3842
by *Trish Wylie*

The shining new stars of tomorrow!

Available wherever Harlequin books are sold.

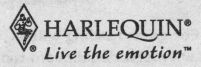

HARLEQUIN®
Live the emotion™

www.eHarlequin.com

HRNTA1204

Enter the compelling and unpredictable world of Silhouette Bombshell

We're pulling out the stops to bring you four high-octane reads per month featuring women of action who always save the day and get— or get away from—their men. Guaranteed.

Available at your local retailer in January 2005:

STELLA, GET YOUR MAN
by Nancy Bartholomew

DECEIVED
by Carla Cassidy

ALWAYS LOOK TWICE
by Sheri WhiteFeather

THE HUNTRESS
by Crystal Green

Sexy. Savvy. Suspenseful.

More Than Meets the Eye

SBGEN2